*Mark Recognized Lucinda in Her
New Disguise as a Spanish Señorita . . .*

She had no experience with kisses and had not known that one—even one of Mark's—could be so devastating. His hands were moving caressingly upon her back and shoulders, sending ripples through her from each point of contact. She gasped as his lips found the hollow of her throat, then began tracing kisses along the line of her jaw before taking her willing mouth another time.

She felt him shudder as her hands slipped up his chest and shoulders until she could fasten them behind his head, her fingers luxuriating in the feel of his crisp hair. One of his hands went to the ties of her mask and she reached quickly to stop him. Even with the paint on her face, Lucinda did not dare to let him see her unmasked. "No." It was only a whisper, but a forceful one.

A HEART IN DISGUISE

MONETTE CUMMINGS

DIAMOND BOOKS, NEW YORK

A HEART IN DISGUISE

A Diamond Book / published by arrangement with
the author

PRINTING HISTORY
Diamond edition / August 1991

ISBN: 1-55773-552-2

Diamond Books are published by The Berkley Publishing
Group, 200 Madison Avenue, New York, New York 10016.
The name "DIAMOND" and its logo are trademarks
belonging to Charter Communications, Inc.

PRINTED IN THE UNITED STATES OF AMERICA

10 9 8 7 6 5 4 3 2 1

Chapter One

"TWO MONTHS!" CAPTAIN Warne caught himself before he made a rash comment. "But—my lord, I cannot. I am on leave, and I must return."

"Your leave can be extended for whatever time *I* shall deem necessary to make my decision," Lord Brayling said testily. "After all, you will find that my name is not without influence, even to the army. My secretary shall write to your commander—"

"No! Er, no sir, if you please. I know my commander and I am certain he would insist that I make the request myself. I shall tell him, of course, that I am requesting the additional time because it is *your* wish. As you have said, my lord, the mention of your name will be sufficient."

The explanation sounded weak, even to the speaker. Was he believed? The captain waited, hardly daring to breathe.

"Very well," the old man said, dismissing the matter with a wave of his hand. "I do not care how it is done, just so long as it is settled."

The uniformed figure visibly relaxed. If the earl had insisted upon writing, the result would have been catastrophic. The general's reply would have been that Captain Warne was not, and never had been, in London, but was at this moment with his troops on the Peninsula. Just as he should be. Further investigation would have revealed that the "soldier" was *not* Captain Lucien Warne at all, but his twin sister, Lucinda.

Not only would that discovery have meant complete disgrace

for the masquerader, but it would have destroyed any chance of Lucien's inheriting his grandfather's money forever.

"As I was saying," the earl went on, satisfied that his word was no longer questioned. "Young Captain Impudence"—he nodded at Lucinda—"you will inherit my title, as the only son of my only son. And whatever property is entailed. But that is little. Most of my fortune came from my mother. And I have called you both here to decide which of you is to have it."

Seated across from Lucinda, Albert Turngren, the cousin she had not known existed, smirked. He had spent the past few years strengthening his position. True, he had not called upon the old man any more often than was needed, but he had been available whenever the earl had summoned him, while the soldier had been larking around on the continent.

Noticing Albert's self-satisfied look, the old man snorted. "Fribble. Only come here when you think I am about to stick my spoon in the wall. You, too." He turned his glare upon the uniformed figure now standing quietly beside him. "Did not come until you were sent for, then took your time about it."

Lucinda thought it best not to reply. The secretary rose as if to go, but his employer growled, "Sit down, Mark. This applies to you, as well as to these two puppies. At least you stayed by me."

"Was I given a choice?" the large young man asked in a quiet tone.

To Lucinda's surprise, the remark caused the earl to throw back his head and laugh heartily, the laugh ending in a cough. When the younger man handed him a glass, he scowled but downed the contents obediently.

"No, you were not," he said. "But I'll give you this much—at least, you never grumbled about your lot. And now to business. Take this down, Mark. Each of the young scamps is to have an allowance. A generous one."

The earl waved away Albert's effusive thanks. Lucinda sat quietly, waiting to learn what strings were attached to the offer.

"And what you do with the money is important. I must warn both of you that hoarding it will mean failure. I wish to know that my money will be spent as I might do if I was able to get about. You are to mingle with the *ton*, as I did when I was a younger man. And the manner in which you comport yourselves will make me decide who is worthy to receive my fortune. Mark is to keep me completely informed of your actions."

He paused to glare at each of his grandchildren, then added, "And if I am not pleased with either of you—and I have no high opinion of the pair of you at this time—every penny of my money shall go to Mark."

When the old gentleman seemed to sag in his chair, Mark went to him at once, but he raised a hand for attention and continued. "You will receive your allowance from Mark today. And I shall talk to each of you separately later on. But it will be Mark who will report on how you spend your time—and my money."

He coughed again and waved them toward the door. Seeing that the old man had exhausted most of his strength, Lucinda only bowed and murmured her thanks for his invitation as she moved away.

Her cousin launched into an effusive speech of farewell and wishes for his lordship's speedy recovery—an impossibility at his great age. The speech was cut off midway when Mark placed a large hand in the middle of the smaller man's back and pushed him out of the room. A servant who had been waiting just outside the door gave them an anxious glance and, at a nod from Mark, hurried into the room, closing the door behind him.

"This arrangement of my grandfather's makes a very nice situation for you, don't it?" Albert said haughtily to Mark. "All you have to do is to turn in an unfavorable report on the pair of us, and you can nab the ready for yourself. How long did it take you to talk him into agreeing to this scheme?"

The secretary bared his teeth—very nice, strong teeth he had, Lucinda thought—at the younger man, much in the same way that a mastiff might act if provoked by the yapping of a small puppy.

"Believe me, you young toadeater, if I knew the sort of a report I should make to keep his lordship's money from falling into your hands, I most certainly would do it. Not because I wish the money for myself, for I do not need it. But because I know you care nothing whatsoever for your grandfather. You have not been in this house six times in your life and would not be here now, except that you have hopes of being named his heir."

His scornful glance shifted to Lucinda.

"Just as you tried to run off this time, using your military duties as an excuse, I suppose there is some slight allowance which can be made for you, since you were born abroad. Still, you have had a good many years in which you might have come here to call upon your grandfather. And would you be here now if it had not been for the hint in my letter that it might be to your advantage?"

Since this *was* the reason she had come—although it was for Lucien and not for herself—Lucinda said nothing.

"Unfortunately, I know no more than either of you about the type of report his lordship expects me to give him. He was quite a Go-among-the-Goers in his young days, according to what I was told by my father. Whether he wishes you to follow his example or to do the opposite is more than I can say. Now, come with me."

He led the way into the library, where he brought out a box and opened it. It appeared to be filled with money, and the secretary handed each of them a large sheaf of notes.

"If you need more," he said, "you have only to inform me. Your grandfather is being quite generous. I was instructed that each of you is to have whatever you require for the next two months."

Albert was riffling through the notes in his hand, whistling softly as he mentally totalled them. "I have often thought the old man was swimming in lard," he said in awe. "But he must be as rich as Golden Ball to be able to open his purse strings in this way."

"Not quite as wealthy as that," said Mark. "However, it is no secret that Lord Brayling is what *you* would doubtless call 'full of juice.' However much you may spend in the next two months, it is unlikely that he will miss it greatly. Unless, of course, you plan to throw down twenty or thirty thousand a night on the gaming tables, as some do. And I hope most sincerely that this is the last of his money either of you will ever see."

Ignoring the secretary's remarks as being beneath his attention, Albert gave Lucinda a sly grin. "A guinea to a groat," he said boastfully, "that it will be *I* who takes the old man's blunt."

Her cousin's callousness shocked Lucinda. She was beginning to feel a grudging respect for the old gentleman, even though he had treated her parents cruelly and herself and Lucien with total indifference. Still, now he was old and far from well, and she did not like the way this little care-for-nobody was speaking of him.

On the other hand, she did not wish her cousin to know her true feelings. He would only sneer at her even more.

For all she knew of such things, indifference of this kind might be the rule among the members of the *ton*. Fishing a small coin from the pocket of her waistcoat, she returned his grin and said, "At such odds as those, I would gladly risk a monkey. Still, as you set the terms—" She held the coin out to Mark, saying, "Will you hold the wager?"

She had not thought it possible that the secretary could look at her with greater loathing than he had shown before, but it seemed that now he did so.

"If I were not under his lordship's orders," he told them, "what I should do would be to take the two of you and crack your heads together until what little brains you may have would be scrambled."

From his expression and the clenching of his huge fists, it appeared that he might yet yield to the temptation and ignore his orders. Albert scurried out of danger. Lucinda followed her cousin's example, although at a slower pace.

When the secretary had seen his lordship's two grandsons out of the house, he returned to his earlier task of handling the old gentleman's correspondence, thankful that these young good-for-naughts probably would not be back at the house for the next two months. It was scarcely to be expected that they would have any true affection for the earl—especially in the case of the captain, who had never seen him—but their impudence toward an old man made him gnash his teeth.

He broke the seal of one letter, read it through, then leaped to his feet and made his way swiftly to the earl's bedchamber. "Read this," he said roughly, for once forgetting the deference he customarily showed his employer.

My lord, the letter began,

I do not feel that it is right for me to address you as grandfather, since you have never seen fit to acknowledge my existence until now. I should do no more now than to say that it is impossible for me to leave my post, nor would I willingly have obeyed your command, or even acknowledged its receipt. It is only that my crack-brained twin, Lucinda, has taken it into her head that this is a matter of an inheritance and that she can cozen you into thinking that she is "Captain Warne." I beg of you, my lord, that you will not deal too harshly with her for her masquerade and that you will send her back to me before she falls into trouble. Your servant, my lord,

Captain Lucien Warne.

Lord Brayling, noted for his high temper, spluttered, "Do you mean to tell me that young jackanapes—"

"If this letter is to be believed, and I see no reason why it should not be, that young jackanapes is the captain's 'crack-brained twin, Lucinda.' "

"A female—daring to present herself to me as my heir—and you will note, Mark, that *he* did not bother to use his title. But this deception—'tis infamous. 'Send her safely back to him,' the fellow begs. Rather, I shall see her exposed for the fraud that she is. We shall see how she enjoys standing in the dock."

Although he felt that boiling in oil was too good for the hoyden who had dared to mock him as well as her grandfather, the secretary said, "If you will permit, sir, I can think of a more fitting punishment."

"And what is that?"

"Let her continue this masquerade until she has made an utter fool of herself, for she can fool no one for long—then tell her that we have known all the while. *Then* she can be sent back to her brother in disgrace."

The earl chewed his lip, his hands closing and unclosing upon the arms of his chair. At last, he gave a bark of laughter. "That will be just the thing, Mark. I have always said you had a shrewd head upon your shoulders."

"When have you said that? I have always heard you curse me for my lack of brains," the younger man said with a grin.

"Well, I say it now—you impudent young snirp. But where is this false captain now? Running about London, I suppose."

"I believe he—she—and a friend are staying at Grillon's Hotel."

"A friend?"

"I should have called him a retainer, but was informed that the captain considers him a friend. A certain Thomas Abbott, I believe."

"Thomas? He dares to come back here, after leaving me to follow my son? That— But you mean my granddaughter is staying at a hotel, accompanied by a man and a former groom at that? I will not have it! If the news leaked out, that would be a scandal." For a moment propriety outweighed exposure of his granddaughter's duplicity in the old man's mind.

"Again—if I may suggest—"

"You are full of suggestions today, are you not? What now?"

"Why not send word to the captain that you wish him to stay beneath your roof for the two months he is in London? So I may observe how he manages the money you gave him."

"Hm—that might be the thing—but he would scarcely believe it if I did not have that other young snirp, Albert, as well."

"I fear that would be necessary. But I shall see that both of them are kept away from you, so they will be no trouble. It will also be necessary, I fear, to have this Thomas Abbott."

The old man was suddenly weary. "Ah well, do as you like. You would do, whether I approved or not. Just do not worry me with the details. But how to plan to make her unmask herself?"

"Easily. I shall see that she is pitchforked into the *ton,* and she will be running back to her brother before we know it."

When Lucinda returned to Grillon's Hotel, she recounted the morning's events with suitable embroidery to Thomas, her companion on this escapade and the nearest to a father that the twins had ever known. When she finished her recitation, Thomas sighed. "Knowing you, Lucinda—and from what you have told me of your cousin—if the secretary *had* banged your heads together, it would have been deserved. I told you from the start, Lucinda Warne," he said sternly, "that you were bacon-brained to attempt so wild a scheme. Lucien told you the same. But of course, you would not listen."

"No one could have turned me from my plan," Lucinda retorted.

"No—and see what has happened. Now we shall have to run for it, and any chance Lucien may have had of inheriting the old man's money will be gone like smoke."

"But that is exactly the thing, Thomas. I *cannot* run away now. But I will own that it seemed easier when we first had the plan."

"When *you* first had it," he corrected.

Lucinda paid no attention to him, remembering back to the day she had thought of the plan. It was the day the letter had come for Lucien, having followed them for some weeks. The army had been on the move, and Lucinda had doggedly followed wherever her brother was sent. It was a letter from England, the first either of them had ever received from their grandfather, and was franked in a hand so shaky that it was barely discernible as that of the Earl of Brayling.

After having read the letter for the third time, Lucien had looked up and said, "This is a curious letter. I cannot fathom any reason for it. But at any rate, it cannot matter, as I can do nothing about it now."

Lucinda had been eagerly waiting for him to read the mysterious letter, but he merely broke the seal on the next envelope. Exasperated, she picked up the discarded letter.

Captain Warne:

This is to inform you that your grandfather, Lord Brayling, has expressed a wish that you should attend him in London at the earliest possible date. You must be aware that his lordship is rather advanced in years and—I am sorry to say this—he is far from being a well man. I may say that I am exceeding his lordship's orders in giving you any explanation, but I feel that it may be to your advantage to come.

"Look," she cried, turning over the page to read the inscription, "it is addressed to 'Captain Lord Lucien Warne.' We always forget, Lucien, that you did inherit Papa's title—that you are a—what is it?—a *vicomte.*"

"They say 'viscount' in English—but it does not matter in the least. I should never use it."

"Then do I have a title, too?"

"I do not think so. Do you want one?"

"Not if you do not wish yours." Reversing the letter once more, she puzzled over the signature. "It is difficult to decipher this, but it looks like 'Mark Warne.' Another Warne. Do you suppose it could be a member of our family?"

"I don't know. Papa had no brothers, you know, only a sister. Any children of hers would not be named Warne. We might ask Thomas if he knows of this one."

"But would you not like to know about your English family?"

Her brother shook his head, but gave her a sympathetic glance. "No. I know you feel that way, but I have never done so. After ignoring us all of our lives, I cannot understand why our grandfather should ask for me now. And why not for you, as well?"

"Maybe he does not know there were twins. Or possibly he thinks I resemble *Maman,* so he would not wish to see me. But I wish you will consider going. You know you can ask for leave if it is a matter of inheritance. Others have done so."

"We have only your imagination to say that it is anything to do with inheritance. No proof. Even if that were the reason, I would not go. I am no vulture to pick clean the bones of an old man, and, more important, Boney is expected to move again soon. I shall write to this Mark Warne and explain."

It was then that Lucinda happened upon the idea which she considered brilliant and which both her brother and Thomas Abbott had told her was harebrained. Slipping away, she had soon returned, clad in Lucien's clothing, announcing herself as "Captain Warne."

Despite her brother's protests and Thomas' warnings of disaster, she insisted that she could carry off the masquerade for the few days it would take to meet his lordship. Then she could claim the call of duty and return to Spain. "Look at us," she declared. "You will see that I can do it."

There was indeed a strong resemblance between the twins. Both were slim, with their mother's dark hair and eyes. Lucinda lacked several inches of matching her brother's six-foot stature and certainly did not have his breadth of shoulder. However, years of exercise had given her a more boyish form than many young ladies of her age. With her hair clipped to match Lucien's, even Thomas reluctantly agreed that many who had not seen the captain might accept the bogus "Lucien."

When all her arguments had failed to convince her brother, she had announced that she *would* go to London, no matter what he might say. Despite his misgivings, Thomas Abbott had agreed to accompany her.

Now that she had come this far, Thomas was speaking of running away. Lucinda shook her head decidedly. "That is exactly it, Thomas. I *cannot* run. If I do so, Lucien's chances will be ruined. Now that I am here, I must carry it through. It will not be so difficult a matter, for there is no one in London who would recognize Lucien."

"There is more to it than that, my girl."

"Nothing so much, after all. The only thing which will be necessary will be for me to show myself from time to time at the races or one of the clubs. Since my grandfather is not a well man, he will not be expecting me to make regular calls upon him, and that brute of a secretary will be much happier if I stay as far from his sight as possible. I cannot tell you how pleased I am to discover that he is no relation of ours. Still, from some of the things he has said, he must have grown up with the family. I wonder that you do not remember him."

Thomas wrinkled his brow and scratched his head, as if by doing so he could stir his memory to life.

"I disremember the name, but since you mention it, I do remember there was a young lad who was always wanting to follow your father about. Made a prime nuisance of himself, he did, for he could not have been long out of leading strings, and your father a young man. A distant cousin or some such relation, if I ain't mistaken."

"He says not. He told Cousin Albert and me that his father had been a foundling raised by Lord Brayling and given his name. When the father died, Lord Brayling had the son educated and made him his secretary."

"Can't say that I remember his lordship taking in any foundlings. But then, I never lived in the house, so it could have been. He—the boy, I mean—would be that young giant who told me I'd best not wait for you this afternoon and that he'd see that you got back here."

"Giant? Mammoth is more like! And rude to everyone—no, I must take that back. He does seem to care for the old man. As he should. His lordship has done more for him than for his own grandsons. And saying he might leave *him* his fortune if he is not pleased with us—"

Seeing that Lucinda's temper was rising, Thomas interrupted quickly, "And what of this other grandson? Your Aunt Sophia's son, I take it."

Anger was forgotten, as Lucinda went off into a gale of laughter. "A Bartholomew baby, Thomas, if ever there was one. He has to be seen to be believed."

"Well, since I did not see him, tell me about him."

"Let me see—a few inches shorter than I, lank brownish hair worn in a tangle, although I suppose it was arranged that way purposely, shirt points so high that he could not turn his head, with a neckcloth so bulky that it looked like a badly bandaged wound."

Thomas joined in her laughter. "Nothing at all like the other one, is he? The secretary? Now, there is a man I suspect I could like."

"And I," Lucinda said grudgingly. "Except that I felt that he looked down on me."

"Well, my lass, from his size, he could do."

"Not on *me*, Thomas. What I mean is on the captain. And you know I will not allow anyone to belittle Lucien."

"I know, but, Lucinda, 'tis time that you looked about for yourself. Four and twenty is quite an age, and you would not wish to end up a spinster."

She laughed and patted his gnarled cheek. "If I could find one who was half so wonderful as my brother, I should take him in a moment. But you know, Thomas, there are none like that. So I am content to go on making a home for Lucien when he is not fighting."

"And if he marries?"

They were interrupted by a servant bringing word that a messenger had arrived for Captain Warne. A moment later a footman wearing Lord Brayling's livery tapped at the door and presented a letter. Although she had seen it only once, she knew it to be Mark Warne's handwriting. The bold letters could belong to no one else.

Lord Brayling has decided that, in order to observe the results of his experiment, it would be best for you and your cousin, Albert Turngren, to spend the next two months beneath his roof. I have explained to his lordship that you have brought a friend with you, so the invitation includes him as well. Patrick, who brings you this letter, has orders to wait until you are packed and to bring the two of you to Grosvenor Square.

When she had finished reading the message, Lucinda gave it to Thomas and bade Patrick await them in the taproom, slipping him a coin.

"Now we are in for it," Thomas said, deep in gloom, as soon as the door closed. "We have no choice but to run for it."

"Oh, Thomas, do not get in the hips," his charge retorted with some irritation. She would not let him know that, secretly, she was as terrified as he.

"Can you give me one reason not to do so?"

"I know I can carry it off. What does it matter if we live here or in my grandfather's house? But I cannot do it without your help. There is no need for you to fall into the dismals about it. Even if I am living in the house, my grandfather will not wish to see me often. And I can certainly fool an old man."

"But can you fool the young one?" There was scepticism in his tone. Despite his earlier reluctant assurances, Thomas felt that anyone who took a second look at her would recognize at once that she was a female. How could they not help doing so?

"Oh, if you mean my cousin Albert, his finery is so blinding that I doubt he can even see beyond it," she said blithely. "He will doubtless not even know I exist. As for that mammoth of a secretary, he will not see past his scorn."

Despite her arguments, Thomas grumbled continuously as he packed their cases. However, since Lucinda was determined to carry out the masquerade, he was left with no choice but to go with her. If he refused she was just stubborn enough to go alone.

During his guardianship Thomas had grown into the habit of reporting to the shade of his old friend and master on their progress. It comforted him, kept Master Philip closer in some way. Thomas spoke to him especially in moments of worry, usually about Lucinda's welfare. "Philip," he said now beneath his breath, "if only you—or someone—would tell me how to deal with her now."

At the very least, he knew that a disclosure of her imposture would result in a scandal which would reflect upon Lucien as well as on herself. Possibly, it would put paid to Lucien's army career. If the old gentleman became very angry at having been deceived—and Thomas had good reason to remember his temper—he might decide to have the girl arrested for her impersonation. Thomas knew he would never be able to face the captain, or himself for that matter, if Lucinda found herself beneath the hatches because he had neglected her.

Chapter Two

BARELY WAITING UNTIL Patrick had set down their cases, Lucinda fell into raptures about her bedchamber.

"Even *Maman*'s second husband, the *comte,* was never able to offer us anything which could compare with this when we visited him," she cried as she whirled about in what Thomas caustically informed her was a distinctly unmilitary manner.

"What does it matter, if no one but you is about to see me?"

"Servants have ways of knowing things, whether they see them or not."

Lucinda ignored him, as usual. She drew appreciative fingers over the carvings on chairs and desk, caressed the heavy gold bed hangings and curtains, and traced the designs upon the ornate bedposts. Then she threw herself upon the bed to bounce on its softness, sighing, "I could never have dreamt—but, of course, you already knew how it would be, did you not, Thomas?"

Thomas paused and shook his head.

"I did not know for certain. But I think this must have been your father's room, for I seem to remember how he described it to me when we were newly come to France. He was homesick at times. How could he help it? This had always been his home."

"Poor Papa. But he was not truly too unhappy, was he?"

"Not after he and your mother were married, although her family had cut her off, too, for running away with him. All they ever needed was each other—and the two of you."

"I wish I could remember him. But we were so young—"

Thomas nodded. "Yes, you could hardly remember. But you would have loved him. Lucien is much like him. As are you— except that both of you have your mother's coloring. Still, as I said, I never saw this room. You must remember, lass, that when I lived here, my place was in the stables and the servants' quarters, never above stairs. I have come up in the world to have a place here—I only hope I do not tumble down just as quickly and end my days in gaol."

Wearying of his gloomy musings, Lucinda demanded, "Is your room as fine as this? Let me see it," and ran to peep into the room next to hers. It was equally luxurious, but done in deep green.

Coming back to stand beside the bed, once more running her fingers over the carving on the posts, she said in a low tone, "Even if I were truly a man, I think I should cry at this moment. Papa's room. Oh, how I wish that Lucien could be here to enjoy all of this. If I manage the affair right, he *will* be here some day—the future master of Brayling House, as he should be."

Once more, Patrick arrived at the door, interrupting them. This time, he bore a summons to Thomas from Lord Brayling. Then he led Thomas off to his lordship's bedchamber.

When Thomas arrived, Lord Brayling chose to be affable, saying only, "Well, Thomas, I had not thought to see you in London again after you left my employ without a word."

"I went because Master Philip was in need of a friend, my lord. And had he lived, we should have returned together— some day."

The old gentleman frowned, feeling that the servant's words implied that the estrangement from his son might have been, in some way, the earl's fault. This he would never own.

"That may be," he said curtly. "But you would have stood a better friend to him if you had managed to prevent him from entering into a disastrous marriage."

"There's no one on earth who could have done that, my lord, once he had set eyes upon the lady."

Lord Brayling uttered a sound midway between his usual growl and a cough. "What did she have to offer a man like my son, compared to the marriage to which he was contracted?"

"She brought him a great deal of happiness, my lord, which—if your lordship will forgive me for saying so—I do not believe he would have had with the other lady. The contract had never been of his making."

"That may be. But had he—died—which doubtless would not have happened had he returned home, 'the other lady,' as you call her, would have remembered what was due to her position as my son's widow. *She*—she has married again, has she not?"

"Yes, my lord. Twice." Thomas wondered how detailed Lord Brayling's reports on his daughter-in-law were. Melanie Warne had never had strong feelings for her children, but had truly loved Philip. Still, she was a woman who could not be happy if she did not have a man to love. Before and after her second marriage, there had been several "protectors." Now she was settled happily and, he hoped, permanently, in the south of France with a man who adored her and catered to her every whim.

His lordship decided to change the subject. "And you have been with my grandson since then?"

With both the children, Thomas thought, but bit back the words. From the day of Philip's fatal accident, he had been both father and mother to the young Warnes. Their French mother, who had no taste for motherhood, had gone off to enjoy life as a widow. Thomas had raised the pair, doing his rough best with them.

Until now.

"Since he was born, my lord," he said, "and saw to it that he was raised an Englishman, which is what his father wanted, for Master Philip never forgot his home."

The old man grunted, but said nothing.

"A finer young man than Lucien you have yet to meet, if I may say so. He may not have your size—no more than his father had—but he has courage enough for two and has distinguished himself more than once in this war. *He* would not say so, but he has twice been mentioned in dispatches." Thomas muttered a silent prayer that no third such mention would be made until he and Lucinda were safely away.

His lordship grunted again, unwilling to own that the information pleased him. Instead, he tried another tack. "Why does he not use his title?"

"Excuse me, my lord, but I think he prefers the one he has earned for himself. 'Twas not easy for him to be accepted by his fellow soldiers. Being half-French, he faced some suspicion at first. And to have earned a captaincy in the field, at his age—"

Lord Brayling grunted a third time and waved a dismissal at the man, suddenly feeling the weight of his years.

Thomas hurried away, certain that the old gentleman had been more pleased with the report about his grandson than he had been willing to own. Everything he had told his lordship about Lucien, he consoled himself, had been no more than the truth. He could not understand how Lord Brayling could be unaware that he had a granddaughter as well as a grandson, but he was happy to have escaped without having dropped a word to the old gentleman which might have revealed Lucinda's secret.

When he returned to Lucinda's chamber, Thomas continued to scold her as he went on with the task of arranging her borrowed gear, hanging the coats in the armoire, sorting shirts and cravats and placing them carefully in the drawers or on the shelves. Lucinda, however, refused to take the bait.

"Stop trying to cast me into despair, Thomas Abbott," she told him gaily, "for you cannot do so. When you remember all the times I have spent with Lucien and the officers in his company, do you think I do not know how gentlemen behave?"

"That is exactly what I *do* think, miss. And I know more about this sort of thing than you. You have seen them only in company and on their best behavior. You do not have any idea of how they go on when ladies ain't around or don't have a brother about to guard them. If you go out on the town with some of the young bucks, there would be things said and done that no young female like yourself ought to know about—much less be forced to take part in."

"You mean about their bits of muslin and—what do they call them—their birds of paradise?" she asked with a grin. "Of course, I know about *that*—young soldiers will let their tongues slip, you know."

As he opened his mouth to roar at her for such unseemly utterances, she placed her fingers on his lips and said in her coaxing way, "Now, do not fly up into the boughs, Thomas. No matter what occurs, I can promise I will do nothing of which you would disapprove." Beneath her breath, she added, "Well, at least *very much.*"

Thomas shook his head, unconvinced by her apparent docility. He knew Lucinda and did not believe her for one moment.

"I should never have consented to becoming a part of this havey-cavey business with you," he grumbled.

"What shall I wear this evening, Thomas?" she enquired, changing the subject abruptly. "While you were paying your respects to my grandfather—and I hope he did not give you the rough edge of his tongue—his secretary sent up word that his lordship had obtained cards for my cousin and me at Lady Leatheringham's rout party tonight. It seems as if she might be someone of importance—I think he said a marchioness. That is the same as a *marquise,* is it not?"

"Did you hear nothing of what I have been saying to you?" Thomas demanded wrathfully.

Lucinda straightened up from the armoire where she had been searching through Lucien's clothes. "I heard you. I only hope that everyone in the house did not hear you as well. And you only say the same things over and over, although I tell you there is no reason to worry. I can do very well. Now, will you please help me? This will be Lucien's first appearance in London, and it is important that I look his best."

Thomas sighed and gave over the battle. When Lucinda got into what he referred to as her "Hey-go-mad" mood, she could never be made to listen to reason. And since he had never seen anything reasonable in this entire affair, it was a waste of time to talk to her.

"Let me do that," he said, thrusting her roughly away from the armoire. "You are making a mess of everything and there will be nothing fit to wear."

Two hours later, when Lucinda descended to the dining room, she was complete in Lucien's best, from buckled shoes to long-tailed coat of crimson brocade. Although these things had been stored, the Parisian styles of several years ago were but little different from those of present-day London. Even before he had entered the army, Lucien had disliked the custom of powdering his hair—a fashion which was still popular in the group of French emigrés, although out of favor among the English themselves.

Lucinda followed her brother's example, thankful that the Prince Regent and his set had declared the wearing of powder or wigs outdated—principally, she had heard, because both were still favored by the King's more staid court, and the Prince's set could not wait to discard what the court liked.

Lucinda's black locks shone as brilliantly as did the buckles on her shoes and the modest pin nestled in the froth of lace at her throat. The wearing of lace, too, was beginning to be considered passé, especially by followers of Beau Brummell. It had still been popular in France, and Lucien had been one who had enjoyed it before he had put away his dress garments in favor of his uniform. Lucinda was happy to have the frill down the front of her shirt, for along with the fact that Lucien's coats did not fit her as snugly as they had her brother, the lace helped to disguise her figure.

She was proud that her legs were slim and straight, so that neither her white satin breeches nor her stockings of striped silk showed a wrinkle. Her white waistcoat was embroidered with a discreet figure in the same color as her coat, and upon each hand she wore only a single ring, one set with a ruby, the other a faithful copy of the signet Lucien wore, one which had belonged to their father.

Watching her descend the stairs, Mark Warne was forced to own that she *looked* the part of a young gentleman. *Acting* the gentleman, however, would be another thing. He would wager that before the evening was done, she would have given herself away more than a dozen times. *If only she does not cause a scandal,* he said beneath his breath, recalling that he had promised Lord Brayling to prevent anything of the kind.

In contrast to the "captain's" restrained dress, her cousin had attired himself for the evening in a coat of a virulent shade of green. Once more his shoulders had been padded until they rose about his ears, and his shirt points were so high that it was impossible for him to turn his head. His lavender breeches were tied at the knee with ribbands, his waistcoat was embroidered in many bright colors, and his cravat was of a wonderfully intricate design. Lucinda thought, however, that its many thick folds about his neck gave him the appearance of being heavily bandaged.

Albert was among the fops who still clung to the use of powder, and tonight his lank hair was covered with such a quantity of the stuff that he was enveloped in a cloud of pale blue whenever he moved suddenly. If the tinted hair had not been enough to mark him as an Exquisite, the number of patches upon his face would certainly have done so. Lucinda told herself that several of them would have been more effective, or at least more practical, if they had been placed to hide some of the spots which marred his sallow skin. His shoes had high red heels and extremely large paste buckles; he sported half a dozen rings set with enormous stones, a variety of fobs and seals, and a quizzing glass whose handle was also set with several large stones.

Choking back a laugh, she asked, "Have I kept you waiting?"

Albert only growled, but a previously unnoticed form moved away from the window and Mark Warne said pleasantly, "Not at all, Captain. We are still in good time. Dinner will be served in ten minutes."

This, then, was at least one reason for her cousin's sour expression. It seemed that Mr. Warne intended to be one of their company this evening. Albert clearly objected to having one whom he considered no better than a servant accompanying them.

Lucinda did not welcome the presence of the large gentleman, for if anyone could see through her disguise, she feared her grandfather's secretary might. Still, when she saw how much the secretary's presence displeased her foppish cousin, she smiled. "I must thank you for your patience, Mr. Warne," she said. "A bit of trouble with my neckcloth, you see."

From the sneering look Albert cast at the neatly tied strip of white with its modest fall, it was apparent that he thought the effort had been wasted. Mark Warne, however, nodded. The chit was wise enough, he thought, to know that—even out of uniform—a soldier would not wish to make himself a figure of fun. Doubtless she was only copying her brother's custom, but it served.

Although Mark Warne was clad in the knee breeches and silk stockings which were *de rigueur* for evening wear, his outfit was of the type of somber elegance Beau Brummell had dictated for English fashion. Both his coat and breeches were of black silk, his white marcella waistcoat bore only the faintest of satin stripes, and his shirt points were of medium height. His neckcloth was arranged with a simplicity that Lucinda thought even she could copy. Like her, he wore his dark hair without powder. Despite herself, Lucinda was filled with admiration for his discreet attire. Indeed, he looked much more the gentleman than did the dandyish Mr. Turngren.

It was a pity, she thought, that his protection of her grandfather made him hold such animosity toward the two heirs. Mark Warne was a man she would have liked to count a friend.

She glanced up at his superior height again. Being unusually tall for a female, many of the men she met little more than matched her height. Rarely did she look up at a man. She sipped at the glass of burgundy he offered her, wondering how it could be that she could both admire and dislike the man at the same time. The question was still unanswered when dinner was announced.

Mark led the way to the dining table which had been set modestly. There were perhaps half a dozen side dishes, no more. All of it looked and smelled delicious, but because of the short notice there were none of the elaborate sauces the cook usually enjoyed creating.

Albert gave a brief sneer at the paltry display, but Lucinda declared, "To one unaccustomed to any but army fare, this is a feast indeed."

It was true that having Thomas to forage for them, the young Warnes had never been on such short rations as some of their friends. Still, there had been many times when they had felt themselves fortunate to have even the plainest of foods, which they gladly shared with some of the soldiers who had less. What would those men not give for a dinner such as this?

"It makes rather a modest showing by London standards, I must own," Mark commented.

"What more could anyone wish?" she asked.

"A great deal more, in many cases. Just ask your cousin. But I assure you that his lordship's chef is an excellent one. I know how delighted he will be to have someone for whom to cook who does not share the earl's digestive ailment. For myself, I am out of favor with him, since I care little for the style of food given me as long as it is in good supply. You may look for him to outdo himself for your benefit after tonight."

"Then we shall doubtless be fat as pigs before we leave here." With a healthy young appetite, Lucinda was able to do full justice to everything offered, from the roast goose and green peas to the meat pie.

Albert, meanwhile, toyed with a few bites, not knowing

whether he should appease his hunger or continue to sneer at what was set before him. Mark—they had progressed to first names by this time—was the good trencherman he had said he was and which his size indicated.

Since the secretary reminded them of their evening's engagement when he passed the bottle, they had but a single glass of claret each. Never having been overfond of spirits, Lucinda was grateful for this, unaware that Mark had used the upcoming engagement as an excuse. He feared the jade might cause a scandal even if completely sober; half-foxed, she was certain to have herself, and her family as well, in the suds.

When they rose from the table, he said, " 'Tis but a short way to Lady Leatheringham's house. An easy walk. Although, if you prefer, I can bespeak chairs."

Never having had the opportunity to be carried in a chair, Lucinda was curious about this mode of transportation. She also wondered about the bearers who could carry Mark Warne's weight. Although quite lean, he was a large man.

She was about to voice a wish for chairs, when she saw Albert's peevish face and decided to thwart him. "Let us walk, by all means," she said. " 'Tis difficult for a soldier to find exercise in the city."

Mark repressed a snort at Albert's aghast expression. The chit had spirit as well as daring. He smiled and watched her stride down the road. She moved much like a young man, doubtless having practiced the real captain's movements. The clothing—her brother's?—suited her very well; she would appear a commanding figure in a gown; probably her height would condemn her to lack partners and to sit with the dowagers at every ball. He could almost sympathize with her—if it were not for the audacity of the game she was playing.

Lucinda was accustomed to walking; still, she found it difficult to match her steps to Mark's longer ones and noted with glee that, in his ridiculous high heels, Albert found it necessary to trot awkwardly to keep pace with them.

A glance at Mark showed that his face was properly sober, and he kept his voice even as he pointed out the houses they passed and named their owners, many of them of the nobility. However, Lucinda had a feeling that he was walking as rapidly as possible and was enjoying her foppish young cousin's discomfiture as much as she. It would seem that his proper appearance hid a sense of humor after all.

There were times, she thought, when she could almost like this very large man.

Chapter
Three

IT WAS BARELY ten. By Society's standards, the hour was not yet far advanced; still, Lady Leatheringham's *soirée* was well under way. "One of my little routs," said her ladyship's invitations, yet to anyone else such a gathering would be labelled a grand ball.

Before the trio had reached her home, they found themselves among many others who had preferred to walk the few steps. Mark took this opportunity to present his lordship's grandsons to several of them. As Lucinda and Albert found themselves accepted gladly for their grandfather's sake, the secretary hoped again that the jade would cause no scandal which would rebound against the earl's reputation.

Mark felt a twinge of unease at his earlier willingness to let Lucinda show herself a fool and then unmask her. But it was only because he had no wish to become entangled in a scandal, he assured himself.

As the trio threaded their way through the guests, vehicles, chairbearers, and link boys packing the streets, they saw the entryway in the distance.

A large canopy extended from the doorway to the street, beneath which a red carpet stretched out to protect the shoes of the dainty from the dirt of the pavement. Once callers had passed within doors, they slowly made their way amid a press of people up an ornate staircase to the ballroom. Here the glimmering of hundreds of candles were reflected in the gilt-trimmed mirrors lining the walls and in the jewels and satins of the guests.

This was the sort of crush which was so dear to her lady-ship's heart. The Marchioness of Leatheringham was a lady of considerable girth, who abhorred any form of exercise which did not have to do with an affair such as this.

"Not," she declared, "that anyone can hope to give an affair to match mine." Had any done so, she would have struggled to have thought of an entertainment more titillating to the members of the *ton,* thus ensuring her reputation.

The late Marquess of Leatheringham had been a gentleman of great energies with a fondness for exploring little-known places in his own country. He declared that even without the troubles which were forever brewing on the continent, it was foolish to waste time touring abroad when there was so much to see at home. He had insisted that his wife accompany him upon all his travels. Although she had cared for him deeply enough to do so without a word of complaint, she announced after his death that she had exhausted herself in keeping pace with him as he climbed mountains and tramped about the countryside.

"I have gone from Lands End to John o' Groats with that man," she declared. "But I never promised that I would do so in his memory. From this moment on, I intend to do nothing which requires the slightest effort."

The cessation of so many years of activity, added to her love of good food, had increased her girth enormously. This, too, was a matter of no concern to her. People could accept her as she was—or they could go elsewhere.

Her ladyship was not boasting when she declared that she could attract a greater portion of Polite Society to her balls and dinners than any other hostess in London. "The best hostess in the *world,*" her admirers called her, for to them London *was* the world, or at least the only portion of it which counted for anything.

Aside from the determination that her parties should con-tinue to surpass those given by any other hostess in the city, Lady Leatheringham had but one other interest in life. That was her son, Edward Fenley, the present marquess.

Despite that young gentleman's exalted title, his friends long ago had dubbed him Neddy the Noddy. Tonight, Neddy stood at her side. Although he fancied himself as a very Pink of the *ton,* he had as little fashion sense as his mother. He was arrayed in evening dress almost as fantastic as Albert's, except that he did not wear high heels. His poundage made them too uncomfortable. The height and stiffness of his shirt points threatened a jawline so fleshy that a few more years would see it develop into jowls. A second chin already appeared above the top of his cravat. Despite this and the great number of rings and fobs he wore—for he was as fond of jewelry as was his mother—his expression, which was one of complete if somewhat sleepy amiability, drew Lucinda to him at once.

He greeted Mark with the warmth of an old and dear friend, exchanged a few pleasantries with the other two, then glanced at the crowd upon the stairs. Seeing that it was beginning to thin slightly, he said, "That is my duty for the evening."

"Now, Edward—"

"No, Mama, do not expect me to dance with any of your finds. You know I do not care to dance and would doubtless step all over their feet. Come along to the card room, Mark. You know the game will not be much—it never is—but it is better than nothing."

Mark nodded acceptance. He could not be expected to keep his eye upon the chit every moment of the evening, and it was doubtful that she would fall into trouble under the wing of her ladyship. Besides, it would be thought odd if he were to refuse his friend's request in order to bear-lead the captain.

"Do you care to join us, Captain?" the host asked. He had felt an instant friendship for the young stranger.

"I wish to introduce the captain to some friends of mine, Edward," his mother said reprovingly. She had accepted his defection from her receiving line, but he must not be allowed to monopolize the interesting newcomer.

Neddy nodded, unsurprised. "I feared that was what you had in mind. Be warned, Captain, you are for it. You will meet all the dowds. But I trust you will be willing to join us later."

Lucinda agreed, watching Neddy and Mark go off arm in arm. Their appearance was as different as their positions and their tastes in dress. Neddy reached only to Mark's shoulder and his own shoulders were so narrow as to emphasize the thickness of the rest of his body. Albert, on the other hand, was completely ignored by the two men.

Wounded, Albert declared in his haughtiest tones, "Having heard much of the excellence of your parties, my lady, I find

myself surprised that your list of guests should include servants."

Lucinda gasped. How dare her cousin be so rude as to criti-
cize their hostess? And to her face?

"My guest list includes whomever I wish to invite," the marchioness told him with equal hauteur. "If I should decide to
invite thieves or beggars, my other guests—even the Princes—
would welcome them. However, if you are referring to Mark
Warne—"

"I am." Albert's head nodded tersely between the shirt
points.

"—Then you should know, young man, that *you* are present
tonight only because Mark sent word, asking if he might bring
you and your cousin. He is my son's dearest friend and a great
favorite of mine, as well as of many of my guests. And he is
far from being a servant. Although he handles many of Lord
Brayling's affairs, he is in fact his employer's cousin."

"Do you mean to say that he goes so far as to claim kinship
with my grandfather?" Albert's sneer was pronounced. "Certainly, you have not been taken in by that tale. I had understood
he does not even know his rightful name—that his father was
a foundling."

Lady Leatheringham laughed so heartily that her turban,
overweighted by its many feathers, tumbled from her head. Lucinda picked it up and returned it to her. Unconcerned by the
mishap, her ladyship replaced it more crookedly than before,
while a number of guests looked in their direction to see what
had so amused her.

"Mark's father a foundling? What fustian! His grandmother
and Brayling's father were twins. Amelia was the elder of the
two by a matter of some moments. If she had been a man, Mark
would be the earl today."

"Then why should he have told us such a Banbury story as
that?" Lucinda asked, a bit vexed to realize that the man had
been making a game of them. "If he is our cousin, why not say
so? And he does use the name of Warne—was his grandfather
also a relative of ours?"

"Not at all. I believe that his name was Scanning, or was
it Scantling? Some sort of odd name as that. Perfectly good
name, of course, but Amelia was always overproud of being
a Warne. She was extremely high in the instep and always con-

sidered it unfair that *she* could not inherit the title. She would not use her husband's name, although I suppose she had a right to feel as she did."

Lucinda shook her head. What other secrets was she to learn about her family? And why had Thomas not known about Mark Warne's parentage?

"Anyhow, she persuaded—more likely bullocked—her husband into talking the name of Warne. Mark has always thought it a shameful thing for his grandfather to have done and, when he was a boy, was forever telling everyone that he did not know who he was."

"That must have caused some comments."

"Not too many. Anyhow we all thought he had been cured of doing so long ago. I can't imagine why he did so—perhaps to keep you on your toes.

His reason was far otherwise, Lucinda thought, but kept silent. It was because *he* thought them both contemptible and did not wish to own to a relationship with them.

"Mark retains the surname Warne only out of respect for his Lordship. Of course, after yourself, Captain, he is heir to the title."

Lucinda was startled to hear herself referred as such. She almost giggled at the thought of herself being addressed as earl. She thought, too, that her ladyship was mistaken. Although she was not familiar with English law, after Lucien the next heir would be her father's nephew, Albert, she reckoned; after all, he was one degree closer than Mark. However, the thought of Albert as Lord Brayling made her choke back a scornful laugh.

"Still, a man who finds it necessary to work for his living cannot be expected to be acceptable as a member of the *ton,*" Albert was commenting. That did bring a laugh from Lucinda, much as she would have preferred to slap his face for his cutting remarks. Although Mark Warne had treated them coolly, it was outside of enough to hold it against him that he must work.

"I fear you must include me in that category, cousin," she retorted. "You must remember I have been earning my living in the army for several years. And it is quite possible that I shall be forced to earn my living for the rest of my life."

Albert put up his bejewelled glass and surveyed his cousin,

much in the manner of one viewing a strange—and unwanted—specimen of animal life.

"Oh, there is no doubt, *cousin,* that *you* will be forced to do
so," he said contemptuously and, without excusing himself, tee-
tered off in search of more congenial company.

"His vulgarity is insufferable," her ladyship said angrily. "I
have told Sophia Turngren she was a featherhead to indulge
him as she does. But will she listen to good advice? She will
not, so he grows worse by the day. In the future I shall refuse
to have the puppy under my roof even for Brayling's sake."

"Please, you must not blame my grandfather for my cousin's
behavior," Lucinda begged. "I gather his lordship knows little
more about Albert than he does about me. We are both to be
inspected by him."

"And I can certainly understand his reason for doing so."
The marchioness gave Lucinda's cheek an affectionate pat. "I
do not think Brayling seriously ill, but one can understand his
wish to meet his heirs. You do not resemble your grandfather
much, though. He was an extremely handsome man in his
youth. I seem to recall that he was even taller than Mark, although I now doubt that he truly was so. You will find, as you
grow older, you often remember things as better than they
were."

Lucinda murmured that her ladyship must have some years
to go before she could be considered to have reached that stage.
The compliment earned her another pat from the marchioness.

"But he had an air that would sweep every woman off her
feet. I am not exaggerating *that.* I can tell you all of female London must have been in love with him at one time. But I think
you may have his spirit. A brave soldier, too, from what I have
heard about you. And certainly Brayling can find no fault with
your manners. I shall tell him that, you may be certain. Now,
permit me to present you to some of our guests."

Lucinda allowed herself to be led about the ballroom, making her bows to a number of the people present, many of them
ladies of Lady Leatheringham's generation. Occasionally, however, a lady would have in tow a young girl who looked hopefully at the handsome stranger. They must be persons of some
importance, but their names were unfamiliar to Lucinda. Only
one name remained in her mind and that one because the dowager said laughingly, "Now, if you were a young female, my boy,

you would certainly be shaking in your shoes at meeting this lady. She is Lady Jersey, one of the Patronesses of Almack's."

"Almack's?" Lucinda inquired politely.

"Lud, boy, you have been far away, have you not?"

"You may forget, your ladyship, that I have never been in London before."

"That is right, I had forgot. But I should have thought the name would have reached you wherever you were. For young ladies, receiving a voucher to Almack's is second only to being presented at court. And I have no doubt that some of them would put it first. Do you not think so, Sally?"

"It is only right that they should do so," Lady Jersey retorted somewhat complacently. "For we are more particular about whom we receive than are Their Majesties."

"However, it is only the young ladies who must be so fearful," Lady Leatheringham soothed. "A handsome young man like yourself—for I must say you *are* handsome, even if you do not resemble Lord Brayling—should find the door open to him, should he not? Sally, this is Lord Brayling's heir."

Neither of the ladies heard her mumbled acknowledgment, for both of them were occupied in trying to dominate the conversation. It was possible that they did not even hear each other.

"We shall be happy to have you, Captain Warne, as long as you appear in proper dress *and* before eleven of the clock, of course. *No* one"—here she glared fiercely—"is admitted after that hour." Lucinda bowed over the woman's hand again, and they took their leave.

As they passed out of Lady Jersey's hearing, the marchioness said, "Almack's, you know, has been named the Marriage Mart by the *ton.*"

"Is that not an odd name?" Lucinda ventured.

"Not at all, since most of the eligible young ladies are to be found there. A voucher may be obtained only from Sally or one of the other Patronesses. And they are very strict about the behavior of those who attend. Which is laughable, when one considers Sally's involvement with . . . although I believe that is ended now. But people do remember such things. And Sally has had her other flirts, as well. As for some of the other Patronesses—well, enough to say that they do not set the proper example which they should. Anyhow, the slightest indiscretion would be cause enough to close the doors forever against the unfortunate girl."

And masquerading about London in her brother's clothing would certainly be thought more than a "slight indiscretion," Lucinda told herself. How horrified all these good ladies would be if they learned the truth. She must make certain they never discovered the ruse. Perhaps Lucien would not come to England for several years—long enough so memories about her looks would be dim.

"You have made a conquest there," Lady Leatheringham was continuing in a laughing undertone. "Not that I ever doubted it, and I hope you do not take too much credit for it."

"Oh, I do not."

"That is well, although you are a handsome young man and Sally is known for her fondness for personable well-behaved young men. Although I suppose I ought not to say this to you, I have heard that she also likes some who are not so well behaved. I do not mean rude ones like your cousin Albert. He would never enter the doors of Almack's more than once. In fact, if he behaved as he has done tonight, they would have no hesitation in asking him to leave. The fact that he is Lord Brayling's grandson would be no defence.

"But, as Sally says, as long as you come in proper dress, which means knee breeches, of course, and on time, Almack's will always be open to you. You should know that Sally Jersey's friends call her 'Silence,' not to her face, of course, although I would not doubt she knows of it, because the word is entirely unknown to her."

Lucinda smiled at that, having noted that Lady Jersey, for all her vaunted talkativeness, had trouble slipping a single word into Lady Leatheringham's conversation.

"Now," her ladyship was asking, "would you prefer to join my son's friends in the card room, or would you care to meet some of the young ladies? I hope it is that, for a number of them have been casting out lures in your direction since your arrival—and I do not believe you have even noticed the poor things. It is shameful for you to ignore them so."

Although he was far from being a gamester, Lucien enjoyed a wager at times, but his sister was well aware that Mark Warne might be reporting whether "Lucien" was acting gentlemanly toward the debutantes. Wondering which choice she ought to make to remain in character as Captain Warne, she glanced about the room.

Candlelight glowing on a mass of golden curls drew her gaze to the far corner of the room where, surrounded by a number of young men, was a lady she thought she had seen before. A second look made her certain, and Lucinda grinned. She had met this "charmer" on her journey across the Channel.

As she had walked along the deck, gazing at the flow of the water, this girl had come by and dropped her reticule, spilling its contents at Lucinda's feet. Recognizing the action as the bid for attention that it was, Lucinda gathered up her things and gave them back to her as a gentleman might have done. They had not exchanged more than half a dozen sentences, the girl's words almost brazenly flirtatious, when an old she-dragon of a duenna had come upon them, snatching the girl away and bear-jawing the stranger for his encroaching behavior.

The girl, who now quite clearly had half the bloods of London at her feet, had not been able then to resist the temptation to add another to her list of conquests. It might prove amusing to pay her back in her own coin.

"There is one I should like to meet, my lady—the one who looks exactly like an angel." She almost groaned aloud at her own playacting. "That golden-haired beauty in the blue gown."

The marchioness followed the direction of the captain's gaze and began to laugh. "You have an excellent eye for a pretty girl, my boy—quite as good as your grandfather's in his youth. Stella Proctor is our reigning collector of hearts, so be warned and do not lose yours to her. However, I feel it is unlikely that you will have a chance there. Her aunt is doubtless hanging out for a duke, since none of the Royals wishes a wife at present. On the other hand, you *are* heir to an earldom, so perhaps you have a chance after all."

"But I merely said that I should like to *meet* her," the captain protested.

Lady Leatheringham laughed again and led Lucinda across the room to make the presentation. After the introductions had been performed, Lady Leatheringham declared, "Miss Proctor and her aunt have only recently returned to England, having dared to spend some time in Paris."

"They are indeed brave to have made such a journey in these times," Lucinda said, adding gallantly, "I am devastated that

I did not know of their journey, for I came that way and would have been greatly pleased to be able to offer my escort to the ladies. We might even have crossed the Channel on the same boat—and I was deprived of the opportunity of meeting them."

The Beauty blushed and dropped her fan in confusion. A number of young gentlemen stepped forward to retrieve it, but Lucinda caught it up, hiding a grin of pure mischief.

It was clear the girl feared that the stranger might say something about their previous meeting and bring censure upon her. Lucinda, however, merely returned the fan and begged permission to lead Miss Proctor out for the waltz just forming. She had no doubt of her ability to play the man's part in any dance.

"Oh no, not a waltz." Stella blushed again, this time with mortification. How could she explain to this new young admirer that, although the waltz was now permitted by the Patronesses of Almack's, her aunt frowned upon this modern dance which allowed a gentleman to hold a lady in so familiar a manner. "I—"

"*All* of Miss Proctor's dances are taken," said a wrathful voice in Lucinda's ear. She turned to face a fair-haired young man, several inches taller than she. There was considerably greater width to his shoulders as well, and his face was one most females would consider handsome were it not darkened by a scowl which matched his tone.

Although Lucinda was certain that the scowl was meant for her alone, Miss Proctor appeared to feel its force as well. In a faint voice, she made Captain Warne known to Lord Byrne. Lucinda gathered the impression that the girl was undecided if she should be proud or resentful of her cavalier's demonstration of proprietorship toward her.

"Perhaps another time, then," Lucinda said, bowing and lightly grasping the lady's hand.

As she did so, she felt the Beauty's fingers pressing hers ever so slightly, conveying an invitation which she apparently did not dare to speak in Lord Byrne's presence. Then, as if dismissing the crowd about her, she allowed her irate suitor to lead her away to await a more modest dance.

Although she was unable to hear them, Lucinda could see the young man speaking, rather fiercely she thought from his expression. Miss Proctor's fan was waving with an agitated force.

"Poor Byrne," Lady Leatheringham commented, having waited nearby to observe the scene. "Heels over head, of course, but he is wasting his time there, although I do not doubt the girl has a fondness for him. Hasn't a feather to fly with—and you may be certain Stella's aunt will put paid to that quickly enough if he should ever declare himself. I wonder that she has not forbidden the girl even to stand up with him, but in view of Byrne's lineage, which is better than her own, that might be too much of an insult even for her to attempt. So, as I told you, your luck is out. At least, for this evening, for you will not wish to brawl with Byrne, the young hothead. Shall I find another young lady for you to partner?"

"Thank you, Lady Leatheringham, not tonight, I think. With your kind permission, I shall join the card room group." Lucinda bowed and turned away, hiding her laughter until she had reached the hallway, out of sight of her hostess.

She knew she had fooled the young Beauty and the others who had been watching them. If Polite Society resembled the army in any way, tomorrow's most prominent *on dit* would be that the new arrival in the city had eyes only for Stella Proctor—which was exactly what Lucinda had intended.

It would be a great help to her masquerade to be counted in the Beauty's train.

Chapter Four

LUCINDA WAS ABLE to control her laughter before entering the card room, where the young marquess waved and called for her to join him. Along with Mark and several other friends, Neddy was playing hazard for the low stakes which were all that his mother would allow—a ruling the guests accepted with reluctance and only because of the other advantages of attending the marchioness' routs.

Had she been given a choice, Lucinda would have preferred to take a place at some other table. She had made up her mind that it would be best for her to stay as far from her grandfather's secretary as possible. Still, she could hardly insult her host, so she moved to the place Neddy made for her beside himself. Having been taught the principles of hazard by Lucien and Thomas during her tomboy years, Lucinda did not doubt her ability to hold her own here. In an honest game such as this one would certainly be, luck counted for more than skill.

Her fortune with the dice varied, first in, then out, then in again. At the end of several hours of play, she found that she was ahead by two guineas and a shilling. She could imagine Lucien's comrades' scorn for the tameness of the game.

Soon thereafter, Mark excused himself. From the play he had watched, he could see that the chit handled the dice as if long accustomed to doing so. In fact, she was more skillfull than most of the men. Had she spent some time in a gaming house, he wondered? After all, they knew nothing of her past. Would her brother have permitted such a thing?

At any rate, he need not hesitate to leave her with this group;

she would be safe enough with this low level of play. However, she must still return home alone. It was reckless enough for a man to walk the streets unaccompanied; if someone should accost her, she could scarcely defend herself.

Resting a friendly hand upon her shoulder—he could have sworn that she flinched when he touched her—he suggested that she should take a chair when she left.

"You are unfamiliar with London, Captain," he said, "and would not know of the street gangs which lie in wait for anyone who appears to have money."

Although grateful for his consideration, she replied lightly, as Lucien would have done, "Every city has them, sir, I am certain."

"Doubtless, but even a soldier should be wary." Mark kept his tone light, but inwardly he seethed. Was the chit ignoring his advice just to keep up this charade?

"Rest easy, Mark," Neddy said. "You can trust us to see that your young cousin is safe from any of the street ruffians—although he may go home a great deal poorer than he is at present."

Mark laughed and tousled Neddy's carefully arranged hair, bringing a protest from the young man.

"If *these* wolves set out to fleece you, lad," he said to Lucinda, "I have no doubt that you will have to summon me—to help you carry home what you have won from them."

His hand rested lightly on her shoulder, this time in a gesture she found comforting, and he exited amid a chorus of friendly insults from those around the table. Mark was reassured; she would not be allowed to venture out alone, and it was unlikely that these fellows would go far beyond the line. If she should hear a word or two that shocked her, that would do her no lasting harm.

After the dice had gone round the table a few more times, the game began to tire. One player after another left to go on to Brooks' or Watiers' or to one of their favorite hells where they could play for higher stakes. As Mark had predicted, Lucinda was the evening's winner, although the gains had been trifling. Madeira was brought in, and the bottle was passed from hand to hand many times.

No one paid attention to the amount the others were drinking, so Lucinda was able to pretend that she was refilling her glass often, while actually not drinking more than a few swallows. She did not trust the potency of the wine and, in fact, did not like the taste of it. The men must not suspect this, however, if she was to keep up her masquerade.

"By the way, Captain," one of the drinkers remarked, "I have a friend who was in your company on the Peninsula. Name of Farlow."

"Farlow?" Lucinda pretended to think. *Had* Lucien had an acquaintance by that name? She had not met him and could not recall Lucien's mentioning the name, but she did not know all the soldiers with whom her brother came in contact.

"You should remember him, I am certain. Of course, he was not there for long. Sent home when he was wounded in battle. Doubtless mentioned for bravery."

"Oh, that Farlow—good man as I recall. There were several fellows of that name, and I did not know at first which you meant." She was determined to avoid this man; even if he were not a close friend of her brother's, he would be able to recognize at once that she was not the captain.

"The two of you should meet soon. I know you must have much to talk about."

"Doubtless." At least, it seemed the man was not here; she was safe for the moment.

Others began to demur that the captain would not wish to think always of battles when there were more important matters in life. The conversation about the table veered around to the favorite subject of the gentlemen: the merits, or the lack of them, of their favorite ladybirds. Lucinda kept her face carefully schooled. This was the sort of thing Thomas had warned her about. Rather than being shocked by what she heard, however, Lucinda was mentally storing up the choicest bits to slip into conversation with Lucien or Thomas at some later time. She almost laughed out loud at the thought.

However, after several minutes of warm comments, Lucinda became bored. To change the subject, she caused a diversion by upsetting her glass, spilling the wine across the table. This action created a great deal of amusement among her new friends.

"Surely the captain cannot be disguised this early in the evening," accused Mr. Redding. He was as match-thin as Neddy was plump, but with a nose of a size which made his friends frequently express their wonder that its weight did not cause him to lose his balance. "What's to become of the country if her soldiers cannot manage to hold their drinks?"

A great number of similar comments came from the others, while Lucinda laughingly protested that the upset had been merely an accident and that she was not even slightly above par, and her new friends continued to insist that she must be. When that subject had been talked over until the jest had worn thin, Mr. Maupin returned to the one nearer his heart.

"Tell you fellowth what," he said, his lisp caused by his protruding teeth. "We mutht find the captain a Thyprian of hith own—only dethent thing for uth to do for a thtranger to the thity. Plenty of lovely oneth to be had, my boy. Jutht do not choothe my Ariel or I thall have to challenge. Thilly name, Ariel, ain't it? But the's a thweet girl, for all of that."

The others, some of them well into their cups by this time, were prepared to set upon Ferdy's suggestion without a waste of time. However, Lucinda had not doubted that some subject of this sort might arise during her stay in London and was prepared to counter their offers.

"My thanks for your kindness," she replied quickly. "At the present moment, I fear I should find your English ladybirds too tame for my taste." Immediately Lucinda regretted her response and hoped her face was not burning.

"What do you mean—they would be too tame?" demanded Mr. Atwood, a sandy-haired young gentleman with bulging eyes and a receding chin. He had imbibed just enough spirits to make him feel quarrelsome. Ignoring him, Lucinda refilled her glass once more, took a sip, and looked at the others with what she hoped would be considered a leer.

"Not all of our time on the Peninsula," she told them, "was spent in fighting, if you must know. For instance, I can recall Ynez—"

The *señorita* she mentioned was actually the daughter of a most respectable family. In fact, Lucinda had met her at a dinner which was given by Lucien's commander. Yet, as she described the flashing black eyes with their incredibly long lashes, the skin like velvet, and the fiery temper the young lady sometimes displayed, Lucinda managed—without saying anything indiscreet, but making suggestive pauses here and there—to give the others the idea that they were being told about a particularly desirable bit of goods.

She consoled herself with the thought that there was not a chance that any of them would ever meet the lady she described, nor would they have recognized her if they did so. Fortunately, neither would Ynez ever know that her character had been so maligned.

To her relief, Neddy and all his friends declared that their new-found acquaintance was bang up to the nines, and when she finally was able to bid her hostess a good night, several of them insisted upon seeing her to her grandfather's house. It was rather a ragged procession, as all of them had imbibed much more than she had done. Lucinda wondered what help they would be if they were accosted by any of the ruffians against whom she had been warned.

Inside, she found Thomas awaiting her and demanding to be told everything that had occurred.

"It was a wonderful evening," Lucinda declared, throwing herself into a chair and stretching luxuriously. "I have never enjoyed myself so immensely. Let Lucien remain in the Peninsula if that is what he prefers. I shall be happy to take his place here forever."

"I knew something of this kind would happen." Thomas shook his head. He continued to growl while he helped Lucinda out of her coat and boots.

At last she cried, "Oh, go to bed. I can do this without your help."

When she finally was beneath the covers, a gentle smile curved her lips before she fell to sleep.

Rising early the next morning, Lucinda determined to explore Brayling House. Had she been given her way, she would have spent many days examining her grandfather's house, for she had fallen in love with the great place. She couldn't wait to discuss everything with Lucien when she returned home. It was annoying that she could not write to tell him how wonderfully she was managing this masquerade, but she could scarcely ask her grandfather to frank a letter to Captain Warne in the Peninsula, when Captain Warne was supposed to be in London and living in his house. All she could do was to store up memories.

Going about the house, she tried to imagine how it must have been when her father and Aunt Sophia were young. Had the children played at hide-and-seek among the many rooms? Had Philip often slid down that sweep of stair rail which tempted her just now—a temptation she put firmly aside as unfitting to one in Lucien's position. She was certain that Aunt Sophia had never slid down bannisters. Undoubtedly, Sophia had been raised a lady and had not been allowed to romp as Lucinda had done under Thomas' strict but masculine tutelage.

At the back of the house was a huge ballroom. Its furniture and chandeliers were shrouded in holland cloth, for it had not been used since the night of Sophia's engagement to Mr. Turngren. Peeping under some of the covers, Lucinda tried to picture the ballroom as it must have appeared then, with its many candles ablaze and with people crowding the room as they had done last night at Lady Leatheringham's.

Perhaps, though, there had not been quite so many people in the room as at Lady Leatheringham's, for in those days the ladies' gowns would have had large panniers and would have taken much more room. The gentlemen's clothing too would have been fuller, with frock coats whose skirts were boned, and with swords at their sides—if they wore swords at dress balls.

Lucinda could almost see how they must have looked, moving gracefully about the rooms in their old-fashioned clothing and powdered hair. She could never have seen them like that, of course, but if Papa and her grandfather had not quarrelled, she and Lucien might have grown up in this house.

"But then, what would Lucien and I have been like, I wonder, with a proper English mother instead of our flighty *Maman* and our dear Thomas?" She had addressed the question to a swathed harp, then jumped at the sound of a voice.

One of the footmen, she believed this one was Charles, stood in the doorway. With an air—not completely hidden—of having run her to earth after a long search, he stated that a gentleman had called upon the captain and was waiting below.

Wondering who, among the new acquaintances she had formed, would have risen at this hour, she followed him and was surprised to find Neddy Fenley awaiting her. She would have thought that he, at least, would have been too indolent to be abroad at this early hour.

The young marquess confirmed this by saying at once, "Glad to find you about at this time of the morning, Captain. Most of my friends ain't, of course. But I suppose the military gets accustomed to such things, which makes me happy that I ain't in it."

Lucinda had to choke back a laugh at the thought of the young man attempting to live an army life. "I wouldn't be up myself," he continued. "Gave m'man quite a shock by coming out at this time. But remembered you said last night that you had a fancy for a rig and a pair. After we left you, someone— can't remember who it was, but it don't matter—remembered that Nat Morely's been knocked into horsenails and that his chestnuts will be up for sale at Tatt's today. It's been kept mum so far—at least, I think so—so if we go early, we should have a chance at them."

"Thank you for telling me this, but . . . I do not wish to insult you, my lord—"

"Call me Neddy. Everyone does."

"Very well, Neddy. But what I wished to ask was if you know anything about horseflesh?" She was eyeing him sceptically. Merely because he was dressed like a macaroni did not mean he did not know his cattle, she was aware. But somehow she doubted his wisdom.

"Not a bit in the world," Neddy said cheerfully. He was too well accustomed to having his friends consider him a bufflehead to take offence at the question.

"Well, then . . ."

"But all London knows about these chestnuts. Regular sixteen-mile-an-hour tits. At least half the fellows I know would beggar themselves for a chance to own them. Shouldn't mind having them myself. But if I did, I would have to enlarge my stables or get rid of some of the cattle I have now, and I don't wish to do either of these things."

"Well, I have been told that I have a good eye for such things, but to be doubly certain that we have made a good buy, we shall take Thomas Abbott with us. He knows more about cattle than L— than anyone I can think of."

Tattersall's was almost as well known on the continent as it was in London. Every visitor to the City who cared anything about horses carried home stories of the place, certain to make fellow horse lovers envious. Richard Tattersall, fired with the wish to attract the most important members of the gentry to his establishment, had caused a sensation by eliminating the drinking bar which previously had been considered to be a necessary part of horse racing.

In place of the common bar, he had set up a beautifully furnished, chandelier-lit room so that gentlemen might feel that they were in the home of some affluent friend. He had also ruled that only the best of horseflesh would pass through his hand. Fortunes were frequently pledged for some of the prime bits of blood and bone he handled, and more than one buck had found himself in the River Tick after settling day at Tatt's.

On certain occasions, the Prince Regent might be found here with some of his racing friends, emptying a glass in honor of some favorite animal. The near-scandal which had caused him to shun the Newmarket races had in no way diminished the Royal interest in the sport. Today royalty was not in evidence, but Lucinda was so absorbed in the goings-on she did not miss his presence.

The marquess' sacrifice in leaving his bed so early was in vain. By the time the trio arrived at Tattersall's, the vaunted chestnuts had been taken away by their new owner. In fact, so many gentlemen had crowded into the famous establishment to bid that the pair had sold for a price far exceeding Morely's debts.

"But I can tell you this much," Neddy commented happily when he heard the news, "all of us know Morely too well for that. He just ain't the kind who is going to worry his noddle about tradesman's bills. Most likely he'll go on throwing them into the fire as he always does and put the lot down on the first race horse or prize fighter that takes his fancy."

"And go home by beggar's bush after all," Thomas commented.

Neddy gazed at him in delight. "Didn't know you was acquainted with Morely—sure I never heard him mention your name. But that's exactly the way he will end up. You can lay your blunt on that. He picks the wrong 'uns every time—absolutely not a bit of judgment about horses or fighters."

He paused for a moment, thinking about what he had said, then added, "Of course, my luck is no better than his—I always seem to pick the wrong 'uns, too. But I can afford to take my losses and Morely cannot. A man shouldn't play if he cannot afford to lose, but Morely will do it. Keeps thinking that this is the time he will win. It never is."

Lucinda exchanged a speaking glance with Thomas, well aware that he would dismiss the young marquess as a cabbage-head. She supposed it was true, but for her part, she found him a pleasant sort of companion. He was much like some of the young officers whom she had met in Lucien's company, and she thought he would prove to be an unexceptional friend, unlike some of the bolder members of his crowd.

The trio inspected one lot after another, Neddy proving that he had told no more than the truth when he owned he was lacking in judgment. He advocated the purchase of a showy pair of such doubtful quality that even their handlers displayed no enthusiasm for them, making Lucinda wonder by what sort of accident had they been admitted to an establishment which prided itself upon offering only the most excellent animals to be found.

"No, Neddy, I do not think those are for me," she told him, kindly refraining from pointing out their defects. Lucinda's heart was nearly lost to a beautiful and well-appointed pair of matched bays. When Thomas advised her to pass them by for a pair of greys, however, she cheerfully agreed to do as he suggested. The bays were good, she was certain, but she had never known Thomas to be in error about horseflesh.

Neddy seemed uncomfortable with Thomas' interference, so Lucinda drew the young man aside. "You must not mind about Thomas Abbott, Neddy," she said softly. "He has been almost a father to me since my father died, and there are times when he forgets that I am no longer a grubby brat."

Although Neddy still appeared doubtful, Lucinda decided that more explanations would serve only to confuse him further.

When they went to Longacre in search of a rig, however, she would not allow Thomas to advise her. Her mind had been set upon the purchase of a racing curricle, for she knew she would never have another chance to own anything so dashing. Ladies—unless they were like Lady Lade, who was notoriously fast—did not drive curricles.

The moment her gaze lit upon the gleaming black curricle with its huge yellow wheels, she knew that it was exactly the vehicle Lucien would have chosen above all others had he been standing in her place. Moreover, she prided herself upon being able to drive any rig her brother could handle.

Thomas accepted her decision, knowing her abilities, but Neddy looked upon the smart vehicle with scepticism.

"Phaeton would be a deal safer to drive," he hazarded, aware of how frequently the two-wheeled curricles came to grief due to the recklessness or inexperience of their drivers. He drove a phaeton and felt that such a vehicle should be sporting enough for anyone. "Not a high-perch phaeton, of course," he warned. "They're inclined to be too top-heavy, if you ask me." Also, although he did not wish to own it to the captain, he found it difficult to get his bulk into the high seat.

"What you are saying is that you think I shall be unable to handle this," Lucinda retorted, stung at having her driving skill doubted. "Come along and I'll show you what I can do." As the marquess showed signs of hesitation, she added, "Hen-hearted, are you?"

"Not at all," Neddy protested with as much dignity as he could manage, knowing the other was right. "Just ain't dressed for driving." This was an obvious untruth, as he had been driving them about all morning. If he hoped that the captain would allow him to escape with such a thin excuse, he was soon shown the error of such thoughts.

"If you feel the need to change, I am certain that you will be able to do so in an hour," Lucinda told him without pity. "I shall drive Thomas home and call for you then—that is, unless you should suddenly remember that you have an urgent engagement elsewhere."

She had allowed a hint of contempt to creep into her voice, and Neddy, thinking that his new acquaintance was certainly quick to take offence, but not wishing to be thought a coward, said with an enthusiasm he was far from feeling, "Nothing I'd rather do than accompany you. But make it ninety minutes. Sometimes takes me half an hour to arrange my cravat."

He reminded himself that while there were a number of his friends who had wrecked their curricles, there were at least as many others who had driven for months without accident. The less lucky ones, he reflected, were often jug-bitten. He did not think Warne was the type to dip too deeply, at least during the day, but he would have to hope that the other remained sober and that he was not the kind of a driver who liked to show off his skill in some extravagant manner.

Since Lucinda had gone out this morning with the intention of making a purchase, she was already in driving gear (as was Neddy, she thought, hiding a laugh at his obvious fear of riding in her curricle). As soon as her greys were brought around and harnessed to the curricle, she tooled her way about the City with Thomas at her side. Both of them were well pleased at the competent manner in which she handled the ribbons.

"They are perfect," she said enthusiastically, as she set her mentor down at her grandfather's house. "You were right not to allow me to buy the other pair, Thomas, and I thank you for doing so."

"You would not have been disappointed in them, Lucinda, for you have a good eye for cattle, as I have told you. These are just a shade the better pair, which is what Lucien would wish to have."

"I, too."

He was happy at her praise, though he knew it was deserved, but kept her back a moment to warn, "Do not be up to any fool tricks now. You handle your cattle as well as a man—better than many—but that does not mean you should try to see how many wheels you can graze just to throw a fright into that young ninnyhammer."

"I will be good," Lucinda promised, just as she had been saying to him for more than twenty years. However, he could see that her eyes were sparkling as she spoke. Watching her guide the pair expertly out of sight, he would not have wagered a groat that she would not have tumbled into some sort of scrape before the day was out, and he sent a silent plea to Philip's shade to keep a watch on his daughter.

Chapter
Five

THOMAS' GLOOM WAS not to lift. When he entered the house, the earl's secretary was coming down the stairs. The man seemed sharp, and Thomas was certain that if anyone in the house could pierce Lucinda's disguise, it would be Mark.

"What have you done with your master?" Mark demanded. The secretary looked at Thomas as if he were still a groom.

"Uh—" Caught off guard, Thomas almost referred to Lucinda as "she." "*He* has gone for a drive about the City with a friend, showing off the curricle *he* has just purchased."

"Curricle!" What could the girl be thinking of to attempt to handle a vehicle of that sort? And why hadn't this man, who appeared to have some influence with her, prevented her from getting it? Driving a curricle took great skill; they were easily overset. "What friend?" he demanded.

Why should it matter to him? Thomas wondered. His duty was solely to report on how the cousins spent their funds. Could their choice of friends matter so much? "One of them he met last night, I suppose. Called himself Neddy or something of the sort."

Neddy Fenley! He almost groaned aloud. That shatter-brained young nobleman was no match for the crazy chit, but at least he could be trusted not drag her into any of the gambling hells. Even so, Mark had qualms. If Neddy had chosen their destination, it was definitely not the sort of place a female should attend.

What if she were to swoon? he wondered; in such a situation even a man could be affected. Her secret could be discovered quickly. Then—scandal! Brushing Thomas aside, Mark ordered his horse. He was off before the other could wonder what was wrong.

By the time Lucinda arrived, Neddy had convinced himself that the captain would prove to be a trustworthy whip. Which gave him time to concentrate on more important matters—his clothes. He had donned his new coat whose multiplicity of capes nearly doubled his size. Since it was a bright yellow in color, it gave him something of the appearance of a giant pumpkin at her side, especially since his large bulk made it nearly impossible for him to move. It was Neddy's first opportunity to wear the garment and the fact that he could wear it today did much to make him forget his apprehension about riding in his new friend's curricle.

Aware that she had practically bullocked the young marquess into accompanying her, Lucinda drove with extra care, and even Neddy was able to enjoy the capable manner in which she handled the greys. He found himself envying the smart way she caught the thong of her whip without taking her eyes off the road ahead. The only time he had attempted such a move, he had caught the thong in a tree branch and nearly pulled himself out of the vehicle.

It was a pleasant afternoon, but driving without a destination began to pall upon the restless Neddy. At last, he said, "Know where we can find a mill this afternoon, Lucien—dashed if that ain't too much of a name for my tongue."

"My friends call me Lu." No one had done so except her brother, but the shortened form seemed equally suited to a man. And it was a name to which she could answer more readily than to Lucien's.

"Lu—That's more the thing, I should say. Never have been one to care for those foreign names, if you don't object to my telling you as much—and a French name, at that, at this time. But then, of course, you cannot help your name—but Lu is better."

Lucinda was beginning to think her young friend had inherited his mother's propensity for chattering as well as her bulk.

"Ever been to a mill?" the marquess continued.

"No," she said quickly.

"I mean, in England?"

"That was what I meant, of course," Lucinda replied, happy that Neddy's thinking processes did not run as rapidly as his tongue. Otherwise, he might have noticed her slip. It was unlikely that a young man of four and twenty had never seen a fight.

"Have heard several people say that this one will be the best since the time Gentleman Jackson met Mendoza. Don't suppose it will be, of course. They say that about every match that comes along, trying to stir up interest."

"Well, it would be useless, would it not, to hold a match if no one wished to see it?"

"That's right, of course. Never thought of it that way, but they have to draw a crowd. Doubt if any of the matches have been as good as that one was—or at least, not many of them. Didn't see it myself. Before my time, of course. Though I have been to the saloons often and have seen both of them spar with the Corinthians who think they are handy with their fives. A few of them are. Your cousin, for example."

"My cousin?" Lucinda could not visualize Albert's even going near a boxing saloon. That he would be able to stand up with a master was unbelievable.

Neddy laughed. "Forgot for a moment that you have two cousins. I meant Mark, not the young gabbler. Mark's a big man, but he handles himself well. Not many can beat him, not even those his size. But what I meant to say is that these two today ought to be evenly matched, and it should be an interesting fight. Care to come?"

His sister knew that Lucien would have agreed to attend a meeting of this sort without a moment of hesitation. He was an admirer of the sport and could be found at any prize fight, even a friendly match between two of the soldiers.

But this was one sport which Thomas had not included in her earlier education. Lucinda was not certain that she would have liked to see such a match, as she had heard that they could be quite cruel and gory affairs. Yet the fact that they were forbidden made her feel that she might have missed something exciting.

Females were strictly prohibited from attending such events, and no amount of coaxing on her part had persuaded her brother or Thomas to relax the rules in her case. Since Thomas had been willing enough to teach her such manly sports as shooting and fencing, she could only wonder about the ban. As Captain Warne, no one could object to her going.

"Yes, I think I should enjoy seeing a bout—in England. It might be interesting to compare the styles of fighting here and abroad." She must hope that no one would ask her to make a comparison.

"Daresay they're handled much the same as the ones you're accustomed to seeing. But at least, it will be something to do until dinnertime. Only hope that neither of them cripples the other. That ain't nice to watch, you know."

"Do you think that might happen?" Lucinda felt an odd lurch somewhere inside.

"Perhaps. Of course, there's usually eye gouging—you have to expect that—but sometimes a man is crippled for life. You know how it is. Some people say that's the chance a man must take if he plans to be a fighter, but I don't think it is necessary for them to go that far."

Eye gouging! Crippling for life! With every word Neddy spoke, Lucinda's enthusiasm for seeing the bout lessened. She had accepted the suggestion, however, so she could see no way of avoiding it now. She might argue that she was not dressed for such a sport, but even as she started to voice this thought, Neddy said, "No need for us to change, as these bouts are held in the country, and everything will be most informal. Daresay we'll find that most of our friends will be in riding gear."

"If that is the custom," she said with a shrug, then wished she had not made the gesture, for Neddy might consider it too French.

By this time, Lucinda would have welcomed any good excuse for avoiding the match, but she could scarcely plead off by saying that Thomas did not wish her to go. Any other excuse for changing her mind would be too feeble. Neddy was far from being needle-witted, but he would certainly wonder if she refused after having said that she wished to see the match.

He would scarcely believe that a soldier would be frightened off by the thought of seeing bloodshed or even of crippling. It would not do for her to offend him and lose the first friend she had made. If she did so, she did not doubt his friends would strike her off their lists as well. It was certain that his mother would do so and would place her in the same category as Albert. Lucinda had no choice but to go through with the arrangement.

Silently, she echoed Neddy's hope that no one would be seriously injured. Aside from the man's suffering, she was not certain what her reaction to such a scene would be. She must not do anything to reflect badly upon Lucien.

At Neddy's direction, she took the road which led them to Hampstead Heath, listening with interest to his tale of the many highwaymen who had used to flourish there, making miserable the lives of all travellers along this road. Just as Neddy was saying reassuringly, "But, of course, there are none such now," a large figure loomed up beside them.

Both Lucinda and Neddy gasped before they recognized Mark, astride a great white horse. Her first thought was what a magnificent animal that was—a perfect match for its rider. It would take a large animal to bear her giant of a cousin. A moment later, she wondered why he was there at all.

"You ought not to spring out of nowhere that way," Neddy accused. "We were just speaking of highwaymen—"

"And I appeared to be one?" Mark laughed. "Most of them, I should have thought, would have been small men who could more easily have disguised themselves when not on the road."

"I had not given the matter much thought," Lucinda said, still worrying about his sudden appearance.

"That may be," Neddy owned. "But when a man comes at you so suddenly—"

"You could hardly say my arrival was sudden, for I saw you some distance away." Since the pair was on this road, there was only one place they could be heading, and he was happy that he had found them before they joined others also on their way to the mill. His plan depended upon finding them alone. Eyeing the pair of greys appreciatively, he added, "You have excellent cattle."

"Yes, and Lu's handling of them is a treat," Neddy told him with enthusiasm. "Why not ride along with us, Mark, if you have not made other plans for the afternoon? We're going to watch the mill. Lu's never seen one."

"In this country," Lucinda added quickly.

Mark fought back his temper. He'd been right. The idiot girl had agreed to accompany Neddy to a mill. Did she have any idea of what she was about to see—two half-naked men beating one another to a bloody pulp? No matter how bold Lucinda was, she wouldn't enjoy that scene.

"Then I am sorry that you are to be disappointed," he said with every semblance of regret. "It appears that someone went to the authorities, and the mill has been put off—until a time when they can hold it safely."

Neddy exclaimed in disgust, and Lucinda did her best to echo his disappointment. Secretly, however, she was pleased. Neddy's remarks about eye-gouging and crippling still rang in her mind. She knew that Lucien would have welcomed the opportunity of seeing the match, no matter how gory, but she herself would prefer to drive about for some time, enjoying her new cattle and rig.

"We shall merely have to look about for something else to do in that case." She hoped that she sounded at a loss for an idea.

Mark came to her rescue. "Well, since you two have no other plans—and if the captain does not object—I should like a ride behind his new cattle." At least, he thought, she could get into no mischief with him at her side. Although he admitted he was afraid to see a female mishandle these prime animals.

"Why—yes, certainly. That is, if you have no objection, Neddy." She was not certain that she wanted the secretary's company, but she could see no way of refusing his request.

"Now, you know, Mark, there is no way the three of us can crowd into this vehicle," Neddy objected.

"Certainly not. If we were both as slim as the captain, it might be managed. As it is, you and I shall merely trade places. you may accompany us on Thunder."

"Oh—oh yes, if that is what you wish. But—if Lu don't mind bringing you home, I'll just ride him back to the stables and find something else to do." It seemed that Neddy was somewhat in awe of the great horse.

He climbed down from the curricle, and Mark took his place with an agility Lucinda thought surprising in a man of his great size. Standing beside the white horse, Neddy seemed about to change his mind, then mounted, waved a hand at the pair of them, and turned back toward the City.

Mark chuckled. "He could never be brought to own to it, of course, but I think my friend is a bit nervous at the idea of riding Thunder."

"I can understand that," Lucinda said, sympathetically. "A brute like that must be difficult to handle."

"Actually, he is as gentle as his owner."

She glanced at him, saw that he was grinning at her, and grinned back. "Yes—that was exactly what I meant. A gentle man who goes about smashing people's heads together."

"Only threatening to do so. And you must own that I had provocation."

"Perhaps, but you could not expect me to stand back from a wager, could you?"

He shook his head, recalling how she had stood upon the stairs, her chin outthrust, matching her cousin's mocking tone with her own.

"If you would like to take the next road to the right, there are several small villages along it," he said. And they would not encounter the others who were bound for the mill, which had *not* been cancelled. "I gather that you have not seen much of England."

"Only on our drive from Dover to London. And often only glimpses of places which looked most interesting. I do want to see it all." When he nodded, she swung the pair around the corner into a narrow lane.

She had not noticed until now, or perhaps he had moved as she made the turn, but it seemed to her that he was sitting rather closer to her than Neddy had. Perhaps, she said to herself, he is afraid that she would throw him out or that his weight upon that side will cause the curricle to overturn when she featheredged a corner. However, he did not appear to be much concerned, but was looking admiringly at the smoothly moving animals.

"You handle them well, Captain." It was true, he thought with some surprise. Her hands upon the ribbons—until now, he had not noticed how much smaller they were than his own— were as steady as a man's; she seemed to be aware of the dangers involved in handling such a vehicle. He was no longer worried that she might overturn them.

"Of course," she told him with a laugh. "With a teacher like Thomas Abbott, I had no choice. He would have boxed my ears soundly if I had so much as scratched the paint off any vehicle as I took it through a narrow gate or had mishandled my cattle in any way."

"You think a great deal of him, do you not?"

"More than you know." She must be careful. If she spoke of their early years, it was too easy to say, "He raised *us,*" instead of "me." To avoid the dangerous subject, she said quickly, "Would you like to try them?"

Now, why had she made such an offer? Lucien would never have allowed anyone to handle a pair of his. Mark was looking at her in surprise. "Do you mean that?"

"Why not?" She tried to sound casual. "Once they have become accustomed to my hands, I should never do so. But they are not so at this time. And I can see that your fingers are itching to take over the ribbons."

He laughed as he took the lines from her hands. "True. I confess that I have a fondness for fine horseflesh. But . . . to be so generous . . ."

Lucinda attempted to sound off-hand. "As I said, if they had time to become accustomed to my touch, I should not do so. But for the present, I am as strange to them as any. And I do not think you will damage their mouths."

"I promise that I shall not." Gently, he maneuvered the pair along the narrow road. Lucinda relaxed, watching as he managed the spirited animals. He was as good as Lucien—well, almost as good. She would not own that anyone could be her brother's equal.

While appearing to give all her attention to the sights he pointed out to her, she managed to study the man. He was large, certainly, but there was no sign of fat. This was a man who kept himself in trim. Well, Neddy had mentioned visits to Jackson's Boxing Saloon.

His hair and eyes were as dark as hers and Lucien's. Odd, because she had noticed in the family portraits that most of the men in the family were fair. Doubtless that dark strain must have come from the grandfather with the strange name—the one she was told Mark attempted to deny because he had agreed to change his name. The difference in coloring would explain his story.

"If it were earlier in the day," Mark said, "I should have suggested a drive to Richmond Park, as it is certainly worth seeing. But it might be best to wait for another day."

"I leave myself in your hands," she replied, thinking that they were certainly large enough to handle an outing or anything else. So large and so capable looking. She had a sudden urge to reach out and touch one of them, but stifled the impulse at once. It certainly was not something Lucien would have done, and it was not wise to allow him to notice her own hands overmuch. She hoped he had not been aware, as she had been, of how her hands had been dwarfed by his as he took the ribbons.

But then, she told herself, my hands are not *much* smaller than Lucien's, so perhaps it was not noticeable.

When at last they returned to Grosvenor Square, Lucinda was able to say with complete honesty, "I thank you, sir, for showing me a bit of my own country. I have often wished to see it, and the afternoon has been most enjoyable."

Mark realized that he, too, had enjoyed the drive. For the first time, he began to believe that she might be able to carry off the masquerade after all. Still, he could put a stop to it any time he chose by assuring her that she had fooled no one. Until he decided to do so, it might be best to keep the earl in ignorance of the fact that his granddaughter had taken to driving a curricle about the City and had been on the verge of attending a mill.

Chapter
Six

LUCINDA DESCENDED THE stairs late next morning to hear Neddy saying angrily, "It ain't like you to spoil sport, Mark. You *knew* that mill had not been cancelled."

" 'Twould have been a most inferior affair, anyhow, Neddy. You would not have enjoyed seeing it. And doubtless you would have lost a great deal of blunt."

"So what if I had done? I can afford to lose as much as I like. And I wanted Lu to see it. He ain't had a chance to see a mill here and 'twould have been a novelty to him."

"I doubt that. Do you think, as a soldier, he has not seen any number of them?"

"Just the same, I don't want you interfering with any more of my plans. He's my friend, and I shall entertain him as I wish . . . with no hindrance from you."

Neddy threw the last words over his shoulder, ignoring Mark's call to him to come back, and stalked from the room, almost colliding with Lucinda, who had reached the foot of the stairs.

"What's amiss?" she asked, surprised that Neddy should be so overset.

"Morning, Lu. Sorry that I cannot stay. Thanks to my friend in there—at least, I *thought* he was my friend—it is now necessary for me to look up a number of people and pay off the wagers I had made on a mill I did not even get to watch."

He strode out the door, and Lucinda entered the breakfast room to find Mark pouring himself a second cup of coffee.

"What can I serve you, Captain?" he asked, apparently not bothered by the recent scene.

"Thank you. I can help myself." She began to fill a plate. "What was it I heard Neddy saying about having to pay off wagers?"

"It seems that yesterday's mill was not put off, and he had laid wagers on it earlier—on the wrong man, of course."

"Oh—then you were misinformed?"

He shook his head. "A fabrication on my part, I confess. You appeared so well pleased with your new purchase that I thought you might prefer a longer drive instead of being crowded with a great number of people, watching two far from experienced fighters pummel one another."

He was correct in that, of course, but Lucinda knew that her brother would not have agreed and would have objected to being deprived of his sport. Men always seemed to enjoy the sight of others belaboring one another. Therefore, as Lucien, she ought to complain about the other's tactics.

"Do you not think that I should have been the one to make such a decision?" she demanded. "After all, Neddy and I had made plans to attend."

"Perhaps you are right that I should have put the decision to you, but I thought you would have insisted upon going rather than disappoint Neddy. Also, I had another reason for stopping you. All sorts of young fellows would have been there—the roads would have been crowded with drivers, many of them whose skill did not match up to their wish to show it. And since your cattle were untried—"

"I have never had any cattle I was unable to handle!" This was true, for she had never owned any animals until this pair.

"There is no need for you to fly into the boughs over my every word." Mark's deception had been planned in good faith, to save her from an unpleasant time, and the young chit's anger was trying his temper. For a groat, he would put an end to her schemes at this moment.

"I am not trying to belittle your driving skill. I have seen for myself that you can handle your cattle well. But even the best of whips have come to grief when meeting with less skilled drivers. I am only telling you that, while your grandfather's condition is not good, I do not wish for you to cause him any undue worry with foolish actions."

The secretary's censorious tone, plus the realization that he was undoubtedly right—and the fact that he had, without knowing that he had done so, saved her from an exhibition she had not wished to see—did not smooth the situation. Forcing herself to remember that the sick old man upstairs was the one who had cut off her father, she was able to say sullenly, "He has not seen fit to worry about me all these years."

"Perhaps if you had been here—"

"You mean he would care more for me if I had hung about, toadeating him as you—"

She broke off as Mark caught her shoulders. "Have a care, bantling, that you do not try my patience too far. I may yet yield to the impulse to give you the drubbing you deserve."

Lucinda was so angered by his patronizing attitude that she could not make up her mind whether to slap him or burst into tears. She knew that she ought not to have accused him of toadeating, as his feeling for her grandfather was unquestionably genuine.

Since neither tears nor slapping would have been a suitable response, she compromised by growling, "Oh, go to the devil," and wrenching herself from his grasp, caught up her hat and slammed out of the house.

Lucinda nearly overturned a trio of young gentlemen upon the front steps as she exited the house. Recovering his balance, Ferdy Maupin lisped an invitation to her to accompany them for a light luncheon, and the other two chimed in, promising her a great surprise.

She was in no mood to go jauntering with them, especially as Roger Atwood was one of the trio. She recalled there had been some mention last night of a friend who had served in the Peninsula and feared she might be forced to meet him. He would certainly know at once that she was not Lucien, and her disguise would be exposed.

Refusal, however, would have meant she must return to the house and, without a doubt, to a resumption of the argument with her grandfather's secretary. It was not that she feared Mark's threats, but that, in her anger, she might say something to give herself away.

Quickly considering her options, Lucinda decided it would be far better for her to remain away from the house until she had recovered her temper. Accordingly, she accepted the invitation and found that her appetite had not been ruined by the quarrel. Instead, she was able to do full justice to what the three bucks called a "light luncheon"—a dozen different dishes, more than enough to feed Lucien and his friends for several days.

During the meal, a number of references were made about the "surprise" they planned for the captain. At first, she feared they intended to bring her face to face with Mr. Atwood's friend—had his name been Farlow, or something of the sort?— but the idea of bringing together two soldiers who had already heard of each other hardly seemed the subject for so much mirth.

The memory of the absent Farlow turned her thoughts in another direction. These young men were healthy enough. Why were they not in the army?

"Doubtless they would be more trouble than they were worth," she said beneath her breath, but had to own this was not necessarily true. Lucien and his fellow officers had been forced to put up with any number of dandies and fops, but there were also many gentlemen—even noblemen—who had accepted the rigors of army life without complaint and who had proven themselves to be brave soldiers.

When the meal had ended, they were on their way to their new destination, which her acquaintances confided was to be the Opera House. Lucinda protested that they would certainly be much too early for the evening's performance. The others hooted with laughter.

"The betht performantheth ain't the oneth you thee from the boxeth, my boy," Ferdy assured her, "but the oneth that take plathe right here."

When they arrived, the other three pulled Lucinda away as she started toward the front of the building, leading her instead around to a door at the side. Ferdy pressed a coin into the hand of the doorman who opened the door for them. They proceeded to the long pink room backstage where the ballet dancers were performing their exercises under the watchful eyes of a number of beaux and amid their loud comments. It was clear that more than one gentleman present had his *chère-amie* among the performers at the opera.

Although the many years she had spent travelling with her brother in the army had made her believe that men discussed their female acquaintances freely when they were alone, Lucinda was deeply shocked at the callous manner in which these men were comparing the attractions—or the lack of them—of the dancers within their hearing. It was as if they spoke of the merits or deficiencies of the cattle which they might view at Tattersalls, she thought angrily, unaware that to many of these females the approval of some titled—or at least, monied—gentleman was their only opportunity to escape from penury.

She was happy to see that the gentlemen who had brought her here had given these girls no more than a passing glance. It was surprising, but at least, she thought, they were more gentlemanly than the others.

Then she realized that she was being led toward a corner of the room where a tiny, dark-haired dancer was standing alone, bending and swaying gracefully to and fro while she studied her reflection in the mirror. Unlike the other hopeful dancers, she looked with annoyance at the gentlemen who interrupted her.

"Thinth you tell uth you don't think you would care for our Englith ladybirdth," Mr. Maupin announced gleefully, "thith ith our thurprithe for you, Warne. *Theñorita* Evita Monteth ith the newetht attracthion at the theatre, direct from Madrid. And, *theñorita*, may I present Captain Luthien Warne, rethently come back from the Peninthula, who hath been telling me he preferth Thpanith ladieth to our own."

Lucinda noticed suspicion in the dancer's green eyes, but thought it could easily be that she was merely angered at being termed a ladybird and being offered by one gentleman to another as if she were a costly gift. She herself should be angry at being so treated, Lucinda thought. To cover her own confusion, Lucinda bowed deeply and observed, "*Seguramente, la señorita no es de Madrid, es de Paraìso.*"

Most females would have been flattered at being told that they must be arrivals from Paradise, but *Señorita* Montez pursed her full lips in distaste. After a moment—an uncomfortable one for Lucinda—Evita caught up a towel, wiped her face, and tossed the cloth to one side.

"I tire of these *ejercicios*," she declared, "even though they are necessary. They are *estupid*. Come, *mi capitàn*, we shall talk together, since you know of my homeland."

Slipping her arm through Lucinda's, she drew her into the

dimly lit theatre, choosing one of the stalls where they could be out of earshot of the others. She then turned upon Lucinda with a furious tirade. Lucinda was happy that the others could not hear her, although the young dancer was speaking in Spanish.

"Now," the dancer demanded, reverting to English, as if to be certain the other understood her, "what sort of jest is this? And what sort are you that you would consent to be a part of it? Because I will have nothing to do with these *estupid* young men . . . because I will not allow them to—I do not know the English for it—they think to make me look a fool. Is that what it is? Do they think I am so blind that I would not know the truth at once? *Capitàn* Warne, who has just returned from the Peninsula. Hah! And in what manner did you serve the army, *Capitàn?*"

Had not the young fools who had brought her here realized that Spain was—however reluctantly—an ally of France and that the dancer might well look upon all English as her enemies, even if she were forced to earn her living among them? She might easily storm back to vent her fury upon the trio for what she considered their trick and, in her tirade, could not fail to give away the captain's secret. Lucinda opened her mouth to reply, but the dancer had not finished.

"Or is it that they seek to give me an insult by thinking that since I would not have one of them—and who would wish any of them?—I would prefer a woman? This is beyond bearing!"

Lucinda gulped in shock. "I must throw myself upon your mercy, *señorita,*" Lucinda said, putting out a hand toward the other.

In as few words as possible, she explained the reason for her being in England and in this disguise. When she had finished, the dancer stared at her for a moment, then broke into full-throated laughter. "This is true? You tell me that they do not see at once that you are a woman? That these—*come se dice?*— these *tontos*—"

"Fools."

"Yes, fools of gentlemen who are so pleased with themselves—they truly believe you are one of them? If you had not told me, I should not have thought even an *Englishman* could be so blind as that. One of my countrymen would have known you as quickly as I did. But this is wonderful!"

"You will not give me away, I beg of you." Lucinda hoped the girl was mistaken about her being so easily recognized by any foreign man; it had not happened before this, so perhaps only another female could see through the disguise.

"Never—never would I do so! Though I choke with my laughter at the thought, I shall watch you play the game with them. Even will I help you as I can. But I think you will agree to help me as well?"

"Certainly, if I can do so," Lucinda promised, too relieved to care what would be asked of her. "But in what way can I help?"

"You must understand that these foolish gentlemen who have brought you here are mistaken when they say I do not have a—a— What is the English word? a—?"

"I . . . I think they say a 'protector.' " Lucinda stifled a giggle at the thought that she was taking part in a discussion of this kind.

"*Sì*—that is it—a protector. At times, the English escapes me. But what I mean is that they are wrong. I do have one— a most wonderful man. I know what you must think, but allow me to tell you—"

"You need not." Lucinda felt uncomfortable. It was one thing to meet such a girl. To listen to the tale of her *affaire* was something entirely different. Gently bred females did not know of such things—or at least they pretended they did not. She had spent more time with the army so was wiser than some, but she was still innocent in many ways.

"But I must. I came here with a company of dancers but was unable to leave when they did, so I must find work for myself. The money they give us here is little—they expect us to find someone to pay our expenses. I did not wish to do this. But then I met my Robin. And I love him. I think it may be that he loves me—not for marriage, of course. You must know that gentlemen do not marry girls from the theatre. The trouble is that, since I have come to London, I have looked at no one but him. So, manlike, he has grown certain of my love, for I do love him dearly, and he has begun to ignore me at times in a most shameful way. I should like very much to teach him a lesson—just a little one—but I do not wish to encourage any of the other gentlemen. As an English gentleman, you will pretend an affection for me?"

Lucinda wondered if she would regret having so rashly given her promise of help. "I should not like the thought of being called out and having my head blown off by a jealous rival," she said slowly.

Evita laughed heartily and caught both her hands. "I promise you need have no fear of such a fate as that. My Robin is a gentle creature. And if he *should* become angry, I shall confess to him that it was my plan to make him jealous. I think he would be pleased at that, for it would prove that I love him. But it will only be necessary to make him think that another believes that I am to be desired . . ."

"I am certain that you would have no trouble in finding a gentleman who thinks that," Lucinda told the young Spanish girl frankly. The dancer was one of the most beautiful women she had ever met. Her midnight-black hair made Lucinda's seem dull by comparison, and her skin was the soft white of a camellia petal, while her tiny but graceful form was well displayed by her exercise costume.

"I could find them if I wish," Evita said with no hint of boasting, "including your three *estupid* friends. They have made that clear enough. But I should not need to tell you that I have no wish to encourage them. They would only believe me to be serious, and I do not want that. I wish only my Robin. And if I looked at one of these, how could I rid myself of him easily? You will help me?"

"I will," Lucinda promised, holding out her hand, which the other grasped. After all, Evita was helping her by not betraying her secret. And what she was asking in return was such a little thing. Why should she not do it? It would be an excellent jest to play upon this "Robin," who would capture the heart of anyone so beautiful as Evita and then neglect her. He deserved to be punished for his effrontery.

Let Thomas scold—and she knew he would do so when he was told of this—but the situation appealed to her sense of fun. These men who brought her here as a jest deserved to have it turned upon them. Also, acquisition of so charming a ladybird would puff up her consequence among the beaux of the City and would lend protection to her role. She was certain that any gentleman—including Lucien—would be proud to be seen with Evita on his arm.

"We have a bargain, then?" the dancer asked. "Good. Now I must return to my work if I am to dance this evening."

She led the way back to the exercise room, pausing when they were in earshot of the others to say, *"Hasta luego, mi capitàn.* You will be here, then, to take me to supper after the performance tonight?"

This had not been decided, but Lucinda bowed low over the hand Evita offered, saying fervently, "I shall be counting the hours—no, the minutes—until then." She was rewarded with a kiss blown from the dancer's fingertips. When she bowed again, there was the reflection of another kiss blown her way before she left the theatre, followed by her envious acquaintances.

"Tell us how you managed that, Warne?" demanded Arthur Taylor, tugging at his carrot-colored hair until he had totally destroyed his fashionable Windswept. "You set up an engagement to dine with the Spanish Venus at the very first meeting, while all the rest of us have been trying to get her attention for months."

"The only word she gave the rest of us," Roger Atwood complained, "was, 'no.'" Atwood prided himself on his ability to charm any ladybird, and he was chagrined that Warne should succeed where he had failed.

Lucinda shrugged her shoulders and winked. "There is no magic to it, I assure you. It is only a matter of knowing what to say to a lady, gentlemen. For I suspect that she has been a lady at one time, and I treated her as such. I have no doubt you were much too abrupt in your dealings with the charmer— at least, when you presented me, I received that impression. These southern beauties—whether ladies or ladybirds—require special handling."

"Didn't I tell all of you that the captain would prove to be a campaigner who knew hith battleth?" Ferdy Maupin said with a laugh. He was well-satisfied with his present light-of-love and knew no jealousy. "Don't take him long to thee what the thituation ith and move in hith fortheth. Then you are taking the Incognita to thupper?"

"Yes, after the performance." After listening to one of Ferdy's long speeches, Lucinda found it difficult to refrain from lisping as he did. "Would any of you gentlemen care to be my guests—for the performance at the Opera House, that is," she added, making them all laugh.

"Yes—and we shall all go to supper with you, as well," declared Mr. Atwood. "I know it ain't the thing, making a crowd when a fellow wants to be alone with a new charmer. But I, for one, would like the opportunity to study the methods which seem to serve the military so well." And see why I do not do as well with her, he thought.

Lucinda was dismayed by this suggestion, as she had thought the two females could plan their future strategy at the supper. Still, it might serve to have the others see them together—she and Evita could talk later.

"I must say I had not intended for others to be along, as it is not the custom where I have been. But since you found her for me . . . well, we shall have to see what my *cariña* has to say on the subject. If she does not object to your presence, I shall not. But you must promise to disappear once supper is over." This brought more laughs and some comments that were too warm for good taste. Well, Thomas had warned her.

She returned to the house filled with good humor. How shocked the three gentlemen would be if they had been told they had taken a female to meet an opera dancer.

Having forgotten her earlier annoyance Lucinda was able to greet Mark Warne in a friendly fashion. Although surprised—and wondering what new mischief she might have in mind—he answered in the same manner, and she decided he might not be so unpleasant a person after all.

On the way up to her room, she decided that since Thomas was bound to learn sooner or later what she was about, she might as well have the pleasure of shocking him. She knocked upon his door and entered, saying lightly, "I must dress with special care tonight, Thomas. I am off to the Opera House with some new friends—and then to supper with a lovely Cyprian."

"What?" Thomas' jaw dropped, as did the boot he had been polishing to a high gloss. Lucinda burst into laughter at his horrified expression. As he fully understood her words, his horror gave way to anger.

Before he could explode, Lucinda said, "Now, do not begin to ring a peal over me before you hear the whole story. This was not my doing—at least, not entirely."

"A likely tale! Or were you merely saying what you did to see what I would do?"

"Not exactly. But as to my adventure—night before last, I tried to keep some of Neddy's friends from presenting me with a ladybird of their choosing by hinting that I preferred Spanish women. I thought that would stop them for, of course, I had no way of knowing there was a new Spanish dancer at the Opera House."

"A dancer! What new scrape will you be getting into now, Lucinda?"

"Well, *I* was not at fault—and even then, I thought I might carry it off. But when they introduced me to her, she recognized me as a female at once, so I had to tell her the entire story and beg her not to give me away to them. That would have been much worse than my meeting her. She thinks it is a grand jest that they do not know me to be a female and has promised to help me. And you know that Lucien would—"

"What Lucien would or would not do ain't the question now, Lucinda. You ain't supposed to know that females of that sort exist. And if you think that either your brother or I would permit—permit you to consort with one—"

"Oh, hide your teeth, Thomas. As for my knowing about ladybirds and such, I have told you before that young soldiers will talk. Not to mention the things that you and Lucien have let slip from time to time—when you forget I am supposed to be a sheltered female. Anyhow, there is no danger of Evita's corrupting me. She is a nice girl."

"Not if she's a Cyprian, she ain't nice. There is no way she could be."

"Well, perhaps I have the wrong word, but I *think* that is what most people would call her. Actually, she is only a poor dancer who was left here when her troupe returned to Spain. Of course, she does have a protector now."

"That is what I was talking about. Females who have protectors ain't respectable."

"Oh, pooh. You know that *Maman* has had several, between her marriages. And even if you thought so, you would never say *Maman* is not respectable."

"That is . . . Well, that is different."

"In what way? A protector is a protector, is he not? Does it matter whether the female involved is a French widow or a Spanish dancer? But I suppose it *is* different. I have known since I was a child that *Maman* is just fond of men, while this girl is doing what she must to stay alive. And she seems to be nice. I am certain she will do me no harm. And it is only for a few days. I am to pose as an admirer to help bring her Robin to heel."

"And if her Robin—whoever he might be—don't care for the attention you are paying to his particular?"

"That is exactly what I mean, Thomas. You—and Lucien as well—use such terms to me, and then tell me I ought not to know what you are talking about. I will own I *was* a trifle worried at first about how this Robin might act, but she assured me that he won't blow my head off. And she'll see that we don't come to cuffs. Just think of the help this will be to my masquerade. You certainly don't want people to think that Lucien is not in the petticoat line, do you?"

"That is neither here nor there. You ain't going anywhere with a female of that sort. And that is my last word!"

Only too well acquainted with Thomas' "last words," Lucinda immediately began to coax him out of his mood. Before long, as she had known he would do, he was helping her to garb herself in some of Lucien's finest clothing, a coat of dull gold brocade over breeches of celestial blue satin, striped stockings and jewel-buckled shoes—all the while issuing his silent pleas to Philip to help him guard this headstrong girl against the perils she was certain to encounter.

Thomas was aware that, with all the gentlemen expecting to see her, there was no way Lucinda could avoid tonight's meeting without the risk of betraying her secret. And, even for her own good, he could not deal her such a trick. However, that did not stop him from muttering about "totty-headed females" and "brats who did not know what was good for them."

Having heard all of this whenever she had done something to displease him, Lucinda ignored the scold. She was resolved that she would enjoy both the performance at the theatre and the one at supper.

Arriving at the supper accompanied by the three young gentlemen, Lucinda pretended to be embarrassed by their presence and apologized deeply for not having come alone as she had wished to do. Recognizing her cue, Evita took to her part with great enthusiasm. At first, she appeared to be angry that the captain had brought friends. But after she pouted for a time while Lucinda pretended to coax, the dancer agreed to accept their presence amiably. Lucinda and Evita spoke to each other in Spanish, and as her companions didn't speak that language, they could only dream about the things the *señorita* was saying.

At one point, Lucinda turned apologetically to the others. "I know you will forgive me, gentlemen, but there are some things which cannot be said properly in English. Is that not the way of it, *querida?*"

"Yes it is, *mi amor.*" And the dancer lapsed again into Spanish.

When the others, disappointed that the conversation was going to continue in a language they did not know and that they would have no details of the captain's success to tell to their friends, reluctantly took their leave, Lucinda and Evita were able to enjoy the laughter they had been forced to hide all evening.

"I think we have fooled them nicely, do you not?" Evita asked.

"Oh yes, they must think the captain is quite a man of the town when it comes to ladies."

They both giggled.

Chapter
Seven

THERE WAS NO help for it, Mark decided. If he was to keep the earl's granddaughter out of trouble, he was going to need assistance. Although his duties were light he could scarcely follow the chit all over London to see that she did not fall into some scrape or other.

He still felt that, given time, she would do something that would reveal herself as well as give him an opportunity to show her how foolish she had been in trying to gull them. Look at her now, for example, careening about the countryside in a curricle, not at all a fit vehicle for a female to drive.

But she does handle it well, he thought. Better than a number of men he knew.

Still, she ought not to go about alone. Look how Neddy had almost taken her to a mill—certainly not a fit place for a female to go.

Of course! Neddy would be just the one. The young marquess might be buffle-headed, but he was a good friend and he could be discreet if sufficiently warned. And no one would think it odd to see Neddy and the captain together.

Later, after searching through a number of Neddy's favorite spots, Mark finally ran him to earth, sitting alone at a corner table at White's. It was much too early for this place to be crowded.

The young man had just paid off the wagers he had lost the night before and, at the moment, was feeling decidedly sorry for himself. Not for the loss of the money—he could afford to lose much more than that. It was the thought that Mark should

deceive him which rankled. Mark, whom he had always considered a good friend.

As Mark approached the table, Neddy looked up at him and
said, "Go away." There was a bottle on the table, but its contents had barely been touched. Neddy was not much given to
drinking.

"Neddy, I must talk to you."

"Well, I do not wish to speak with *you.*"

As Mark took a chair, Neddy started to rise, but Mark
caught his wrist. "Neddy, I need your help."

Neddy had never refused a plea for help from any friend but
he was surprised that Mark should need his aid. "In what
way?" he asked sceptically.

"I think instead of attempting to explain, I should allow you
to read this." Mark took out Captain Warne's letter and passed
it across the table.

Neddy read the missive slowly, then went through it another
time. "Is this true?" he asked at last.

Mark nodded.

"Then Captain Warne—"

"Is not Captain Warne, but his sister Lucinda."

"Do you mean that a female—" Neddy's voice was rising
and Mark signalled him to lower it. "That . . . that it was a
female who was driving me about yesterday? That I was about
to take a *female* to a mill?"

"Now you understand why I stopped you."

"I'm happy that you did. Why, if I'd taken . . . I must find
her at once and apologize for suggesting such a thing."

Mark stopped him once more. "No, Neddy—you do not yet
understand. We do not wish her to know that we know about
her."

"We?"

"Yes. I was forced to tell his lordship what the captain had
written."

"And the earl did not put a stop to his—I mean her—oh,
you know what I mean."

"He would have done, but I persuaded him to let her go on."

"You mean that he approves of his . . . his granddaughter . . .
going about in a racing curricle? Such a vehicle ain't fit for a
man to drive, let alone a female."

"You must own, Neddy, that she is a good driver. Better than you, in fact.

Neddy bristled a bit, then grinned. "Well, I own, I'd not attempt *that* vehicle. But *does* he approve?"

"Well, in fact, I have not told him about that. I should not wish to worry him unduly in his state of health."

The marquess stared at him. "If you ask me, Mark, your attic is to let. How can you keep a . . . a female . . . from getting into some scrape or other? You cannot follow him—her—all over London."

"That is where I need your help. It would look odd if I suddenly began bear-leading a grown man—or what everyone thinks is a grown man. But she has made friends with you. You could help me to keep an eye on her."

"Oh no—not in any way. You know I ain't in the petticoat line, Mark."

"Of course you are not. But I do not wish you to allow her to discover you know she is a female. Treat her as you would a younger brother."

"Never had a brother."

"A young cousin, then." Mark was becoming exasperated, but dared not show it; he needed Neddy's help. "Or a green young man just come to town. Just go about with her as you would if she were the real captain. And if there is any trouble, come to me."

Neddy looked obstinate for a moment, then nodded. "I suppose I could do it. But it will be difficult not to let something slip." He sat for several moments, turning the matter over in his mind, then grinned. "It would be quite a feat, would it not—to hoax a hoaxer in that way? You can depend upon me, Mark."

Mark gave a long sigh of relief. If Neddy looked upon it as a game, he would certainly keep an eye on the girl. And *he* could return to his work free from worry. Not entirely free, he amended; he must keep the earl from learning about his granddaughter's curricle. He would not object to her driving about as long as she did it sedately, as a lady should. The thought of this girl doing anything sedately made him grin as he returned to the house.

*　　　*　　　*

While the captain pursued her evening rounds of balls, routs, even an occasional appearance at Almack's, her daytime schedule had changed. Since Evita was at the Opera House almost every night, and consequently did not care to rise until mid-morning, the late afternoon and early morning hours were not theirs. However, each morning, promptly at eleven of the clock, Captain Warne's dashing new curricle could be seen outside the lodgings which *Señorita* Montez shared with several other dancers.

One of the envious crowd of urchins was permitted to hold the grays while the captain gallantly handed the charmer to the curricle's seat. Shortly thereafter, the pair would be found tooling through the Park under the scandalized eyes of any strait-laced members of the *ton* who might be abroad at this hour instead of at the fashionable one of four, as well as beneath the admiring gaze of some of the beaux. On these occasions, Evita usually displayed some new trinket, such as a fan or a frivolous new bonnet.

"You must make me a few gifts, I fear, just for the show," the girl had decreed at the start of their *"affaire."* "Your friends and mine will think it odd if you do not. But since this only a jest, I do not wish that you should give me anything which is costly."

Lucinda agreed. She was willing to spend a certain amount of money in order to keep up her masquerade but she was loath to part with more than was necessary. It seemed unfair to her grandfather. He might, of course, be expecting her to spend extravagantly. It would help if she had some way of learning what he wished, but, according to Mark, the old gentleman himself was the only one who knew that.

The results of her economy were amazing to the young bucks who watched her progress. Many a gentleman had discovered that the pathway to the affections of his *chère-amie* must be paved with expensive gifts, so they looked at the captain in envy. Such trifles as a ruby necklace, a carriage and pair, or a house of her own—if not all three—were expected by the average light-of-love. Those who dealt with the captain knew he was no nip-farthing, so the economy must be practiced by his companion. They could only stare in awe at the soldier who was able to hold the Spanish beauty without lavishing a fortune on her.

After having made certain that they had been seen in the park, they would continue to drive about until it was time for Evita to go to the theatre for rehearsals. Often, they would search out some little-known inn for a luncheon and a laugh over the day's events. Lucinda was happy for this chance to see even a part of her father's homeland, for her only other excursion had been the one with Mark. Evita was willing to go wherever the other wished. She only drew the line at being dragged through art displays or museums.

"I do not care for the things of long ago," she said when Lucinda suggested viewing the Elgin Marbles. "I live for the now."

Not having been present when his friends took Lucinda to the Opera House, Neddy did not learn of her newest escapade until he heard discussions of the captain's success with his Spanish ladybird. As soon as he understood all the details, Neddy hurried to inform Mark.

" 'Twas none of my doing," he said, his words falling over one another in his excitement. "I was not there. 'Twas Maupin and Atwood—and it might have been one or two others—who took her there."

"Lucinda?" Mark was alert at once. "Who took her where?"

"I told you—those—some of the ones she met at the ball at m' mother's. They took her to the Opera House."

"Nothing wrong with that, is there?" Mark asked with a laugh. "I own, some of the farces are a bit bawdy, but—"

"Not a *performance*. They took her backstage. Introduced her to one of the dancers . . . and your make-believe captain is now driving her all about the countryside."

That brought the larger man to his feet. "Do you mean that Lucinda is actually being seen in public with a performer from the Opera House?"

"Haven't seen 'em myself, but I hear that they drive in the park every morning between eleven and twelve. Odd hour to go there, but—"

"That young idiot!" He caught up his hat and strode out of the house so rapidly that Neddy had trouble keeping pace with him.

"Where . . . are you going . . .?" he managed between gasps.

"To the park—to see this for myself."

"But— But, Mark—" Neddy was sputtering by the time

Mark halted, "you can do nothing here. So—" They were standing beside one of the popular drives, one that Lucinda was certain to take if she kept to her schedule.

"What I should like to do would be to drag her out of that curricle and shake some sense into her."

"But . . . but think of the scandal! You know everyone would expect him—her—dash it all, how am I to keep it straight?— to challenge you to a duel if you did that."

"I know. That is what I should *like* to do. But I shall wait until she returns home, then tell her that her little game is at an end."

Neddy felt a stab of pity for Lucinda. He had become fond of her, despite the scandalous way she was behaving. Still, Mark was right, of course. She could not be allowed to continue. If word got about of what she was doing, it would reflect badly upon all of them—Mark, the earl, her brother.

The two men did not have long to wait before the familiar curricle came in sight. Lucinda was clad in pearl grey, her hat at a rakish angle. Beside her, the petite dancer looked like some bright-plumaged bird. As Mark watched, Lucinda tooled the vehicle expertly through a group of young horsemen who had come at that unusual hour to observe the captain's success with the hitherto unobtainable Spanish ladybird. Suddenly, Mark felt his anger dissolve. And when Lucinda broke off her exchange of quips with them to bow low to a disapproving dowager and exchange smiles with her charge, he gave a shout of laughter.

"Did you see that, Neddy? There is not a buck in London who could have handled that better. She has their manners to the life."

"Yes." Neddy was slightly envious. He had never been able to cut such a dash. "But what are you going to do?"

"I? Not a thing." Mark laughed again. "Of course, she may get her eyes scratched out when that little spitfire with her learns how she has been gulled. But I should wager my girl can take care of herself."

"Your girl?"

"Uh—well, what I meant was his lordship's girl. Still I cannot help feeling an interest in her welfare."

"Oh . . . yes." Neddy was not certain he understood at all. Mark had sounded—well, different—when he had said, "my girl," but doubtless he had meant nothing by it. They watched the curricle out of sight, then strolled back to the house in Grosvenor Square.

Neddy pleaded another engagement and left. Mark watched him leave with a sigh of relief. The words had slipped out, surprising him as much as they did Neddy, and anyone who was more needle-witted than his friend would doubtless have commented upon it.

Certainly, he had never thought of the . . . the wench . . . as "his" girl. Far from it! It was only that he felt it would be necessary to keep this latest mad behavior of hers from her grandfather. If the earl learned the truth, he would immediately order the girl to return to Spain.

Even to himself, Mark disliked to own the truth—that he did not wish to see her go.

Unaware of the danger she had narrowly escaped, Lucinda continued to be seen about London and the nearby countryside with her new companion. On one of these visits, the dancer remarked that she would be free that evening, as there would be a masquerade at the Opera House.

"A masquerade? That sounds most exciting. The only one I have attended was a dull party of people who knew each other despite their masks. This would be something entirely different. Let us go—that is, if you would care for it. Is it the sort of affair your Robin would attend?"

"I do not think he would be there. But it is not the proper thing for you to do. I do not mind if we go or not, but an affair of this sort is not for you, *mi amiga.*"

"Whyever not?"

"You cannot know—there will be people of the roughest kind there this evening, and it will become *muy degradable* as the night goes on. There are masquerades which are given by members of your class. They are not so bad, but ladies do not attend masquerades of this kind."

"You sound exactly like Thomas Abbott," Lucinda complained. "Both of you forget that I am not Miss Lucinda Warne at present, but a captain in His Majesty's army."

"You pretend the part very well, *mi amiga*—and your pretense is clever enough to fool your *estupid* friends. But beneath that *capitàn's* coat, you are a lady, after all. And you would be shocked by much that occurred."

Lucinda shrugged. "Oh well, if you do not care to go with me, you need not do so. I can get up a party of my friends. *They* will not object to my company."

"You are impossible," Evita cried, throwing up her hands. "That would be the worst of all—to go with a crowd of young men. You would be drawn into all kinds of sordid matters. If you must go, I shall go with you. But you must promise me— if the crowd gets too unruly, you will leave."

"Oh, I promise." Why should she not, for she was getting her own way once more. And what could there be about a masquerade that could be so terrible?

That night, under the glare of the lights, the Opera House looked more tawdry than when performances were taking place, but the masquerade itself was a colorful affair. Lucinda was happy that she was wearing a mask, however. It somewhat disguised her eyes, which she did not doubt were sparkling with an excitement her brother would never have shown. Lucien was more accustomed to such things, she supposed. At the same time, she could see at once why Evita had not wished her to attend this event.

One portion of the crowd was made up of Cits. The two young females would have had no objection to these, for most of them were sober people who enjoyed a quiet supper and drank sparingly, content to watch the goings-on about them. A few of the other younger men, however, were aping the actions of the beaux who were here, partaking freely from various bottles and flirting with all the females in a manner which bade fair to become dangerous before the night was over.

Lucinda and her companion had been there less than half an hour when she noticed one masked and costumed gallant who made his way somewhat uncertainly to one of the tables and attempted to coax a girl to come out onto the floor with him to join in the rowdy dance which was taking place. An older man, apparently her father, rose from his chair and caught the celebrant in both hands. Raising him above his head, he threw the other into the midst of the swaying crowd, then herded his family together and left. The young girl threw anxious looks over her shoulder as she went, doubtless bemoaning the loss of her only chance to mingle with the *ton*—or, at least, with whatever part of it which was here tonight.

The buck was shaken by his fall but unhurt. Scrambling to his feet, he drew his clothing together and shouted an insult after the departing group, then turned to pursue a scantily clad nymph. She made a pretense of eluding him but soon was persuaded to accompany him into a curtained alcove.

There seemed to be a number of these curtained rooms, set aside, Lucinda supposed, for dallying couples. They were not a part of the everyday Opera House furnishings. Unused to anything of this sort, Lucinda would have like to peer into one of them to see how they were furnished, but Evita drew her firmly away. Since most of the rooms were clearly occupied by this time, Lucinda made no protest.

Most of the females in the milling crowd were costumed and masked, but the extreme freedom of their actions labelled them as members of the frail sisterhood. At least, Lucinda supposed that was how such creatures would behave. The only ladybird she had met was Evita, whose behavior was always decorous, if her words were sometimes otherwise.

With the secrecy afforded by a mask—and perhaps a costume as well—a lady *might* take the risk of attending, but her reputation would be damaged beyond repair if she were found out. It was obvious why no gentleman would bring his wife or sister to such a place.

Many of the gentlemen present wore evening dress rather than costumes, and a few had even dispensed with masks. Still, there were costumes aplenty about the hall—sheiks and pirates, cavaliers and naval officers. Whether or not they were gentlemen could not have been told by their behavior. Some of them took advantage of their disguises to make outrageous suggestions to their partners. Most of these were greeted with shrieks of laughter, or occasionally with a slap which was more provocative than punishing.

Almost unheard in the din, the musicians labored at their melodies. Many of the dances were no more than romps, but one or two were more decorous. Lucinda danced one of these with Evita. Being told that her way of waltzing was gentlemanly enough to fool anyone, she led out an houri she had recognized, despite her costume, as a dancer from the theatre.

The girl also recognized her partner from the fact that Evita

was present and preened herself, thinking that she had a chance
of winning away the Spanish girl's protector. An attempt upon
her part to dance rather closer than propriety indicated was
foiled by Lucinda, who had no intention of allowing the other
to press against her. The houri was forced to admit defeat
when, at the end of the dance, the captain bowed and went back
to his own box.

Lucinda returned just in time to discourage an obviously
foxed young sprig who was balancing precariously on the edge
of the box, trying to fondle Evita and much too far gone in spirits to see that she had moved far out of his reach. When her
escort suddenly tapped him upon the shoulder, the young man
was so startled that he tumbled off the ledge, under the feet
of two wandering couples, bringing them and several others
down into a noisy heap, from which order was not restored for
some time.

As she resumed her seat beside the dancer, Lucinda laughed,
"If I were the true Captain Warne, I think I should be quite
jealous." She was not surprised that Evita attracted attention,
for her costume was that of a noble lady of Spain, although
a close inspection would reveal that it was more than slightly
shabby.

A mantilla of spidery black lace fell from the high comb in
the back of her hair, emphasizing the camellialike quality of
her skin, which had not been harmed by the paint she was
forced to wear when she was performing. Indeed, not only her
costume, but her bearing, was that of a great lady. Lucinda
found herself wondering if the dancer might have come from
some important family. She put the fancy aside at once, for how
could a great lady have become a ballet dancer, one who had
needed years of training? She supposed that it was only Evita's
ability in acting a part which gave rise to the thought.

Aware that Thomas would never have permitted her to attend such an affair, Lucinda had not attempted to procure a
costume, but had contented herself with wearing Lucien's so-
berest evening dress of black satin coat and breeches, plus the
mask which Evita had obtained for her.

She congratulated herself that she, at least, could not be recognized and was in a mood to argue when Evita laid a hand
upon her arm and said, "I think, *mi amiga,* that it is best for
us to leave soon."

Lucinda could scarcely understand what she was saying, for the shrieks and roars of the crowd had been rising steadily as both the men and their companions drank more and more. Just before their box, a harem lady, whose face was heavily veiled but who was scantily covered elsewhere, snatched off a scarf which had comprised a large part of her costume and flung it about the neck of her companion, tying it in a large bow under his chin. He shouted something into her ear and led her toward one of the curtained alcoves.

Wishing that her mask covered her entire face, for she felt that she must certainly be blushing at the sight of such immodesty, Lucinda changed her mind and nodded agreement when Evita suggested that they leave. Picking up the dancer's cloak to place it about her shoulders, she thought it would have been of more use had she given it to the half-naked harem lady. It would have been wasted, she knew, for the creature clearly did not mind baring so much of her body.

"I can see why you did not wish me to come," Lucinda murmured, guiding her companion to the door. As they passed out upon the steps, several voices hailed them, and they turned to face a quartet of young gentlemen who had just descended from a hackney.

"What, not going already, are you Warne?" called Roger Atwood, apparently already somewhat the worse for drink. "The party is certain to go on until morning and you would not wish to miss that, for it gets better by the hour."

While Lucinda searched for a good excuse for going, the Spanish girl said quickly, "It is I who am to blame. All this noise, it gives me—how do you say?—*dolor de cabeza.*"

"Headache," Lucinda translated, thankful that Evita had provided them with a good reason.

"Yes—the headache. So I have asked the *capitàn* to take me home."

"Don't thuppothe, in that cathe, that we'll thee you any more tonight," Ferdy Maupin put in.

He leered at Evita in a manner which made Lucinda wish to hit him with something. How completely like a man to put the worst possible connotation upon everything! Although two of Ferdy's companions laughed loudly at his remark, the other followed their example a bit uncertainly. Mr. Atwood caught him by the hand and drew him forward.

"You remember Farlow, don't you, Warne?" he enquired. "I told you I knew him. Lieutenant George Farlow, who was with your regiment in Portugal."

Chapter
Eight

GRATEFUL THAT SHE was standing far from the flicker-
ing torches, and for the fact that she had not yet removed her
mask, Lucinda turned toward the young man, wondering what
it was that caused *him* to appear so ill at ease.

"Certainly I remember him," she declared, deciding that
boldness was her best course of action. She could only hope
that he would not see through her masquerade as easily as the
Spanish girl had done. She had never met him, but he may have
known that Lucien had a sister. At least, he would know that
she was not Captain Warne. "If I were not otherwise engaged,
this evening, Lieutenant, I should like to reminisce with you
over the times we have spent together," she added, determined
that they should never meet again if she could manage to prevent it.

"I . . . I should have liked that very much, Captain," the
young man stammered. "However, I do not wish to keep you
now. Perhaps we shall meet some other time." He edged away,
as if wishing to keep his friend between him and the captain.
At the same time, Mr. Maupin and Mr. Atwood were clamor-
ing for the others to come along lest they miss some of the entertainment, so the quartet passed indoors.

"That young man—he knows your brother?" Evita asked as
their hackney drew away from the Opera House.

"I fear that he does. I shall have to be careful not to see him
another time."

"It seemed to me that he was also not anxious to meet the
capitàn."

"I hope that is true," Lucinda said fervently, "for it would be disgraceful if I were to be unmasked now when everything has been going so well. You were right, Evita, I ought not to have come here tonight. Yet I supposed that I should have had to meet him sometime, for his friend seemed so anxious to bring us together."

"Then perhaps it was for the best that it happened tonight, as you were masked when you met."

"Yes, that was a good thing."

"So it is over. Forget about it now, *mi amiga.*"

Lucinda would have liked to take her friend's advice, but it proved impossible. As she descended to breakfast the following morning, she was told that Lieutenant Farlow had called, asking if he might be permitted to see Captain Warne.

"A soldier friend, I have no doubt. I have shown the gentleman into the library, Master Lucien," Fenton told her with a smile. The old butler had become quite fond of "Master Philip's son" and treated the captain as if he had known him from childhood.

Wishing that it might be possible for her to run out the door and far away, Lucinda moved toward the library. There was not the slightest doubt that one of Lucien's fellow officers would see at once that she was not the captain. It had been dark last night, and she had been masked; now she must face him in daylight. She wondered for a moment if she could convince him that there were several Captain Warnes, but Lucien was so unusual a name for an English soldier that she knew there would be no hope. Squaring her shoulders, she opened the library door.

"Lieutenant Farlow?"

The slim young man got to his feet and whirled to face her. "I . . . I wish to thank you, sir, for not unmasking me before my friends."

This was a *volte-face,* indeed, almost the very words that she might have used to him. Wondering if this was some sort of game on his part, she said as lightly as she could, "But it was I who was masked, not you."

"Yes—yes, of course, captain, but I think you must see what I mean." His tone was desperate. "*You* certainly must have known, the moment we were introduced, that I had not been at Bussaco. But I assure you that it had never been my intention to claim any glory for my actions."

Lucinda shook her head. With every word he spoke, the mystery deepened.

The young man continued, "It happened this way. I fell ill upon the ship before we reached the Peninsula and was delirious all the time I was there. By the time I recovered my senses, the battle was over. I was still so weak, however, that I was sent home with the wounded. My family had not been notified of my illness, of course, and when I arrived home, I discovered that they thought I was in action and they had been telling their friends about my bravery under fire."

He paused, as if seeking words to excuse himself. "They were so proud of me that . . . that I did not disabuse them. It was a shameful thing for me to have done. But you do not know, Captain, how such lies can build up once you begin."

"Do I not?" Lucinda said fervently, feeling weak-kneed with relief. All her worries of the past days had been for nothing. "But did not some of your friends have questions about the battle? How could you answer them?"

"The wounded men—some of them—talked to me while we were on our way home, and I learned enough that I was not entirely ignorant of what had happened. When I came to a point I did not know, I merely said it was something I did not wish to remember. You need not tell me how contemptibly I have behaved in keeping silent,—"

"I should not refine too much upon it," Lucinda said, thinking that his deception was certainly no worse than her own—and his reason a better one. "You were not to blame that you had not been in the battle, although you may consider that you were one of the fortunate to have missed it." Lucien had come through without a scratch, but not all of their friends had been so lucky. "I understand that your only reason for keeping quiet was to spare your family the pain they would have suffered had they learned of your illness. You may depend upon it that I shall say nothing."

Lieutenant Farlow stayed several minutes more, stammering his thanks, then left. Lucinda went in to breakfast, surprised to discover that relief over her escape had given her an unusual appetite. She was unaware of the sharp glances Mark gave her from time to time.

He had come through the hall in time to witness Farlow's fervent handshake and hear him say, "You cannot know how your words have changed my life. Since I left the Peninsula, I have felt myself under a cloud. You have made me another person."

These were scarcely the words of a casual acquaintance. And the man, too, had been on the Peninsula. Was he perhaps an old interest of the girl's? And what did he mean that her words had changed his life? Mark had a distinctly uneasy feeling.

The only remaining bar to Lucinda's complete happiness now was her uncertainty about Lucien's safety, but she knew that he could not write to her as long as she stood in his shoes. And she still hadn't figured out a way to write to him.

She had sent Lucien a brief message when she knew she would be forced to remain in London but had not given him any of the details of the matter, not wishing to worry him. No word of any further engagements upon the Peninsula had come to London, so she must suppose he was well.

She would not have owned it to Thomas—who would have declared, "I told you"—and had only hinted to Evita that she was beginning to find the life of a London buck less satisfying than she had expected. When she saw all of these young men frittering away their lives and thought about Lucien and others who were in danger, she found it difficult at times to say nothing.

Still, she was determined to go through with this for Lucien's sake, and she would do so. It couldn't be much longer now. Soon she would be happy to be free of this disguise, but she would miss London. And Evita, who had become her confidante. And even Mark. But she would *not* miss her cousin Albert.

Her involvement—as it appeared to others—with the dancer did not prevent her from being invited to most of the events of the *ton*—no more than the possession of a *chère-amie* would have been held against any of the other beaux. A few of the highest sticklers might scoff at the blatant manner in which the captain paraded his interest in the female, but much could be forgiven the probable heir to Lord Brayling's fortune.

She received invitations to every ball and card party. Hostesses always welcomed an unattached gentleman. This was especially true when the gentleman was polite and charming and could be relied upon for several duty dances and even a supper with one of the less popular young ladies. Lucinda pitied these young ladies and—although she would much prefer to wear a beautiful gown and be partnered by some beau—she had become aware that standing up for a dance with "Captain Warne" served to bring these wallflowers to the attention of other—and more eligible—partners.

At some time during the evening, Lucinda would make one of the crowd about Stella Proctor, ignoring Lord Byrne's scowls and apparently basking in the light of the Incomparable's smiles. The Beauty accepted this admiration as her due, pleased to see that Byrne had not been able to drive away the captain as he had done with several other more fainthearted swains.

Stella and the wallflowers were not the only ones who found the "heir" attractive. At one ball, Caro Lamb lisped a greeting and spent considerable time wondering if it might be to her advantage to encourage closer attention. Would Byron be moved to jealousy at seeing her with a man who was younger, one who was equally dark, equally handsome—and one who could lead her out for a dance, as well? There were times when the lady thought that Byron relied too greatly on his lameness to excuse himself from unwanted duties. After a time, however, she decided against the idea. Byron had no need to curry favor; he would doubtless only turn to someone else, and she would find herself in the cold.

It was impossible for Lucinda to attend every function to which she was invited these days. However, she did attend as many as she could, hoping that this was what his lordship expected of Lucien. She had not seen her grandfather since the day of her arrival. She was certain that Mark carried regular reports upon both cousins' behavior, but if the earl had given any indication of his feelings about his two grandsons, Mark did not relay them. She could not know how many of her escapades Mark kept from the old man's ears in order to protect her from his wrath.

To her surprise, Lucinda met Neddy Fenley at most of the affairs she attended. She had supposed from his conversation that he cared nothing for balls. Nor did he, but he was bound by his word to Mark to help keep watch over the girl. "Why did I allow myself to be bullocked into this?" he often asked himself, as he dragged his way through another boring evening.

He suggested no more such escapades as attending mills, knowing Mark would have his ears if he did so. Unaware of his reasons, Lucinda was grateful to be spared such sport. Only Mark's intervention had saved her the last time, and she found she was no longer curious enough about them to regret missing such fights. It seemed to her, however, that the marquess was also doing his best to steer her away from some of the gaming hells and other rowdy establishments his friends appeared to enjoy. Could it be that he found himself pinched in the pocket?

She was not the only one who noticed that he was shunning such places, and Neddy's friends began to speculate as to the reason for it. Although Lucinda might think otherwise, no one who had known him for years would believe that anyone so well to pass as young Leatheringham could have drifted into Dun Territory.

"You don't thuppothe he'th in love, do you?" Ferdy Maupin hazarded.

"Neddy—in the petticoat line?" said Roger Atwood, astonished. "Never saw him give any female as much as a second glance, did you? Besides, what's being in love got to do with a fellow not wanting to play cards?"

"Have you notithed Byrne lately? Wager he wouldn't know a winning hand if he held one."

"Oh, I own Byrne's a hopeless case—cannot see a thing except the Incomparable. But take a look at Warne. He seems to be running well in the race for her favors, and it has not ruined his game."

"That ith becauthe he doeth not have to worry. Hith fortune ith running well."

"But they say, 'lucky in love, unlucky at cards.' Warne proves it ain't true."

It was true that Lucinda's good fortune at dice and cards seemed to be fairly uniform. Even at White's, where the stakes were extremely high, she had lost only a little more than she had won. "Even Grandpapa could not object to that," she said to herself. "If it does not happen too often."

She had been badly dipped one evening at a private house to which Roger Atwood had taken her, over Neddy's strenuous objections. However, she suspected that the cards had been fuzzed and refused to go there a second time.

"The dealers must find another pigeon to pluck," she declared, ending the matter.

The jest of attempting to vie for Stella Proctor's favor was beginning to pall.

The truth was that the entire masquerade was beginning to pall. As Lucinda watched the young ladies in their modish gowns, flirting over their fans or dancing with the gallants, she longed to be one of them once more, as she had been at home.

"I'll wager that if I were properly gowned, I could make black hair as fashionable as yellow and take a number of them away from the Beauty," she said beneath her breath, barely able to keep from tapping her toe to the strains of the waltz being played by the fashionable orchestra. She watched a very short young lady trying to match her steps to those of her much larger partner, then saw with surprise that the gentleman was Mark.

He danced well—especially for such a tall man, she admitted grudgingly to herself. But then, she thought critically, his partner was too short. He needed someone taller.

Like yourself? something within her asked, and she pushed the thought aside. *She* certainly had no desire to dance with *him*. Still, she knew she would be able to match his steps better than that tiny thing could do.

She had known that Mark appeared at the functions from time to time; although he was not a rich man, he was stylish and quite presentable. Alfred, however, was a different matter. Many hostesses were offended by his manners.

At one affair, Mark had detached Lucinda from a group of her acquaintances and led her across the room to where a slim, dark, soberly dressed gentleman appeared to be giving another a set down for some deficiency in his costume.

"George, I should like to present to you one of Lord Brayling's grandsons, Captain Lucien Warne," Mark told the gentleman. "And, Captain, this is my good friend, George Brummell."

The Beau! Lucinda swallowed hard. Even on the frontier there were many who spoke of him and his dicta about fashion. He turned and looked at the figure before him, his gaze going from head to toe, while others standing nearby wondered what his verdict might be. Tonight, Lucinda was garbed in a dark blue brocade coat, with a modestly figured waistcoat, neat cravat, and white breeches. There was a slight shudder when the Beau's glance reached the buckled shoes.

After a moment, he said, "The captain has some excuse for what he wears, of course, not having had the good fortune to spend much time in the City. Doubtless, he will soon learn what is acceptable. At least, I can see that he has the good sense not to weigh himself down with gauds, but—take a word of advice, my lad—*no* jewelry of any sort—and I should say that the best thing you could do would be to toss that entire rig in the dust bin."

Lucinda gasped at his condemnation. She considered her outfit extremely nice. Albert, who had seen the group and wished he might be a part of it, came up in time to hear the Beau's last words, but not to realize who was speaking.

He smirked, saying, "How right you are. I have been telling my cousin for some time that what he wears ain't fit to be seen. I'll take him to my snyder any time he likes. And he could do a lot for you, too," he added, eyeing Brummell's clothing. "Why, in that get-up, you look like a plaguey Methodist."

Everyone who heard him waited expectantly for one of the famous set downs, but it seemed that, for once in his life, Beau Brummell was left without words. He did, indeed, survey the young man from his loosely powdered hair—green this evening—past his apricot-colored coat and green-and-coquelicot-striped waistcoat to his lavender Inexpressibles and high-heeled shoes. Putting his hand over his eyes for a moment, as if to blot out the painful sight, the Beau then turned to Lucinda and said, "Did I hear him call you *cousin*?"

Lucinda laughed, understanding the reaction of England's First Gentleman of Fashion to Albert's multicolored display and forgave him completely for the mild criticism of her own attire. After all, everyone knew that Brummell was a fanatic on the subject of simplicity in dress.

"I beg of you not to hold that against me, sir," she pleaded. " 'Tis merely an accident of birth."

"Not an accident, my boy," Brummell said, at last making a recover. "Whatever gave birth to such a monstrosity as we are seeing could only be called a catastrophe."

A laugh went up from everyone within hearing. Albert

moved away, aware that he had been insulted, but not quite certain how it had come about. He had made the offer in good faith and had expected it to be appreciated.

He did not know until someone told him that the man had been the famous Beau Brummell, but it made no difference. It was plain to see that for all that some of the *ton* considered him to be the arbiter of London fashion, he needed someone to take him in hand. If he could only know how insignificant he looked in that black suit without so much as a single fob or seal to set it off. It was truly pitiful.

Of course, it must be remembered that Brummell had been a nobody until the Prince took him up and made so much of him. And it was well known that the Prince—now the Prince Regent—was not at all particular in choosing his friends. How like that frumpish Warne to hang out with someone like Brummell and with their grandfather's secretary.

"Like will seek like," he muttered. *He* would never lower himself to make such an offer a second time.

Despite his anger and contempt for the hostesses who did not invite him to their balls, Albert viewed his cousin's popularity with secret envy and schemed for some way to outshine him. He considered himself an accomplished whip, an opinion not even his doting mother could bring herself to share. With this in mind, he had purchased a racing curricle and a pair of fine but mettlesome bays. The first time he saw them, Thomas whistled to show appreciation and wondered aloud about who had chosen them for him.

"I know the young snirp fancies himself as a down-the-roadster, but I'll wager he has no more judgment in the choosing of horseflesh than your friend Neddy."

Lucinda laughed. "You'll get no wager for me on that point, Thomas; you may take my word for it that he is far worse. I saw the pair Albert had in mind in the beginning—all show and no bottom."

"How did he happen to change?"

"Mark was able to talk him out of it and persuade him that he ought to take these instead. As Albert makes no distinction between a secretary and a groom—neither of them rating as a person with him—Mark was told to go out and buy whatever he chose. After all, grandfather is paying the shot."

"Your grandfather's secretary is twice the man that Albert is—and I don't mean only in size."

Secretly agreeing, but unwilling to own it, Lucinda remained silent.

"I cannot understand why you should have taken him in such aversion as you have done."

Not aversion, Lucinda told herself . . . something much different, something she did not understand. "Mark Warne is a great bully. He thinks his size gives him the right to order everyone about."

Now, why did she say that? she wondered. It was not the way she saw the large man, at all. He was *not* a bully. In fact, he had been kind to her in many ways. Not at all the sort of person he had seemed at their first meeting. He had not censured her actions for many days.

"You mean that he would not permit you to ride rusty over him as Lucien's fellow-officers have always done," Thomas told her with a grin, ruffling her carefully arranged hair. "You must remember, girl, that you know you for a lady; he does not. That is why he treats you as he does. Better than you deserve, at times. Mark's still a good man."

"Enough about him," Lucinda said, unwilling to own that there had been any change in her feelings toward the man. "He does not matter. The important thing just now is this race with Albert."

Her foppish cousin's conceit in his driving ability had led him to think he could outshine his cousin in this field and bring some of her friends to his side. He had challenged her to a curricle race.

"I cannot like the idea of you racing him."

"Lucien would—"

"How many times must I tell you that you need not do all that Lucien would do just because you are standing in his clothing?"

"But, Thomas, he challenged me before my friends. You would not have them think I was afraid."

"*I'd* never think it—you haven't the sense to be afraid, even when you should be. But since you've accepted in public, I suppose you must go on with it. His cattle are as good as yours, for which he should thank Mark Warne. But I fancy he'll prove to be cow-handed."

"He hasn't had the benefit of such a good teacher as I have had. If he had learned from you, I might worry about my chances."

Thomas acknowledged this tribute to his driving skill with another grin. It was wiped away by another thought.

"From London to Newmarket—'tis a long, tiring way. I wish you had chosen a shorter route, child."

"It was Albert who named it, not I. He has heard of the famous whips who have set records along that road and hopes to beat them. I could hardly refuse. As I said, everyone was urging me to accept and would have thought it strange if I chose an easier route. Anyhow, I think I am as strong as he, and I'll wager he will find himself lurched before he's halfway there."

"Mind that you do not do the same."

The advice won him a pained look from Lucinda. "Thomas, you know I care too much for my greys to risk them in any way. Also, I shall have another reason for driving carefully, for I shall be carrying a passenger."

"A passenger in a race. Who?" he demanded, and she gave him another grin.

"Who else?"

Thomas glared at her. "That female from the Opera House? There are times, Lucinda Warne, when I am sorry you are too old to be put over my knee. I vow that you have windmills in your head. 'Tis one thing—and bad enough, considering who you are—to carry that female through the park every day. But to jaunter about the country with her—"

Lucinda laughed and said, "You must remember—I am Lucien, not Lucinda," then went off to pick up her companion and make her way to the starting line.

Chapter
Nine

CURRICLE RACES BETWEEN gentlemen had become so common that they were merely another event on which to place wagers. Conditions and course were often varied, and even the Royal Dukes had tried their skills from time to time. They did not participate often, for it was difficult to find competitors who matched their weight and every ounce counted in such a race.

Interest in this race was higher than most, however, for it was whispered that it was—at least on the part of Albert Turngren—a grudge match. Wagering had originally been heavy in favor of the captain; he was popular with the crowd, and his driving skills were well known.

The odds began to change, however, when the two vehicles appeared and it was seen that the captain carried a companion. Albert, of course, was driving alone and had even left off his many fobs and rings, having heard that gentlemen sometimes felt the weight of such gauds might make a difference in their chance of winning. If this were true, the presence of Evita in the second vehicle, slight as she seemed, might be enough to give him the victory.

The captain's friends felt much the same. Even Neddy was driven to protest, "Really, Lu, you cannot do this—it ain't fair to those of us who have already put our blunt upon you." He felt guilty because he had not yet been able to reach Mark with the information about the race, although what Mark could have done to prevent it was beyond him.

Lucinda leaned down so that only Neddy could hear and said in a low tone, "After all, I had to give the poor fellow some sort of handicap. As it is, I have no doubt that I shall pass him before we are halfway there. Your wagers are safe enough."

Friendship for the girl battled against better judgment and, since the marquess had never been overburdened with the latter, friendship won. He offered another wager upon the greys, finding his friends willing to give him much better odds than he would have received half an hour earlier.

Had anyone told him that he would be expecting a female to win in such a race—even if one had dared to enter—Neddy would have laughed. However, he knew Lucinda's ability. Also, he consoled himself with the thought that if it proved that she had erred by bringing the ladybird, at least *he* could afford to lose.

It did appear that he had made one of his customary bad bets when, at the drop of Roger Atwood's handkerchief, Albert brought his whip down sharply upon the backs of his gleaming bays and they leaped ahead. Almost leisurely, it seemed to the crowd, Lucinda dropped her hands and the greys moved forward at a brisk trot.

Evita grasped Lucinda's arm so tightly that she caused the horses to swerve, bringing a groan from some of the crowd. "Make them hurry," the dancer exclaimed in a near-panic. "Your cousin beats us."

Lucinda carefully brought her pair back under control before slanting a frowning glance at her companion. "Do that one more time and I shall set you down." Her voice was stern. "That is the way to get us overturned," she said through gritted teeth.

"But I wish you to win."

"There is no need to worry; I shall win. Thomas taught me quite well. We have a long way to go before this race is ended, and if Albert springs his cattle in that fashion at the very start, it will not be long before we pass him."

By the time the next and steeper hill had been gained, only a few lengths separated the vehicles; Lucinda urged her pair forward. Sweeping past Albert, who again brought his whip down on his nearly exhausted pair, she once more slowed her own horses to their earlier easy stride.

Glancing over her shoulder, Lucinda was compelled to pull her vehicle far to one side to pass an Accommodation Coach which was lumbering along the crown of the road, its driver unwilling to give way. In order to pass, the curricle almost went into the ditch.

Evita shrieked. She shrieked a second time as a crash sounded behind them.

"What was that?" Lucinda asked, not daring to take her gaze off the road.

"It is your cousin! He tried to pass the coach in a narrow spot and overturned himself. I cannot tell, but I think he may be hurt."

The race was over. Easing her pair to a walk, Lucinda searched for a place where she could turn her own vehicle, well aware that an attempt to turn too sharply could overset the delicately balanced curricle. She was forced to drive nearly a quarter-mile more until she found a place where she could turn about safely.

By the time she returned to the scene of the accident, Albert was struggling to his feet, and a passenger from the coach had gone to the bays' heads and was quieting them. With his own team brought once more under control, the coachman began berating both racers as care-for-nobodies who endangered the safety of his passengers.

"That will be quite enough," Lucinda told him so sharply that he was silenced for a moment, recognizing the tone of Quality and impressed by the speaker's outfit, from curly brimmed hat to gleaming Hessians. All bespoke a man of means, and it was unwise for a coachman to antagonize such a one.

Ignoring him, she said to her cousin, "We must call an end to the race for today and take you back to London. Do you think you will be able to drive?"

"I—I don't know," Albert replied, holding his head with his hands. "What—what happened?"

"What happened, you young rattlepate," the coach driver shouted, having regained his breath and being reminded by the complaints of his passengers that he had as much right to travel the road as any gentleman, "is that you nearly wrecked us all by your rackety driving."

As his head cleared, Albert took exception to the man's words and tone, and began to argue hotly with him. The young man who had been holding the bays—a country lad, Lucinda thought, having seen many of them under Lucien's command—jerked his head in an effort to bring her closer to him.

"If it would please you, sir," he said in a low tone, "I could drive your friend back to London. I am travelling that way and, although I own I have never laid ribbons over the backs of such a fine pair as these, I can handle them well enough if we do not have to go too fast. I have never driven a curricle, you see, and I think they might prove a bit hard to manage."

However inexperienced a driver he might prove to be, Lucinda was convinced that, since he cared for the animals, he would doubtless handle them better than Albert would.

"You are very kind to make such an offer," she told him. "Get up, Albert, and stop arguing with the coachman. This young man will drive you home."

Turning her back upon him without waiting to see his response, she was equally stern with the driver of the coach. "This road is not for you alone. If you had given way a bit, this need not have happened. I passed you myself, so I know you were taking more than your share of the road. However, since no one was seriously injured and no damage was done to your coach, let us hear no more about it. Get out this gentleman's luggage, if you please."

She removed the sting from her words by fishing a coin from her waistcoat pocket and tossing it to him. Looking at the glint of gold in his palm, the driver was immediately all smiles and assurances that no harm had been done. He hastened to bring out the required bag, meanwhile admonishing those passengers who were complaining about the delay to close their boneboxes if they did not wish to be set down here and now, no matter what the waybill might have to say.

When the drivers reached Grosvenor Square, Albert, without a word of thanks to the young man holding the lines, stumbled up the steps of the house, leaving Lucinda to see to the care of his bays.

She turned them over to one of the grooms, telling him to check them carefully and tend to any possible injury. Then, sensing that, unlike the coachman, the young man would be insulted if she offered to pay him for his trouble, she suggested that she should take him to his destination. He declined graciously, declaring that this was only a step away and that it was a rare privilege to be permitted to drive such a prime pair. Catching up his pack, he strode off whistling.

Lucinda drove after him to express her thanks for his kindness and to apologize for her cousin's rudeness. To herself, and later to Evita, she declared that the lad had behaved in a much more gentlemanly manner than Albert had done. At Evita's lodgings, she apologized again, this time for the shortness of their outing.

"Not that I can be unhappy that the race was cancelled," she owned. "It is odd, but I do not take such an interest in these things as I once did. But when Albert challenged me, what else could I do but accept?"

"Nothing, of course. But I enjoyed what there was of the race. I can see that you would have won easily had we kept on. And it was exciting—especially when your cousin overturned himself. Do you think he was truly hurt?"

Lucinda laughed at the other's idea of excitement. "I do not think so—merely shaken. It was only his pride that was hurt."

"And he has so much of that, it must have been a great bruise."

"It would be. I shall probably find him fabricating some tale to explain why he was not at all to blame for what happened. Poor Albert—he so wishes to do something that is noteworthy, and nothing develops as he planned. I suppose it is due to his mother's spoiling him, as Lady Leatheringham says, making him feel he is more important than he truly is. I am more concerned about his bays than about him, but I do not think they sustained any hurt. Still, I think it is best that I return home now to see what is occurring. *Hasta luego,* Evita."

Resetting her hat at the correct angle, Lucinda turned her greys in the direction of her grandfather's house. As she entered the door, she found that Albert, as she had been expecting, was giving Mark his highly colored version of the accident. He did not seem any the worse for his upset, except in his temper.

"The fool of a driver swerved the coach just as I started to pass him. There was no chance that I could miss him." He looked up to see Lucinda and called out, "You saw what happened, didn't you, cousin?"

"No, I saw nothing. You forget that I was ahead of you at the time."

"Then you had already passed the coach?" Mark asked with

interest. They exchanged grins as she nodded. "And you had no trouble?"

She shrugged, thinking it ill mannered to lay the blame on Albert. "I must own that the fellow was taking more than his share of the road, but it was certainly not enough to give me any trouble."

"You nearly grazed his wheel as you passed him," Albert said sullenly. "Doubtless that was what unnerved him and caused him to swerve."

The idea that anything another driver might do could unnerve an experienced coach driver would have been laughable at some other time, but the unfairness of Albert's comment stung.

"Are you trying to say now that *I* was at fault because you had an accident?" she demanded. "Why, when I passed him, there was *this* much space between our vehicles."

She flung out her hand to indicate the distance, just as Albert moved in her direction. Her hand struck him across the face, and Albert turned pale and fumbled for a handkerchief. A moment later, he left the room muttering something unintelligible.

Lucinda looked after him in dismay. "Now he will doubtless go about saying that I intended to strike him."

"No need to worry, little man," Mark assured her gravely. He was relieved that she was unhurt after her adventure. "If he should decide to challenge you, I promise I shall stand your second."

"A duel—with *Albert*? What should we fight with—pea shooters?" She burst into laughter, and Mark joined in.

At times such as this, when she forgot what she thought of his overbearing ways, Mark could be the most pleasant of companions. Much as she disliked to say it, he *had* been pleasant to her more often than not. When he had been harsh, usually she had been to blame. She disliked owning she had been at fault, but it was true. Besides, there was something . . .

After a moment, wondering what was going through her mind to account for her quickly changing expressions, Mark asked, "What actually *did* happen during the race?"

Lucinda shrugged. "As to the accident itself, I do not know. He had sprung his cattle at the beginning—and I must say, cousin,"—Mark gave a slight start at hearing himself so addressed; he had never wished for her to consider him a relative, at first for dislike, now for . . . for some other reason he could not explain—"that you did those bays an ill turn when you persuaded him to take them."

"I must plead guilty. But if you could have seen the animals he wanted—"

"I did see them, but they would have been a match for his driving skill, having already been ruined. The bays are too good for him. I only hope he does not do them any hurt."

"I had not considered that. Perhaps now that he has lost the race he will permit me to take them off his hands."

"I wish you will do so. If I offered to take them, he would consider it an insult and would refuse to part with them. Anyway, as I was saying, they were tiring badly when I passed him, just before the coach arrived. It was taking more than its share of the road, to be sure, and doubtless Albert was angry because I had passed him. If he used his whip as he did earlier, perhaps the bays jumped and he lost control of them. He was so certain that he would be able to beat us that he would have disliked our going ahead of him."

She paused, aware that Mark's expression had become stern. "Why so sour, cousin?" she asked in an effort to bring back the earlier pleasantness. "Do you disapprove of racing?"

"Hardly that, for I frequently indulge in the sport when I have the time to do so, even though my size is sometimes a handicap, depending upon who my opponent chances to be. But I do not enjoy it if a female is involved." He saw her start and knew she must be afraid her secret had been discovered— as it was certain to be soon, he thought, if she continued to do such madcap things. "I understand that you were carrying a passenger at the time."

For a moment, Lucinda had forgotten that someone must have told him that she was accompanied by Evita. Happy that he had meant the dancer and not herself, she grinned. "Yes, Evita Montez, from the theatre. She thought she would enjoy a race, and I always enjoy her company. You are not going to tell me that it is of my companion that you disapprove?"

Mark laughed, although he longed to tell her how greatly he disapproved of such a companion for her. But he could hardly do that without telling her he knew of her masquerade. And if he did so, she must go away. "Up in the boughs again over such a slight remark? You have a peppery disposition, but

I suppose you know that. The only thing of which I disapprove
is that you were putting a female in danger." There! He had
managed to deliver a scold without telling what he knew.

"There was no danger—not to us!"

"May I remind you there are always other drivers on the
road? You might have met another as reckless as your cousin.
As for your ladybird, you must remember that I have never
met her, so I cannot judge her in any way. But if you have used
the same good judgment in choosing her as you did when you
got your greys, I must salute your taste."

Why did he have to make such a remark? The feeling of com-
panionship she had thought was growing between them
dimmed.

As lightly as she could manage, she said, "Thomas Abbott
helped me to choose the greys."

"And of course, you chose the—er—lady yourself." Neddy
had told him how it had happened, but he wondered what she
would say about it.

"Do you think I would allow anyone else to take over so
pleasant a chore as that? But, in fact, it was the *lady* who chose
me—over half the beaux in London, who would be at her feet
if she would only permit it."

Why would the dancer have done such a thing, he wondered.
Lucinda might fool someone at first acquaintance, but she and
this Evita had been together day after day. Did the dancer suspect nothing? "That proves that the *señorita* is a rare creature,"
he commented. "And that you are more fortunate than most.
Unless, of course, it could be that she has heard of your possible
prospects."

"It is not for the future, but for the past, that she chose me—
at least at first. Because I have some knowledge of her homeland."

This was not entirely a lie, for Evita did enjoy talking to
someone who had seen her native Spain.

The little liar, Mark said to himself, uttering a hearty laugh.
Lucinda saw him raise his hand and feared he was going to clap
her on the back, as it seemed her acquaintances were forever
doing. At the last moment, however, he changed his mind and
touched her on the shoulder, giving her a slight but friendly
shake. "Enjoy your conquest, little man." Then as she started

to leave the room, "What—are you so anxious to return to her already?"

She was forced to laugh with him at that. "No, but with the race cancelled, I am left somewhat at loose ends. I had an invitation to Lady Tornway's dinner and ball, but had sent regrets, thinking I should not return in time. I shall not go to the dinner now, of course, as that would overset her plans, but I may perhaps attend the ball, after all. I do not think she would object if I did so. Do you intend to go?"

"No. I had also sent regrets. Your grandfather has not had a good day, and I should prefer to stay nearby."

"Is he worse?" Lucinda was contrite. It was so easy to forget about the old man when she never saw him. "I had no idea. Ought I to go to him? Or would my presence be bad for him?"

"No, it is better for him to remain quiet at such times as this. He has such spells now and then. The doctor tells us there is no need for concern, but I feel that I ought not to go away at this time."

Lucinda nodded. All the anger and bitterness she had once felt for the old gentleman upstairs was washed away in her concern for his present state of health.

"Since you have no definite plans for the evening," Mark suggested, thinking this would be a good opportunity to have her to himself without interruption, when perhaps she might even let something slip about herself, "how would you feel about spending an evening at home? I have heard you are better than a fair hand with the pasteboards, and I always enjoy a good game of piquet."

That man! One moment he was censuring her for something; the next, asking her to play cards with him. Lucinda hesitated, turning the idea over in her mind. She was so bored with the thought of pretending to be the gallant to a number of stupid misses. On the other hand, could she risk an entire evening in such close contact with Mark? Still—he had not penetrated her disguise in the past weeks. It was unlikely that he should be able to do so now.

Chapter Ten

"WHY NOT?" SHE agreed. "I shall try my fortune against yours."

"I hope that is merely a figure of speech, little man, for I have no fortune."

Why had he begun calling her "little man" so often? True, he was of greater size, but she knew Lucien would have objected to the term. She did not. "Nor have I. The army does not pay that well."

"And you have not set your sights upon your grandfather's money?"

Yes—but not for myself, only for Lucien, she thought. He *must* have it. Still, she was able to say, "I believe you have as much chance of getting it as I." Far more, in fact, she thought.

"That's as may be," he said noncommittally. He was thankful that Albert had other plans and would not be with them this evening. It would be much more . . . comfortable . . . with just the two of them.

He was an unusual man, Lucinda thought, studying him as he turned away to order the meal. He could be autocratic one moment, kind and considerate the next. And he made her a prey to conflicting emotions, as well. There were times when she found herself disliking him so much that, if she had indeed been a man, she would have been tempted to plant him a facer. At others, she found herself liking him very much.

Perhaps too much.

They spoke of various trivial matters during dinner, such as the places she had seen since her arrival. Mark told her of others which sounded interesting, and Lucinda privately vowed to see them before she left.

Near the end of the meal, he said, "I have been thinking of going to the races at Newmarket next week. Would you care to keep me company, since you missed getting there today?"

Lucinda's eyes glowed. Even on the continent, England's Newmarket races were known. What a thrill it would be to tell Lucien that she had seen them. She admired the beauty of a good horse, but watching the races did not appeal to her as it would have done to him. Since he could not see them, she would go in his place.

"Many of the fellows we know have friends living in the vicinity of Newmarket and rack up with them during the season. But when I go—I do not always do so—I prefer to stay at an inn." He watched her in secret amusement, wondering how she would respond.

An inn! The glow faded from Lucinda's eyes. She could not go to an inn with him. If a great crowd attended the races, as she supposed they would, there would be no way to obtain a room to herself. She would be forced to share with Mark and possibly with several others. It was impossible.

"I do not doubt you will consider me an unnatural sort of Englishman," she managed at last, unaware of the truth of her words, "but racing as a sport has never held any great interest for me. I have seen any number, of course, even some between our soldiers, many of whom are racing-mad. But I prefer to do my gaming with a deck of cards."

"As you will." The great shoulders shrugged.

"I trust I am not oversetting any plans of yours by my refusal?"

"Certainly not, Captain." Had she imagined it, or was there a hint of stiffness in his voice? "Although I should have enjoyed having your company. As I said, I may go, or I may not. If I do not, do not blame yourself." Of course, he would not go— he could not leave her on her own with only Neddy to watch her. Besides, it was almost certain Neddy would wish to go. So *he* must stay to play watchdog. Surprisingly, he found that he did not mind the task as he would have done some weeks ago. Quite the opposite, in fact.

Rising, he said, "Since you prefer the cards, shall we have

a game of piquet? I shall just step up and see how your grandfather is doing, then join you in the library."

"But may I not see him?"

"No." More gently he added, "I am sorry, but when he has these spells, it is best that he be kept as quiet as possible. When he is feeling better, I know he will welcome a visit from you."

"Of course. I should not wish to disturb him. But if you speak to him, please tell him that I am sorry to hear he is down pin."

Mark nodded and strode away, while Lucinda made her way to the library. He was very considerate of the old man, she thought. And not just because he was being paid for his services or because the earl was his great-uncle. He truly cared for him.

She began to wonder if much of the friction between the two of them might not be, as Thomas had declared, her fault. As resentful as she was of anything that might belittle Lucien, she doubtless read disparagement into what had been intended as friendly advice.

Mark's return put an end to her self-chastisement. "He is resting well," he reported, "but not yet asleep. I gave him your message, and it pleased him."

"I did not say it for that reason—"

"I know you did not, which made it the more pleasing." In a way, he could understand her earlier resentment of the earl and was happy that it had vanished. His hand rested lightly on her shoulder for an instant, then he drew up a chair opposite hers. Fenton came into the room with a tray bearing a bottle, several glasses, and two decks of cards.

"Sherry, Captain?" Mark asked, filling a glass and handing it to her. "I have noted that, like me, you tend to stay away from the heavier wines." Sherry was not too strong a drink for a female, yet one which an officer would not despise, he thought.

"Thank you." Lucinda took the glass, hoping he had not noticed much more about her. She eyed him with caution, but Mark had taken up the cards and was intent upon shuffling them. He dealt them out, and Lucinda, examining hers, declared, "A point of five."

"Good."

"A point of five. I score five. A tierce."

"How high?"

"Queen."

"Not good."

So it went through several games. Mark was a slightly better player, but Lucinda won almost as often as she lost. Now and then, Mark added wine to her glass, seeming not to notice that she only sipped from it, as he, too, drank sparingly.

As one game ended, Lucinda reached out to gather up the cards scattered across the table and glanced up to find Mark studying her. A twitch of her hand sent several cards off the edge of the table and both bent to retrieve them. She caught up the cards and Mark's hand closed over hers, sending a lightning shock through her entire being. Confused by her reaction, she drew her hand from his and began stacking the scattered cards. She played badly after that, unable to keep her mind focussed. When she had been capotted for the second time, Mark declared, "I think it time we called the game to a halt. I am for an early bedtime, and I think you must be the same."

As they rose from the table, Lucinda, in an effort to hide her troubled thoughts, said, "It is unfortunate for you, cousin, that we were not playing for stakes. You would have won quite a share of my allowance."

"No matter," he told her with a smile. " 'Tis the game itself that is important. I am content to be the winner."

Despite his declaration of a wish for an early bedtime, he sank back into his seat as Lucinda went upstairs. He shuffled the cards and laid them about in aimless patterns, wondering why he should be so happy just to have spent a quiet evening with a girl he had considered a shameless hoyden only weeks ago. At last, he flung down the cards, exclaiming, "Warne, you are behaving exactly like an idiot," and made his way to his room.

Mark was closeted with his accounts when Lucinda left the house next day. She was content not to see him, unable to explain to herself her newly sympathetic feelings toward him. Now, lounging in a chair at Evita's, she ran her fingers through her hair, disturbing its careful arrangement, and grimaced as she studied the girl opposite her. "That gown suits you so well, Evita, that I must own I am quite jealous."

Evita twirled about, the better to display it, pleased at the compliment, knowing there was no jealousy here. "You will not be shocked if I tell you it is a gift from my Robin?"

"Certainly, I am not." Lucinda thought of the many intimate gifts *Maman* had accepted from gentlemen through the years and smiled. "He is quite generous, your Robin. I am happy that you are seeing him again."

"Yes—now and then he remembers me. I think I owe you much for that. But, although he is bringing me gifts, he goes often to visit with some other." The dancer fingered the shimmering satin which displayed her graceful figure so well. "Perhaps in time, the thought that I have another 'admirer' will bring him back to me for good."

Lucinda laughed. "Knowing the *ton,* I am certain he has been told about our every meeting. And although you do not mean it in that way, you do have an admirer. I admire you greatly."

"I do not see how you can say so. Most ladies of your class look down upon me. Or pretend that they do not see me at all, which is worse."

"But I am nothing like most ladies of my class, as you must know. Else I should never have thought of this . . . this masquerade. Oh, Evita, if you only knew how tired I am of all this! How I wish that I could attend a ball as *myself,* in a beautiful gown!"

"I do know it, Lucinda. I have seen how—tedious, is that the word?—you find your role. Especially of late." Suddenly, her black eyes sparkled. "Will you put yourself in my hands? Completely?"

"What do you have in mind?"

"No—I shall not tell it. You must wait and learn. Will you do it?"

"I . . . I suppose so." Certainly, Evita would never do anything to harm Lucinda's position. The dancer knew how greatly the other counted upon her masquerade to influence the earl in Lucien's favor. And with only a few weeks to go . . .

"*Bueño.* Then return here tonight and you shall learn what it is."

"Tonight? Do you not have to perform?"

"No, for tonight I shall play the—the—*como se dice?*—when one does not work?"

"The truant?"

"That is it. I shall be the truant. So you must come to me tonight."

Mystified, Lucinda agreed and left.

When she and her two cousins gathered for dinner, she looked at Mark in surprise and said, "I did not expect to see you here. I thought you had planned to go to Newmarket."

"I said I might go and I might not. I decided against going."

"Grandfather? He is not worse?"

"Nothing of the kind. I merely found it would be less enjoyable to go without company. That is all."

"You mean that you turned down an opportunity to go to *Newmarket?*" Albert said enviously. "I should have agreed to go at once," although none of his few friends had suggested his going. He looked hopefully at Mark, then glowered as the secretary refused to take the hint. Albert considered Mark beneath him, but would have accepted his company for such an outing.

How can he? Lucinda wondered. He treats Mark as if he were a servant, then expects favors from him. Aunt Sophia must indeed have spoiled him to make him so . . . so thick-skinned. It would have done him good to have spent several years under Thomas' rule.

As if the smaller man had said nothing, Mark turned to her, asking, "Shall we have more piquet tonight? I shall give you a chance to redeem yourself."

She wanted very much to be in his company, but she was suddenly shy of spending time alone with him. "I must beg off for this evening, cousin. I should be happy to oblige, but I have made other plans."

Aware that Mark was not going to extend to him the invitation his cousin had rejected, Albert sneered, "Piquet—and for chicken stakes, I'll wager."

"Then you would lose," Lucinda retorted. "For we had no stakes at all."

"Even worse. You should come with me, coz. A friend is going to take me to a new hell where he has promised the play will be interesting."

Mark scowled, then shrugged. Albert's "friend" had been introducing him to gaming establishments where the play was deep. Either the cards were fuzzed and the dice loaded, or the younger man was merely an inept player. Twice he had asked—demanded would be a better word—additional money. Still, the earl had said to let him have what he wished for the next two months. And if the old man thought a halt should be called to the young snirp's spending, he would say so.

At least, the girl had better sense, he thought, as she shook her head at the invitation. "Thank you, but I find I do not care to play with sharps. And as I said, I have other plans for tonight."

The lamplighter was beginning to make his rounds when Lucinda arrived in Evita's rooms. Wishing neither to have her cattle standing or to own to Thomas what she was doing—she did not know what it would be, but she was certain to object—she had taken a hackney.

Evita opened the door, her eyes shining. "Look," she exclaimed, pointing to the bed. Spread across it was a lovely gown of emerald satin. At one glance she knew that it did not belong to the dancer.

"For you. For tonight," she explained.

"What—? Where did you get it?" Lucinda demanded, rubbing appreciative fingers over the lustrous cloth.

"I hired it. You do not object to wearing a hired gown, do you?"

"It is not that, but—" Lucinda knew that stage finery, while it gave the appearance of being costly was actually quite shabby when seen too closely. This was nothing of the sort.

"I know a dressmaker who provides gowns for those who are invited to perform at affairs of the *ton*. They must appear at their best at such times, but they cannot afford to purchase such things. So they go to her. Put it on quickly, Lucinda. I think it is exactly your size. We are going to Vauxhall tonight!"

"Vauxhall? Oh, I could not. If I were seen—"

"I have thought of that as well." Evita brought out a beautifully styled wig of dark auburn and a green egret mask which exactly matched the gown. "There will be many there tonight who will be masked, so you will not be noticed. Oh, you will be noticed, of course, but not *recognized*."

As Lucinda hesitated, she went on, "You need not worry. It will not be like the masquerade at the Opera House."

The lure of the beautiful gown was enough to overcome all

Lucinda's objections, and she quickly doffed her male attire. With a few deft adjustments, made by Evita, the gown was pronounced a perfect fit by both girls. The auburn wig and the mask completed the transformation. No one, she was certain, would think the tall, elegant lady was Captain Warne.

"You are beautiful," Evita told her.

"It is the gown that is beautiful. And the hair. But, Evita, you must allow me to give you what it cost you."

"But I wish to do something for you, *mi amiga*. You have done so much for me."

"My dear friend, just the opportunity of wearing so lovely a gown, even for a few hours, is more of a treat than you can know. I should not insult you by the offer of payment, except that I know you are not too plump in the pocket—I mean, you do not have much money," she explained to the other's questioning look, "and my allowance from the earl is more than I can spend."

"But my Robin—"

"He may be generous, but you can scarcely expect him to pay for this escapade, my dear." Lucinda turned about, studying her reflection in Evita's stained mirror. The gown fitted itself about her, showing a form more feminine than she recalled. The neckline was not extremely low; indeed, compared with many she had seen at balls, it was demure. However, after these weeks when she had worn Lucien's shirts and coats, her throat and shoulders seemed quite bare. She felt as if she should be covered and was relieved when Evita draped a light shawl about her.

It was amazing how greatly the auburn wig transformed her appearance, and with the feather-trimmed mask hiding all except her mouth, it was unlikely that she would be recognized, even by the captain's friends, should she chance to meet them. She smiled with delight at Evita, whose small form was clad in ruby satin, much less discreet in cut than Lucinda's gown.

"We shall have a wonderful evening, shall we not?" the dancer said, slipping her arm into the taller girl's and leading her away.

Lucinda had visited Vauxhall in company with some of her male friends, but it seemed a different world tonight. The glitter of the many lamps and the far-off sound of music transformed it into a dream world. The two young females were ogled by wandering groups of bucks, whose advances were skillfully parried by the Spanish girl. It had been decided that, in case they should meet someone who knew the captain, Lucinda should pretend to be fresh from Spain and know no English.

Some of the remarks tossed their way, complimentary as they might be, were rather warm, and it was difficult for Lucinda to keep a vague smile upon her lips as if she could not understand what was being said.

"I had not expected that you would be so slurred," Evita whispered.

"They do not matter," Lucinda told her softly. "It is so wonderful a feeling to be out of those hateful male clothes, even for this short time, that it is worth the price. And they think I do not know what they are saying." She winked mischievously at her companion. "However, I shall be careful not to allow any of them to persuade me to accompany them down one of those dark walks."

"On no account must you do that," Evita agreed, and they continued to stroll along, admiring the colored lanterns and the crowds of people moving about. In the boxes, most of which were occupied by members of the *ton,* some of the ladies were masked, some were not. Nearly all of the gentlemen had dispensed with masks. Here, the babble of many voices almost drowned the efforts of the orchestra.

"It is almost as noisy here as it was at the masquerade at the Opera House," Lucinda said in a low tone, hearing an occasional squeal from the darkened walks and the sound of male voices slurred by drink.

Evita nodded, then stopped as a hand clamped itself about her arm and a voice exclaimed, "Eve—it is you, is it not? What are you doing here tonight?"

"Oh—oh, Robin. I did not think to see you. I play the—I forget the word—but I do not work tonight so that I may show the park to my cousin Margarita."

"Your cousin?"

"*Sí*—my cousin Margarita, who has just come from Spain. She speaks no English, so let me tell her about you."

She repeated the remarks in Spanish and Lucinda turned to face the gentleman, happy that her mask could conceal her surprise. Evita's Robin was none other than Lord Byrne, Stella Proctor's persistent, but unfortunate, suitor. She ought not to be surprised, she thought. Many gentlemen had both a wife and a mistress. Lord Byrne might not achieve the bride he wanted, but he could be certain of Evita's devotion.

"I must speak to you . . ." he was just saying, when a large man appeared at his side and cut in. "Do not be selfish, Byrne. Introduce me to your friends."

At the sound of his voice, Lucinda gasped, but managed to hide her face behind her fan until she had regained her composure. Of all the people in London, to meet Mark Warne *here*!

Mark had wondered for a time when Lucinda had been so firm about her engagement for the evening. Many of the captain's friends would have gone to Newmarket, but some were still in London—and who knew what mischief they might lead her into, without either Neddy or himself to watch over her.

Tonight was to be a gala night at Vauxhall, just the sort of affair which would appeal to some of the young bucks. They would ogle the young ladies, doubtless drink more than they should, and indulge in who knew what sort of antics with the light wenches along the dark walks.

It was no place for his girl to be. To himself he now owned he always thought of her as his, although she might never know it.

He had wandered about Vauxhall for some time, searching vainly for the well-remembered figure. In the distance, he espied two females walking together. The smaller one looked familiar and he moved closer, recognizing her as the dancer he had seen in Lucinda's curricle the day he had watched them in the park. He thought she was employed at the Opera House. What was she doing here?

The taller female turned to speak to her companion, and Mark caught his breath. He had never seen Lucinda in women's clothing, but he knew her at once. That line of jaw and chin, the way of moving her head, gave her away to anyone who had observed her as carefully as he had.

He eyed the green-clad figure appreciatively. She was slim, of course, but certainly not the maypole he had once imagined her. A delightful armful, in fact.

When he saw Byrne accost the smaller form and speak to her earnestly, he approached and said, "Introduce me to your friends."

Byrne had not noticed anyone but the Spanish girl. Now he

whirled about to face Mark. Seeing who it was, he managed a smile and said, "Very well. Evita Montez, *my* friend. And this—"

"Is my cousin Margarita," Evita said, ignoring Lucinda's tugging at her arm. "I am sorry, *Señor* Warne. She knows no English."

"I am sorry to hear that, for I do not speak Spanish. Will you convey to her how happy I am to meet her?" He caught Lucinda's hand and bowed over it.

Evita repeated his remarks in Spanish. Lucinda, fearing that even in a strange tongue, the sound of her voice might betray her, merely nodded. Leaning down, she whispered in the other girl's ear, "I must leave here *at once!*"

"My cousin thanks you for your kindness," the dancer said, her eyes sparkling. This was a situation to please her heart. From Lucinda's conversations, she had learned enough about her friend's feelings toward the large man. More than Lucinda knew she was revealing, possibly more than she herself knew of it.

Lucinda tugged at Evita's arm again, but the dancer ignored her. On her other side, Lord Byrne was repeating, "Eve, we must talk," and his voice drowned all else for her.

"Perhaps," Mark Warne said tactfully, his gaze fixed on the figure in the green gown, "your cousin might walk with me to admire the lights while you are talking."

"Yes, oh, yes—that would be wonderful." In her delight at Lord Byrne's presence, Evita forgot that her "cousin" was not supposed to understand English.

Lucinda bent down another time and said in a fierce whisper, "Evita, I cannot. You know that I cannot go with him. I must not. Tell him it is not proper."

"But you must go," Evita told her in rapid Spanish. "I must know what my Robin wishes to say to me—and I fear he will not speak when the two of you are here."

Chapter
Eleven

MARK APPEARED TO take it for granted that Evita was giving her cousin permission to accompany him. He hoped that was what she was saying, for—permission or not—he meant to have the girl to himself. Despite Lucinda's hesitation, he took her hand, but a moment later, his arm encircled her waist as he began to draw her away, not in the direction of the lights, as he had said, but toward the paths where there was more darkness between the lanterns. From the pitchblack areas beside the paths came sighs and giggles which told of lovers who had sought the darkness.

More than anything, Lucinda would have enjoyed such a rendezvous with Mark, but she dared not, fearing that she would betray herself. "No, *señor, no puedo*," she said, pitching her voice higher than usual, a sense of near-panic aiding her to distort its sound. "*Debo que quedarme con mi prima.*"

What good was it to protest, to tell him she must stay with Evita, when he could not understand her? If only Evita had not told him she spoke no English! "*La musica està alla*," she said desperately, gesturing toward the sound. He could certainly understand that much. If she must spend this time with him, she would have enjoyed a dance, especially a waltz, since he danced so well.

A dance, however, was far from Mark's thoughts. "It sounds better from a distance," he said, drawing her along the path. Aside from digging in her heels, Lucinda had no choice but to go where he wished. In the dimness, he turned her to face him. The warmth of his hands burned into the flesh of her bare shoulders.

Then his hands were cupping her face, his thumbs drawing caressing circles upon her cheeks below the mask, taking turns in outlining her lips, sending shivers to every inch of her. She put her hands against his chest, attempting to push him away. "No," she whispered, "n—"

The word was cut off as his mouth captured her own. His arms had dropped to encircle her waist and shoulders, holding her tightly against him. Without their support, she doubted if she would have been able to stand, for her senses were reeling.

She had no experience with kisses and had not known that one—even one of Mark's—could be so devastating. His hands were moving caressingly upon her back and shoulders, sending ripples through her from each point of contact. She gasped as his lips found the hollow of her throat, then began tracing kisses along the line of her jaw before taking her willing mouth another time.

She felt him shudder as her hands slipped up his chest and shoulders until she could fasten them behind his head, her fingers luxuriating in the feel of his crisp hair. One of his hands went to the ties of her mask, and she reached quickly to stop him. Even with the paint upon her face, Lucinda did not dare to let him see her unmasked. "No." It was only a whisper, but a forceful one.

"And why not?" Mark's voice was husky. From the moment he had recognized her green-clad form this evening, he had known this was what he wanted—to hold her, to kiss her, to tell her of his feelings. This was the perfect time to end the masquerade, now when she was willing in his arms. "You are so very lovely, but I want to see your eyes, kiss their lids, see that you feel as I do. If only I could make you understand—"

Even if she had been the girl he thought her, one who knew no English, Lucinda thought, his tone was unmistakable. She must do something to distract him from his wish to see her entire face. "*Y tu eres muy guapo, mi amor,*" she murmured, daring to touch his cheek, to allow her fingers to trail across his lips as he had done with hers, till he crushed her against him once more, his mouth taking hers with a passion which sent sparks of flame racing through her veins. Now she knew why she had become dissatisfied with her masquerade, why she wanted to be a woman again. She had wanted Mark—*Mark*— to hold her as he was doing now, to kiss her, to tell her she was beautiful to him. In another moment, she would be telling him who she was, begging him to forgive her deception.

Evita darted out of the shadows. "*Venga, Margarita!*" she cried. "*Venga immidiamente!*" She tugged at Lucinda's arm, pulling her from Mark's embrace. "We must leave—at once!" she said to him and began to run, drawing the other after her, ignoring Mark's shouts to them to wait.

"What is it?" Lucinda cried, gasping for breath, attempting to stop Evita's headlong rush. "What has happened?" Why did you take me out of Mark's arms, she wanted to say. Just when I was about to tell him . . .

Evita hailed a passing hackney and pushed Lucinda into it, giving breathless directions to the jarvey. Once they were under way, she said, "Forgive me, *mi* Lucinda, for hurrying you away. I should never have interrupted you at such a time, but it means my life. Robin has said that he will come to me in an hour, and I have promised him that I shall get rid of my cousin by that time—find her some other place to stay the night."

"But why should we hurry so madly if you have an hour? Perhaps there is another room in your lodging where I could go. If he should come before I am gone, I shall just bid you 'Good night,' and leave."

"Have you forgotten?" Evita wailed. "We have left the *capitàn*'s clothing spread all about my bedchamber."

"Oh, yes—it would never do for him to see that. We must remove all evidence of the captain's presence. Cannot the driver go faster?"

It seemed to both girls that the journey would never end, but at last they were scampering up the stairs to Evita's room.

"There is no time to search around for another room for you. You must change and leave here at once," Evita ordered, fumbling with the fastenings of Lucinda's gown while the other removed her mask and wig, and wiped the paint from her face. As she struggled into Lucien's garments, Evita caught up "Margarita's" costume and hid it behind her own clothing.

"The best of fortune to you, my dear friend," Lucinda told her, opening the door. She knew most young ladies in Polite Society would be shocked at the mere idea of an assignation,

let alone practically taking part in one. But they had not been
raised as she had, with the memory of *Maman* and her friends.

As Evita's door closed behind her, she heard the lower door
open and a heavy tread beginning to mount the stairs. It would
not do for her to meet Lord Byrne upon the stairs, especially
with her half-buttoned coat and untied cravat giving evidence
of her hasty dressing. Byrne must have known the name of
Evita's other "admirer," and he would be enraged to find
"him" slipping from her room in this fashion.

Fortunately, there was another floor above, and Lucinda
hastened up past the bend in the stairs, waiting until the door
below had closed behind his lordship. She buttoned her coat,
ran her fingers through her hair, and struggled to arrange her
cravat.

"I cannot do better than that," she muttered, tiptoeing down
the stairs to the street. "And what does it matter? There is no
one to see Captain Warne slipping out of his ladybird's home
to escape a rival."

Overcome by the absurdity of the situation, she leaned
against the building, laughing until her sides ached. Not that
there would have been anything laughable had she been caught
by Lord Byrne. Doubtless, she would have had to choose between facing him, pistol in hand, one morning or revealing her
masquerade. The first might well cost her life, the second would
certainly be the end of her reputation. And of Lucien's, as well,
which would be worse.

Still, the evening had been worth the danger—dressing for
the first time in weeks in a beautiful gown, even the ogling by
the bucks at Vauxhall, the ecstasy she had felt in Mark's embrace. At least the oglers had shown her that she was attractive,
although some of them were so deep in their cups that their
comments must be discounted.

Mark had called her beautiful. Mark . . . If only he could
have said such a thing to *her,* rather than to "Margarita," who,
for all he knew, was no better than she should be—one who
would permit such liberties from a stranger.

"Poo," she said aloud. "Why should I want *Mark Warne*
to think me beautiful?" Liar, something within her clamored.
You know you would prize that more than anything.

Aware that, despite her efforts, she must still present a dishe-
velled appearance, she decided to walk home rather than to hail

a hackney and arouse speculation even in the mind of a stranger. The moonlight was certainly bright enough to discourage footpads. And she had much to think about.

When had the resentment she had first felt toward Mark changed to this . . . to this— "Admit it, Lucinda," she said aloud. "You are in love with the man. It makes no sense, but it is true. You love him—and he does not even know you exist." She sighed and wished she had never begun this foolish disguise. If she had stayed at Lucien's side, she would have been safe from this love which could bring her nothing except unhappiness.

The footman who admitted her to the house was too sleepy to notice anything amiss in her appearance, but as she crossed the hall toward the stairs, Mark came to the door of the library and hailed her. She did not see the glint of amusement in his eyes as he observed her. So the game was to continue, he thought. He had hoped that, after this evening, Lucinda would be willing to confide in him. But he had been wrong. She looked every inch the rake who had barely escaped being caught.

"But then, what could I expect?" he said beneath his breath. "That she would come in boldly in her green gown—perhaps even with the mask and wig."

Lucinda had not expected that he would still be about and felt herself flushing as she recalled how she had been held in his embrace a short time ago. He did not seem to notice, however, and merely said, "A good evening to you, Captain. Will you join me in a drink before retiring?"

She would have preferred to refuse and seek the privacy of her room, but he seemed to have taken her acceptance for granted. Leaving the footman to hold the door for her, he returned to the library. She came cautiously into the room, but he was standing by the drink table, his back to the door. "A brandy, Captain?" he asked.

"Thank you," she managed, although if she must drink with him, she would have preferred something less potent. How well would the brandy sit with the flame that seemed to course through her every time she glanced at him?

Nodding dismissal to the footman, Mark handed her a glass and said, "I observed your little ladybird tonight at Vauxhall. At least, I think it was she. But you would seem to have a rival for her charms."

How could he have recognized Evita? When had he seen her? At least, he would never know her "cousin." "You mean Byrne?" she said lightly. Sipping her drink and feeling its fire slip down her throat, she went on, "Yes, we seem to be in conflict in several areas. But I do not worry. I saw them together—for a moment—but I was otherwise engaged." And would he not be shocked if she added, "With you"?

What would she say, he wondered, if he told her that he knew well how she was occupied. "Then you were there also?"

"For a time." Fortified by the brandy, she decided to be daring. "You did not see me, then? I caught a glimpse of you, but did not wish to interrupt, as you were strolling with some carrot-top. Too much of a Long Meg for me. I am surprised that you were able to tear yourself away from her so soon."

" 'Twas the other way around, I fear. She tore herself away from me—without giving me an opportunity to arrange another meeting. Not that I could have done so, anyhow, for neither of us spoke the other's language."

"I can see that would pose something of a problem." She was shocked. She did not think Mark was the sort who would boast of his exploits, even with a . . . a "Margarita."

She was right, for he only said, "Quite a problem, for how can one say what he feels? I mean, he can do so, but if the words are not understood . . . Still, there are times when words are not so important." He smiled, as if in memory of the encounter.

"True," Lucinda said, feeling that further words would choke her.

"And you—you seem to have had an enjoyable evening." Mark's hand flicked the disordered cravat.

She choked a bit on her drink, recalling her struggle to get into these things before Byrne should arrive, then started to make a light reply. She was left speechless when Mark went on, "Most enjoyable, I should think it," and reached out a thumb to brush the corner of her mouth, once more sending unexpected sensations through her.

Then she saw in horror the red lip-paint on his thumb. How had she missed that? He must suspect something. Still, perhaps there was no reason for him to do so. She had sometimes seen her brother return home with just such a telltale stain. And there were other red stains upon Mark's handkerchief when he drew it out to wipe his thumb. She hoped he would not notice they were the same color.

Apparently he had seen nothing. "Rest well, little man," he said. "May your dreams be pleasant."

"And may your fortune be better next time," Lucinda managed to reply.

"Had you watched longer, you might have noticed that I had no cause for complaint. I could hope that I might see the charmer again. But if not . . . 'twas a pleasant enough interlude."

A pleasant enough interlude! Lucinda made her way up the stairs with her head high, pleased that he could not see that her lip was caught between her teeth to stop its trembling or that her eyes were moist. Those moments she had spent in Mark's arms were a bit of heaven for her—a heaven she knew she could never again attain. And to him they were merely a pleasant interlude, a moment or two of dalliance with a Spanish ladybird. It was an effort to restrain herself from running to the haven of her room.

Mark stood in the doorway, hands thrust into his pockets, grinning after her. It was time, indeed, to end this charade. He would follow her, tell her that he had known it was she all the time and resume those wonderful moments at Vauxhall.

Vauxhall! His grin faded. Why had she been there? Whom had she intended to meet? Certainly, she had known who he was when he held her in his arms. But in Vauxhall, masked and gowned as she was, would she have gone equally willingly to some other man's embrace?

Mark Warne was easily the second most miserable person in London that night.

Mark's wishes for pleasant dreams for her not coming true, Lucinda awoke to find her pillow wet with tears. The servants must not be left to wonder, so she tossed the pillow carelessly against the washstand, then toppled her pitcher of hot water over it.

"Why should I care what *he* likes?" she asked herself defiantly as she dressed. "The only thing that matters is that I can finish the two months and convince grandfather that Lucien is the proper heir for him."

Nothing else must be allowed to matter. Least of all her aching heart.

Deep in thought, she descended the stairs and entered the breakfast room, colliding with Albert, who was just leaving. The force of the collision made the young man stagger backward and, still angered at the thought of the poor showing he had made in the race, he cried, "You did that deliberately. Just as you struck me the other day. Do you think yourself so important merely because, in a short time, you can go back to your army and strut about in a uniform? A lot you know about real fighting."

"What are you talking about?" Lucinda demanded.

"You—and your ways. You have been like that ever since you came. Knocking a fellow about, pushing him out of your way . . . and . . . and *everything*."

By this time, he had convinced himself that it was entirely his cousin's fault that he had had the accident during the race. Also, it was his cousin who was to blame for so many of the hostesses' turning a cold shoulder upon him. As much as he pretended they were beneath his notice, it galled Albert to be overlooked when his cousin was invited to these functions.

"Let us see how much of a fighter you are," he taunted. "Come down to Jackson's Saloon with me, and I'll paint your eye just as you did mine." He had never been inside the sporting establishment, but he made himself believe that it was his cousin who would shy at going.

"Gentleman Jackson's?" Mark asked, emerging from the breakfast room and looking critically at the two figures before him—first at Albert, who looked at the moment a great deal like a highly colored bantam cock, prancing about and crowing his defiance to the world, and then at his taller, but quite slim cousin. To those who knew no better, Lucinda would appear to be a better fighter than the other. And knowing, as he did, her reckless acceptance of any dare, she might well agree. He must stop her before she did so. "I suppose you might go down there—that is, if you do not object to being made laughing-stocks. Jackson will not hesitate to tell you that neither of you would strip to advantage."

On the verge of declaring to her cousin that she was certain she could draw his cork a second time as easily as she had done before—only, this time, she would do it purposely—Lucinda was brought up short by Mark's comment. Naturally, she had never been permitted to enter a boxing saloon. And no one had suggested taking her to such a place since she had come to London, if she did not count the mill.

Even so, she ought to have realized that the gentlemen who frequented such places could scarcely stand up to fight in their tight-fitting coats and breeches. They would have to remove a part of their clothing if they did not change entirely. She doubted they would be allowed any privacy for changing, or at least, there would be servants to assist them. Unwittingly, Mark had saved her from embarrassment, if not from discovery. For that she could forgive him—well, almost—for saying that last night's encounter was just a "pleasant interlude."

What was she to do now? She could not avoid Albert's direct challenge without appearing a coward. Lucien, of course, could have milled him down, but she could scarcely begin a brawl beneath her grandfather's roof—and she could not do so elsewhere.

"I have heard it said by some of my men," she said to both the others, "that here in England, it is the custom for even men of quality to fight with their fists. You must realize, of course, that it is not the custom where I was raised."

"I thought you would not do it," Albert jeered.

"In my home, a blow is used only as a challenge. Even then, a slap is considered sufficient. To strike another with a fist would be thought uncivilized."

That should put paid to his ranting, Mark thought, admiring her wit. Albert's sneer remained, however, and Lucinda knew she must do something about that.

"It is possible that you would be able to pummel me, although I beg leave to doubt that you could come near enough even to touch me. Still, I refuse to indulge in so plebeian an encounter. Would you consider, instead, crossing blades with me, cousin?"

"I would," Albert said so promptly that Lucinda was startled. She had not expected him to agree. In fact, she would not have thought he knew which end of a sword was dangerous. In any case, she was certain she would not be in any danger from him, for she had been well taught. Lucien was a master swordsman and had drilled her till he owned she was nearly as good as he. It seemed that her tomboy years were to stand her in good stead another time.

That's thrown the cat amongst the pigeons, Mark thought. What are you going to do now, my girl?

She turned to him. "Where shall we find a fencing academy?" He would be the one to know, and she would put no faith in any place recommended by Albert. In a fencing saloon, she would not be expected to remove more than her coat and perhaps her boots.

"There are several good ones about the City. I can provide you with their direction. But why should you go out? You can have your match here, just as well." Here, where I can come to your rescue if need be, he silently added.

"Here?"

"Why not? Your grandfather planned at one time to have an armament room and began a collection of weapons. Later his interest was turned to other things, but there are several excellent pairs of foils among the weapons he did purchase. Since he did not care to continue with his plans for the room, the weapons have been left in the library. Perhaps you have noticed them there. You may try your proficiency against one another and—if you will allow—I shall challenge the victor. Although I must own my skill with the blade is limited."

As Mark moved ahead of them into the library, Albert grimaced at his broad back. Lucinda sensed that he was about to make some comment about fencing's being a sport for gentlemen rather than for servants and forgot her earlier comments against the use of fists. Thrusting one before Albert's face, she whispered, "Say it—if you wish to feel the weight of this again."

Albert had nearly convinced himself that the reputation of his cousin's bravery was a myth—and he was certain that the captain's reason for suggesting this match was that he was afraid of a battle of fisticuffs. As a consequence, the other's threat of violence was enough to startle him into silence.

In the library, Mark brought out the earl's collection of weapons of various ages, some of them, as he had said, excellent specimens. He selected a pair of foils and placed them upon the table, then showed them a pair of duelling pistols.

"After you have finished your exercise with the blades, you

may enjoy a test of these. At targets, of course, not at each other. I do not think your grandfather would approve of *that.*"

"But 'twould be a way of narrowing the race for the old man's blunt," Albert said with a snicker.

Mark looked at him as if he would like to use one of the pistols over the other's head. Lucinda hoped he would not; the instrument was much too fine to be damaged. After a moment, Mark shrugged and placed the weapon beside its mate.

His businesslike method of arranging the match was such a contrast to his ardent behavior of last evening. But then, she was not the same, either. What would he say, Lucinda wondered, if he knew *she* had been "Margarita"? It did no good to think of such matters, so she pushed them aside.

Taking up one of the pistols, she balanced it in her hand, admiring its weight as well as the beauty of the chased design upon its long barrel and the gold inlay upon its grip. "It is beautiful," she commented. "There is nothing I should enjoy more than trying it."

Not to be outdone, Albert agreed, although his own talent as a marksman was, like his other sporting talents, far below his belief in them. Mark loaded the weapons and laid them aside, giving orders to a servant to have targets set up in the yard behind the house.

"Also, see that his lordship is informed of what we are about to do," he instructed. "He is better today, but we do not wish him to be disturbed by the sound of the shots."

Having determined that the foils were evenly matched for weight and length, Mark offered one to each of them. Albert, of course, refused to accept Mark's judgment and insisted upon measuring them himself. Watching him throw aside his brocade coat and kick off his high-heeled boots, Lucinda knew her threat had angered him, but she did not mind his ill humor. In fact, she preferred it to his natural hauteur.

It was stupid of Albert to continue to treat Mark as an inferior when they knew he was as much a Warne as they. It was only the fact that the title must pass through the male line which had prevented him from being the Earl of Brayling instead of their grandfather. Still, as she followed her younger cousin's example and rolled up the sleeves of her shirt, she could not help feeling a bit of pity for Albert, much as she disliked his dandyish ways and resented the rudeness he often displayed.

She had seen other young men of his kind. They always wished to make a good showing, but always fell short of their object. Despite that, the overindulgence of their parents caused them to grow up with an exalted opinion of themselves and the belief that it was impossible for them to be defeated. Those who went into the army would soon be shown the error of their ways by their fellow-soldiers. It was a pity that Albert had never before come against this kind of treatment. It would have done him a great deal of good.

It was past time, she thought, that someone administered a lesson or two. Nothing would kill his pride more quickly than to learn that, for the past few weeks, he had been consistently defeated by a female. At least, she would spare him that knowledge. And despite her desire to discipline him, she had determined to allow him to win this match or, at least, to make a good showing.

It would have to be carefully done, so that he would not realize what she was doing. She believed her skill was enough even for that. After Thomas had taught them all he knew of the sport, Lucien had studied with some of the best instructors on the continent. She had wanted to do the same, but they would never have taught a female. She gave her brother no rest until he had taught her every trick he knew. In return, he had drilled her mercilessly, saying, "If you are determined to be a fencer, then you must be a good one."

Why she should attempt to save Albert's pride, she did not know. *Perhaps* he would be a bit less disagreeable if he won.

"I am ready when you are, cousin," she announced.

Chapter
Twelve

THE GIRL HELD her foil as if she knew how to use it, Mark thought, watching the pair face off. She had handled the pistol in the same manner, although he would be willing to wager she would close her eyes when she fired it.

As the cousins began their match, his amusement gave way to admiration. She actually knew what she was doing with the blade—which was more than he could say for Albert. Could this actually be the same person he had held in his arms last evening at Vauxhall, whose lips had been so warm and willing under his? He shook his head and concentrated upon the match.

Lucinda soon found that her wish to have Albert make a good showing in this affair could not be realized. His fencing ability was as poor as his skill in handling his horses.

He was too eager for a win, and he was making sloppy mistakes. Whoever had taught him must have been a butcher, or else he was ignoring everything he had been taught. Smoothly, she parried the slashes that passed as lunges and withheld her own thrusts which could easily have penetrated his clumsy guard. The best she could do was not to disarm him too soon.

Then he made a vicious slash at her face, which she quickly parried. As her own foil forced his thrust aside, she completed her lunge, the button on her weapon striking him directly over the heart.

Mark had been startled by Albert's savage thrust, but settled back to watch admiringly as Lucinda parried it and struck home. He was on his feet again a moment later.

Unwilling to own that he had been fairly beaten, Albert started forward as Lucinda dropped the point of her blade as a signal that the fight had ended. His blade swung in a dangerous arc toward her. She dodged and tried to bring up her own weapon again, but Mark quickly caught the younger man's wrist, halting the blow, then took the foil from his hand.

"It seems that my challenge must go to you, Captain," he said. "Do you accept?" He smiled, thinking it would be one thing for her to cross blades with that foppish boy; to meet a man, even in a friendly bout, would be another matter. How would she avoid it?

He blinked when she said, "Gladly," and took her place before him.

Long ago her brother had told her that the larger a man was, the worse his chances were of becoming an expert fencer. "Watch them," he had said. "They are too slow in their movements, as well as presenting too great a target. An agile man can make rings about one of them and strike whenever he wishes."

She had believed it to be true, for she had watched Lucien prove it more than once with opponents of greater bulk than he. In that case, she would win this match as well, but she did not want to defeat Mark. How could she fight him this morning—after last evening? Then she remembered that his kisses had not been for her, but for "Margarita," and her resolve hardened.

By the time they had exchanged only a few passes, she knew that victory was far from certain. She did not know whether Mark had purposely understated his skill with a blade. What she did know was that he was certainly an exception to Lucien's remarks about the clumsiness of a large man.

Of course, she thought, she ought to have remembered that Mark was *never* clumsy. She had seen what a good dancer he was, how well he moved at all times. Now he gave the appearance of moving slowly, even lazily, yet every thrust of her foil was turned aside and, several times, a counter-thrust almost reached its target.

In his turn, Mark was surprised. He thought she looked well in the earlier match only in comparison with the ineptness of her partner. Now he was forced to own that she had been well taught in the handling of a blade. Was there no end to the unwomanly skills she possessed? And yet, last evening . . . He quickly brought his thoughts back to the present in time to parry an unexpected thrust.

Lucinda may have learned all her brother's skill, but she never had his strength. And Lucien at his best would be no better than this large man. She knew she was overmatched. Secretly, she was happy that he would win, but she was not willing to concede the bout. Stubbornly, she continued to fight until, with a movement almost too slight to be seen, his blade caught hers and sent it spinning from a hand which was numbed by the force of the blow.

Mark allowed the point of his foil to drop and stepped back, waiting for her to retrieve the fallen blade. She did so, but knew it was useless to continue the match. Instead, she sketched a salute to the victor.

"I acknowledge myself fairly beaten," she owned. It was an odd thing, but she did not mind allowing that he was her master—at fencing.

"Hardly a fair match," he said generously. She truly had given him a better bout than he had expected. "There were several points which were in my favor. My reach is considerably longer than yours, for one thing. Also, I challenged you when you were tired from your previous bout. Shall we try again some other time, when you are fresh?"

"I should like that." She tried to keep the eagerness from her voice for, although she welcomed any activity with him, she knew Lucien would not be *that* eager for another match. "But I doubt I shall make a better showing then. And it is not merely because your reach is longer. I have crossed blades with only one person who *might* beat you."

It was clear that he was pleased by the compliment for he knew she had been taught by an expert. Her brother, he wondered, or another? "And that one?"

My brother, she thought, but said, "He is an officer with whom I crossed blades now and then on the Peninsula. It would be a pleasure to watch a bout between the pair of you."

Certain now who her teacher had been, he said, "If he is an English officer, I might have the privilege of meeting him one day. But of course, if he is Spanish or Portuguese—for I think it unlikely that you would have met with any French officers."

She had met with any number of them when she was much

younger, during visits to *Maman* and her husband of the moment. But she had never been allowed to fence with any of them nor with any others, except Thomas and Lucien.

"Oh, he is English," she said. "But I do not think there is a chance that the pair of you can test your skill against each other."

It certainly would not happen if she could prevent it. With a great deal of practice, she had copied Lucien's style very well. There were differences, however, which—slight as they might be—would be detected at once by a fencer of Mark's ability. It might be several years before Lucien was able to return to England, but it was unlikely that his style could have changed so much. Mark would not be fooled.

When the time came for Lucien's arrival in London—unlikely to happen until he came into his grandfather's title—she would have to warn him about meeting Mark with a blade. In fact, it would be best if he had as little contact as possible with the man. Mark's eyes were sharp enough and his memory good enough to tell the difference between them. The difference in height was only a few inches and might be overlooked, but the breadth of shoulder and the difference in musculature were things a man did not ordinarily develop after he had reached four and twenty.

"The gentleman I mentioned," she said, "had studied with an Italian master. I'll wager you did the same."

"Yes. In this, as in all other things, his lordship insisted I learn from the best masters to be found in the City. They were Italian. And your style, as well, is unmistakably Italian."

She bowed, as if in assent, thinking that was a tribute to her brother's skill as a teacher, and in a way hers as his pupil, to have learned the various tricks and movements he had been taught by Maestro Giacomo.

While the others were fencing, Albert wandered about the room. No longer being the center of attention piqued him, and he was angered that Mark had taken the foil from him so easily. After all, his cousin had only slipped by his guard, using a trick, and he should have been given an opportunity to retaliate.

He looked casually over his grandfather's collection of books. He was not bookish, and any interest they held for him was in the chance that they might be valuable pieces of merchandise. A collector of Lord Brayling's stature would doubtless have purchased a number of fine editions during the years, and he had heard that sometimes such things were worth a great deal of money. He could not understand why people should be interested in *books,* especially in old ones, but he did not doubt the tales he had heard.

If he inherited—*when* he inherited, he amended, for there was no reason why the earl should not prefer him to the half-French soldier (and he dismissed as ridiculous any thought of Mark's getting the money)—he would lose no time in getting as much for the contents of the library as he could. Such wealth would be better spent on new horses or fine clothing. These were the things his peers could see and envy.

The duelling pistols next claimed his attention. He did not doubt that they, too, were valuable objects, with their long barrels and inlaid work. Was it truly gold? He had never heard of the maker, but he was certain any number of the habitues of Manton's would like to have them.

Still, he thought he might keep them. He'd always wanted to own a pair of really fine pistols. It was the only wish his fond mama would not allow, for she feared firearms of any sort. He took one of them from the case and examined it, imagining himself the winner in some affair of honor as he sighted along the barrel at the two fencers.

Mark turned, saw what he was doing and, dropping his foil, leaped toward the younger man. "What do you think you are doing, you fool?" he shouted. "Did you not see me load those just moments ago?"

As he grasped the barrel of the weapon, Albert tightened his hold upon it. "You snatched my foil," he said angrily. "You are not going to take this away from me, as well. My grandfather shall hear how you treat me."

Albert struggled for possession of the pistol, but his strength was no match for Mark's and it was wrenched out of his hands. The sound of the shot was echoed by Lucinda's yelp of pain as she clapped her hand to her side. It had felt as if a red-hot iron had been dragged across her ribs. Both men stared at her.

Albert uttered a moan and crumpled to the floor.

Mark said stupidly, "You have been wounded."

Fighting an urge to throw herself upon his massive chest and burst into tears, Lucinda managed to draw herself together and say, "So it would appear. However, it is naught but a scratch.

Thomas will see to it if you will be kind enough to call him for me."

"But you might have been killed." What if she had been? What would he have done? "Let me—"

"I do think I must go and change my shirt." Her arm felt like fire, and she did not know how she could speak so calmly with that terrible pain. "I fear this one is ruined. 'Tis a good thing I had not had time to put on my coat or it would have been spoiled as well. And then his lordship would doubtless think me out of reason extravagant." Was she babbling, she wondered.

If so, Mark did not appear to notice. "But—but—allow me to help—"

He seemed to be in such distress that she wondered if he, like Albert, was one of those who could not abide the sight of blood. However, it had not affected him to the point of swooning, she was happy to see. Uncertain as to how much longer she would be able to stand, and fearing that Mark was about to pick her up, she put out a hand. She would have liked nothing better than to have him do so—but once in his arms, held against his chest, he would know at once that she was a female.

"Thomas," she begged. "Just send him to me. Up to my bedchamber."

"Yes, yes, of course. I shall find him at once." Mark almost ran from the room. If only he could care for her—but he could not bear to expose her when she was acting so valiantly. He'd fetch Thomas.

Lucinda made her way dizzily up the stairs, clinging to the rail and hoping she would not fall before she reached the safety of her room.

She decided Mark was agitated from fear that her grandfather would think him to blame for the accident. After all, he had been the one to load the pistols and leave them on the table. Still, how could he know that even Albert would be so foolish—?

It could not have been planned between the two of them. Or could it?

When Thomas reached her room with Mark on his heels, he found her lying across the bed, her hand pressed to her right side. He closed the door against the other man, then looked at his charge. The wound seemed to have stopped its bleeding, but Thomas insisted a doctor should be called.

"No," Lucinda cried, attempting to sit up and biting her lip at the pain caused by even that small movement. "There must be no doctor. You know that, Thomas. He would be bound to talk. There would be a scandal, and Lucien's career would be ruined."

"Your life is more important than Lucien's career! And besides, you know I cannot take care of you—"

"I know— You're going to say I'm a female. That's just the reason why there can be no doctor. How many times have you dressed me when I was small? After all these years, are you going to worry about my modesty? That's nothing but fustian," she said crossly, pulling herself to her feet. Thomas acceded to Lucinda's wishes and ripped her shirt off, uncaring for the damage to the cloth. "And, it is not as if it were a matter of my life. The bullet merely cut the skin. I have been hurt worse than this many times—you remember when I fell from the hayloft?"

"This is different—"

"No—I forbid you to call a doctor. You have tended me through all the scrapes and bruises I have taken in my life— and better than any doctor could have done. You can handle this, as well."

She sank back upon the bed and Thomas, muttering, pulled the edge of the undervest up several inches to bare the wound, grimacing when he saw it. The bullet had struck her lowest rib a glancing blow and had travelled along it, tearing the flesh. Although not deep, it was an ugly sight, and he set about cleansing it and preparing a dressing.

During her childhood, Lucinda had always been one to make a great outcry over the slightest bump or bruise, a habit she had never completely outgrown. Now, however, she bit her lip to keep from uttering a sound. Also, Mark might still be waiting near at hand and, if he heard her, might well come into the room. To Thomas, her unnatural silence was more worrying than complaints would have been.

There was no way she could keep her mind from straying to distressing thoughts. Certainly, the pistol must have been fired by accident. Still, she had to remember that, if Lucien were eliminated, Albert would be nearer to getting their grandfather's great wealth. . . . The younger man had been the one who fainted at the sight of her blood, but that did not mean he had not planned to shed it.

Mark had certainly appeared to be concerned. But was he? He had declared when they first arrived that he did not know what plans Lord Brayling had made for the disposition of his fortune, but that might not be true. And he *had* been the one who loaded the pistols.

After last evening, could *Mark* have considered such a thing? But then, Mark did not know that she had been at Vauxhall. He thought she was Lucien, of course. Could it have been that it was not Albert, but Mark, who had meant for her—for Lucien—to be killed?

She moaned. Thomas said apologetically, "I'm sorry if I'm hurting you, lass. I'm being as gentle as I can."

"It does not matter," Lucinda said weakly. How could she tell him that the pain in her side hurt far less than the ache in her heart?

It was impossible to keep the tale of the accident from Lord Brayling, and it was nearly enough to drive the old man into an apoplexy. He struggled to rise from his chair and, when Mark put out a hand to help him, he struck it angrily.

"If I had my strength," he shouted, his face almost purple, "grown man or not, you'd receive the thrashing of your life. To have done anything so idiotic—"

"I know," Mark said humbly. "The blame is entirely mine. The pistols should not have been loaded so soon, but who would have expected that even Albert would have so little sense—"

"It is clear that *you* did not. And how is the girl—what is her name?"

"Lucinda. And I do not think it was too serious. She would not allow me even to assist her to her room—merely sent me after Thomas."

"You mean that Thomas Abbott is caring for my granddaughter? Fetch a doctor for her at once—the best to be had!"

"Yes, of course. I shall do so at once."

As he turned toward the door, the old man had not yet done with him. "What were you about, anyhow? Pistols, swords—have you forgotten my granddaughter is a lady?"

"If you will permit me, sir, she seems to have had a most unladylike upbringing. She handled the blade expertly; far better, in fact, than her cousin."

"That I can easily imagine. But what are you doing standing about here chattering? Go and fetch that doctor at once!"

Mark thankfully made his escape and sought out Thomas, who had just come from Lucinda's room. "Have you summoned a doctor?" he asked.

"No, sir. Master Lucien prefers—"

" 'Master Lucien' be hanged! Do you think we do not know 'tis his sister in there?"

Thomas gaped at him.

"Close your mouth man, we have known from the beginning. But that is of no matter now. We must summon a doctor—his lordship's orders. I should have done so anyhow."

"But Lucinda—"

"We can make up some tale for her. But, man, you *cannot* care for her."

"That I know, sir. But the girl is stubborn. Still, as you say, she must have better care than I can give her. I fear that she is already in a fever."

The wound had not been a deep one and, under Lucinda's orders, Thomas had tried every remedy he knew to care for it. Still, it had been extensive, and Lucinda had lost more blood than she realized. Too, the pistol ball was old, and who knew how it might have soiled the wound. Worse, as soon as Thomas had left her alone, with orders that she must try to sleep, she had burst into tears and cried until her eyes throbbed and her throat ached, so great was her fear that it had been Mark who had intended to shoot her.

These conditions sent her into the high fever Thomas had feared. For several days, she hovered between waking and coma, tossing and muttering in the dreams which tormented her and kept her from resting as she should.

The doctor admitted that Thomas had doubtless done the best he could, but looked grave over the fever. "She must have care. Someone must be with her at all times."

"I can care for her," Thomas declared.

"And I," added Mark.

The doctor shook his head. "It would be best under the circumstances to have a female in attendance. Perhaps one of the maids."

"We have no maids. This is an all-male household."

"Then perhaps I should find you a nurse."

"Listen to me, doctor," Thomas said, "I have cared for this girl since she was a babe. I can do so now."

Mark seemed about to speak, then drew the doctor to one side. "Let the man have his way," he advised. "I shall be here and, if necessary, can bring in help, whether he wishes it or not. I have his lordship's authority."

"Well, in that case . . . I cannot like it, but if Lord Brayling wishes it this way—" He took his leave, promising to look in again on the morrow.

When he had gone, Mark said, "You must allow me to help you in caring for her."

"Mr. Warne, I cannot. Lucinda would—"

"You must!"

The urgency in his tone made the older man look at him carefully, then nod. "But not when she is awake."

"No, we shall allow her to play out her game. 'Twill only be a short time more in any case. Her grandfather will see to that."

"I am surprised that he let it drag on this long if he knew the truth."

"That was my doing. I begged him to let her go her way. I thought to trap her into owning up to her masquerade, but it seems that I am the one who was trapped."

Thomas studied him for a moment, then grinned. "Well, I must get back to Lucinda, sir. I'll let you know when you can be of help."

Coming out of her wandering for a brief moment, Lucinda thought she saw Mark bending over her, looking anxiously at her. She knew it was not more than a dream, for when she said, "Mark, I knew you would not—" and reached out her arms toward him, his face disappeared, to be replaced by a bearded one she did not know.

Displeased by this turn her dream had taken, she made a petulant attempt to push him away and slipped once more into the darkness in which Mark alternately tried to protect her from Albert, or threatened her with the pistol or with a blade he wielded so dangerously. She tried to run from him, but could only stand and wait for the attack which never quite reached her before another dream chased it away.

Whenever he was permitted inside the room, Mark sat beside her. It was he who held her in his arms and persuaded her to swallow the unpleasant draughts the doctor had left for her. Her babblings during these times brought a pleased smile to his face and caused him to hold her more tightly than was necessary while he murmured words he knew could not penetrate her fevered dreams.

There were moments when Lucinda half-roused to feel the comforting arms holding her and imagined that it was Mark's voice she heard urging her to take her doses. She knew it was only her longing for him which caused her to see him here. Thomas would not have dared to allow him to enter her room until she was completely conscious, fearing that she might betray herself.

The dreams, which seemed to follow the swallowing of the bitter draughts, were disturbing and unsatisfactory; at times, they were even frightening. However, she was finally convinced that—if indeed any attempt had been made upon her life— Mark was not the one who was responsible. She was not concerned that Albert might be guilty; her only worry had been about Mark. Freed from fear, she drifted into a deep sleep, to finally awaken weak but clear-eyed and with only a slight feeling of stiffness in her side.

Chapter Thirteen

"AWAKE AT LAST, are you?" Thomas asked heartily, rising from a chair at the bedside. His appearance belied his manner, however. He looked worn. "I must send word to your grandfather at once. He has been much worried about you, my girl—insisting upon being told about your condition several times a day."

What of the others, Lucinda wondered, what of Mark? Had he, too, asked—perhaps not daily, but from time to time—how she was faring? She looked sharply at Thomas, wondering if she had spoken aloud during the times she had been dreaming, but if he had heard anything, he gave no sign. His only expression was one of relief at her improvement.

She hoped she had said nothing. Thomas must never know—indeed, no one must ever know—how her earlier dislike for her grandfather's secretary had turned into love. She could not understand how her feelings could have changed so much. It had happened, she was certain, even before those moments in his arms at Vauxhall. She knew, however, that if Thomas even suspected how she felt, he would chaff her about it, reminding her of the disparaging things she had said about Mark in the past.

"You see, Thomas, I knew you would be able to pull me through without summoning a doctor." As she spoke, she remembered the draughts she had taken—if indeed, that was not part of her dream—and looked at him closely.

He looked so guilty that she said reproachfully, "Oh no, you *did* summon someone—and after I told you how important it was that you must not. How could you do that, risk Lucien's future?"

Thankful, at least, that she did not suspect how much time Mark had spent with her, Thomas said, "There was no risk involved. And yes, I did call a doctor. I should do the same ten times over before I could chance losing you." As she opened her mouth to scold him for betraying her disguise, he added, "You were in a worse way, child, than you know. There was a time when your fever was so high . . . And no need for you to give me the rough edge of your tongue for calling him. He'll say nothing. He and your father were boys together, and he was happy to be of help when I explained the story to him."

Nothing of the sort was actually said, but the doctor was left with the impression that Lucinda was a spy who was carrying messages from someone in the Peninsula to an equally important personage in London.

"Well, there is no help for it now," Lucinda said. "But I wish you had not done it."

"I'd do it again," Thomas retorted. "You have no idea of how ill you were."

"I know I had all sorts of nightmares." Not that all of the dreams were bad, certainly not the ones about Mark's being with her. She supposed the doctor was the bearded man she had seen now and then, bending over her, urging her to take her medicine. It had only been the vagaries of the female mind, something to which she had never before been a prey, which caused her to imagine Mark had been there as well.

She hoped she had not spoken any of the thoughts going through her fevered mind—her hope that Mark would come to love her one day and how useless were such hopes because he did not know she existed. Besides, he preferred women like that shameless "Margarita," who would come to a stranger's arms and welcome his kisses.

If she had said anything—well, doctors were supposed to be discreet. She would rather have borne the fever and the pain with no help than to risk Mark's discovering how she felt. Then she laughed at herself. How could he think anything of the kind when he believed she was Lucien?

The thought that her secrets—both of her identity and of her love—were safe made her feel more cheerful. Now that she was fully awake, none of her earlier fantasies made the least sense although there were times when they had been most pleasant. She was thinking it was time she called upon Evita to explain her absence, when there was a discreet knock upon the door. Patrick conveyed Lord Brayling's satisfaction that his grandson was better, and wished he would call as soon as he felt able to do so.

"Please send word to his lordship that I shall be happy to wait upon him at once."

Thomas protested. "Exertion at this time might bring on a relapse. Your grandfather will understand if you send word that you must wait until you have gained more strength."

Patrick was looking from one to the other in a curious fashion which would have earned him a reprimand from anyone else. Under the circumstances, Lucinda could not blame him, but she ordered him sharply to deliver her message.

The footman departed, shaking his head over the strange ways of foreigners, for although the captain was the earl's grandson, he was half-French by birth and seemingly wholly so in his outlook. That was their republican nonsense, where a servant might bring himself to argue with his master and the master to permit such impertinence.

The captain did call Thomas Abbott his friend, and he was permitted to live above stairs. Still, Patrick had heard that the man had been a groom before he went to France with his lordship's son. And now he waited upon the captain. In Patrick's eyes, that made him a servant. Thomas may have been English-born, but he had spent so many years in France that doubtless he had picked up some of their plaguey ideas. Let anyone in *this* household attempt to argue with his lordship or countermand an order he had given and see what would happen.

When the door had closed behind the footman, Lucinda said, "Thomas, you ought not to argue with me before the servants. They do not know what to make of it, since I am supposed to be your master."

"Now, Lucinda—"

"I know, Thomas—you do it out of love for me and my well-being. But it looks odd to people who do not know how you have raised and cared for the two of us all these years. Since I have been here, I have seen that most people treat their servants as if they were not people at all."

" 'Tis the same everywhere. Even in France, for all their talk of equality."

"I suppose so, but we must observe the rules while we are here."

She was determined to coax him into permitting her to make the visit. At last he relented, as she had known he would, but refused to permit her to dress.

"The wound is healing, but too much strain might cause it to open again," he said, bundling her into Lucien's dressing gown and half-carrying her—despite the fact that she was taller than he—along the hall to her grandfather's room.

Lord Brayling gave Thomas his fiercest scowl as he settled Lucinda into a comfortable chair and took his place behind her. The man had entirely forgotten his place during the years of living abroad. Had even refused to summon a doctor for the chit until Mark had bullocked him into it.

Thomas ignored the scowl, well aware that it was the old gentleman's way of covering his emotions. He had no intention of leaving the girl alone here in her weakened condition. The earl might well begin scolding her for her reckless behavior, unbecoming to his granddaughter. Lucinda was not yet strong enough to be told they had known her secret from the beginning.

Lucinda could scarcely conceal her dismay when she looked at her grandfather. He appeared much older and weaker than when she had seen him last. His face seemed more shrunken, bringing his beak of a nose into greater prominence than before. And his eyes were duller than she recalled.

Thomas had told her the old gentleman had been concerned about her, but she had discounted that, thinking he had never cared for his grandson; why should he do so now? She saw that she had been wrong. Could worry have caused so great a change in him? Did he know the reason for her illness, or had they kept it from him? Did they not know a frail old man would be overset by such news?

She was so sorry that she'd been the unwilling cause of his suffering, that she was tempted to throw herself upon her knees beside his chair and confess her masquerade. When she thought, however, of all she had undergone these past weeks to ensure Lucien's inheritance, she steeled herself to silence.

After all, she told herself, the knowledge that he had been deceived would only disturb him further.

For several moments, the old gentleman studied her without speaking. Fighting down something he had not known before, the wish to take this young creature in his arms and comfort her—after giving her the scold of her life for having tried to deceive him—he finally said gruffly, "So you have recovered, have you?"

"Completely, sir," she assured him. Could it be that he cared more for his grandchildren than he was willing to own?

Laughing, then wincing because of the pain caused by her laughter, she said, "After all, being wounded is something a soldier must expect. Such things happen. Although I must confess I did not expect such a thing to happen in London." She hoped that making a jest of the matter would relieve his mind, but it was the wrong thing for her to have said.

"You think it might not have have been an accident?" he asked so sharply that she knew his reason for concern. He feared that one of the others might have tried to kill her for the inheritance. If that had been the reason behind the shooting, he must be blaming himself for having placed temptation in their way.

Remembering how often this same disturbing question had occurred to her in her fevered moments, Lucinda shook her head.

Now she was able to say lightly, "I am certain that it was, sir. How could it have been anything else? I know that Albert"—she must not mention that there was a brief time when she had wondered if Mark could have been the culprit—"could never have hit me if he had been trying to do so. It is only that a loaded pistol is too dangerous a toy to fall into the hands of a foolish child."

His lordship gave a deep sigh of relief, as if she had been able to banish his doubts, then tried to dismiss his feelings by saying harshly, "If I supposed there was to be any trouble over my money, I should . . . I should throw it into the sea before any of you should touch a penny of it."

Although he tried to control his feelings, his voice had trembled. Lucinda felt a wave of sympathy for him, a feeling she would never have expected to possess for the man who had so cruelly disinherited his son and who had ignored his son's family these many years. For the first time, she thought he might have regretted what he had done. With the Warne stubbornness, which she could understand, having a good share of it herself, he would never bring himself to own that he had been at fault. The nearest he could come would be to give his grandson a chance to inherit the money.

"Oh, my dear sir," she said earnestly, "there has been no trouble at all. You must believe that. Albert is only given to acting heedlessly, and I'll wager Thomas has lost count of the times I have earned a bear-garden jaw from him for that same fault." Thomas touched her shoulder, and she knew he must be smiling. "But it was only heedlessness on Albert's part, nothing more."

Her answer apparently satisfied the old gentleman, but he seemed to be completely exhausted by her visit. He waved a dismissal. Rising to leave, Lucinda impulsively bent down to press a kiss upon his hand. Male youth no longer expressed its respect for its elders by such a gesture, but she knew it had been done when Lord Brayling was a young man, and he would recognize it as it had been meant—concern for him and not for his money.

She decided then she must write to Lucien and tell him that their grandfather was not the ogre they had thought him—when they thought of him at all. He was merely a lonely old man who had broken his ties with his son in a moment of anger and had not known how to mend them.

As short as the journey between her grandfather's room and her own was, Lucinda meekly obeyed Thomas when he ordered her back to bed. After several hours of sleep, however, she felt so much improved that she overrode his protests, dressed, and made her way down the stairs.

It was time, she thought again, that she should order out the curricle and greys to make a call upon Evita. The dancer would not have been informed of her injury and would be wondering why her friend had not called upon her for some days. By the time she had reached the bottom of the stairs, however, Lucinda realized that any sort of outing would require a great deal more strength than she presently had. The call must wait.

She stood in the lower hallway, supporting herself by clinging to the newel post, wondering if she would be able to return to her room without calling for someone to assist her. "Thomas will give me a scold and tell me he was right all the time," she said to herself.

Raised voices from the small drawing room claimed her attention. Mark's voice was stern and commanding, while it seemed that Albert's customary hauteur was merely an attempt to cover his uneasiness. Curious, she walked slowly to the doorway and clung there.

The secretary was standing over her smaller cousin, looking as if it required the greatest effort on his part to keep himself from laying hands upon the younger man. It was no wonder that Albert was nervous under that threat.

Glancing up, Mark spied Lucinda and forgot what he had been saying to Albert. Fighting down an impulse to pick her up and carry her across the room, he put a hand upon her arm, offering his support to a comfortable chair, where he arranged cushions at her back.

At his touch, her already weakened knees felt as if they must be melting, and Lucinda had been happy to cling to his strong arm. Albert remained sprawled upon the sofa, looking sulkier than usual—if such a thing were possible—and made no move to help. She felt that his and Mark's altercation might have had something to do with her.

When she looked up to thank Mark for his help, he was looking gravely down at her. Their glances crossed, and, recalling the manner in which he had figured in her fevered dreams, she could feel her face growing so hot that she was surprised he did not notice.

He did not comment, so he must have attributed the flush to her efforts to come downstairs. His solicitous attitude did not change. Seeing that she still lacked a pillow at her side, he went to the sofa, pushed Albert out of the way, and brought her the one the younger man had been using.

There was so much more he wished to do for her. If Albert had not been present, Mark was certain he would no longer be able to prevent himself from telling her he knew the truth and declaring his feeling for her. That troublesome cub, however, must never know his darling's secret. Nothing would have pleased him more than to blast it all over town, thereby creating the scandal everyone was trying to avoid.

"Are you certain you are strong enough yet to be about, Lucien?" It was the first time he had called her by her brother's name, but he thought it safe to do so; it was so near to her own. "Have you recovered?"

There was such deep concern in his voice that Lucinda felt her throat close. Although Thomas had not mentioned that Mark had asked about her well-being, she was certain he must have.

It was several moments before she could recover enough to give him a light-hearted answer, "Oh, completely. You can always depend upon Thomas Abbott to take the best of care. He has done so for as long as I can remember."

She hoped that no one had learned about the doctor's visits. Or if they knew of him, that they did not know his direction. He might have the best of intentions about helping her for her father's sake, yet might accidentally give her secret away. No one must be allowed to speak to him.

"Although," she went on, "I could not guarantee that I should be able to stand up with Gentleman Jackson for a bout, at least for the next day or so."

"It is satisfying to learn that you are well again, coz." Albert's voice was filled with spite. "Now, perhaps my grandfather's secretary"—Lucinda noted that he never said "our grandfather," as if unwilling to own their relationship—"will no longer feel under any obligation to read me lectures on my carelessness."

An imp of mischief made Lucinda enquire, "Oh, is that what I heard as I was coming downstairs?"

"I do not doubt it. He has been doing so continually all the time you were abed. Although I still consider that he was more at fault for what occurred than I by trying to take the pistol out of my hand. If he had not twisted it about as he did, it would not have discharged."

He might have been right about that. But Albert's finger had been on the trigger, and it was also possible that only Mark's grasping of the pistol when he did prevented her from being wounded more seriously.

Albert had taken out his snuff box and a tiny silver shovel—the latest conceit among the fops—scooped up some snuff and inhaled it as if he enjoyed it. He did not, but one must follow the mode. Then he fastidiously whisked away several grains which had fallen upon his coat of coquelicot brocade, worn with a green-and-white-striped waistcoat and amber breeches.

This task completed, he added, "And you have no idea what the sight of blood does to a man of my sensibilities."

She had seen what it did to him, but she was stung to anger by his remark. He did not feel the slightest hint of remorse for his part in an accident which might well have cost her life. Indeed, his only pleasure in her recovery was that he would no longer be lectured about the affair.

Lucinda's reply was sharp. "For that matter, *coz,* I can certainly assure you that taking a pistol ball in the side did little good to my sensibilities, either. Merely because a soldier is accustomed to bloodshed, he does not wish it to be his own."

She heard a snort of laughter and turned her back on Albert to catch the look of deep appreciation in Mark's eyes. Paying no more heed to Albert, she said, "I paid a brief visit to grandfather this morning. At his request, of course. I was grieved to see that he was looking so unwell."

"He has been much concerned about you these past days, as we all have been." Mark's glance flicked to Albert, then away, dismissing him as of no consequence. "There was no way we could keep the news from him. He cares for you deeply, child." That last word was an error; would she, in her role as the captain, not resent it? How much longer must he put a guard upon his tongue?

First "little man," now "child." Doubtless, Lucinda thought, Lucien would have resented being spoken to in such terms by one who was little older than himself, even if he were larger. For herself, she was beginning to treasure the words from him, although they were not intended for *her.* She sensed he was not using the words scornfully; instead, they were terms of friendship. Perhaps even affection. A man could feel such affection for another, as Lucien and Thomas felt for each other.

He was careful never to use such terms in public, she noted. They would prove embarrassing to any man and especially to a soldier of Lucien's experience. Color flooded her face anew as she wondered how deeply her grandfather—or anyone else—would care for her if they realized the manner in which she had been deceiving them.

"I am very sorry to have been a cause of concern," she said, rising unsteadily to her feet. Mark was at her side in an instant, offering an arm.

She was happy for his support, even more happy that she

could cling to him while mounting the stairs. If only she could tell *him* the truth! But such a thing was not to be thought of for a moment. He would feel duty-bound to tell her grandfather at once. Too, he would despise her for her unfeminine behavior in masquerading this way.

When they had reached her door, he said, "In fairness to your cousin, I must own that he has some reason for blaming me. If I had not tried to take the pistol from him, perhaps it would not have discharged."

"Perhaps it would not, but there is no way of knowing. If it had done, when he was pointing it as he did, I should be dead by now. At least, you turned it aside so that I was only grazed. I feel that I owe you my life, cousin, and I thank you for that. And for your support at this moment." To herself, she added, and for the chance to be near you for a moment, just to touch you.

If he'd truly saved her life, then it should belong to him, should it not? Mark said to himself. What would she say if he told her that? "You may command me at any time, little man."

His tone had been so warm that, as soon as the door had closed behind him, Lucinda found herself sobbing helplessly. Having heard the voice in the hallway and recognizing the reason for her unhappiness, Thomas seated himself and drew her down upon his lap, as he had done when she was a child. Holding her tightly, he said in a scolding tone which did not hide his deep concern, "I knew I ought to have insisted that you remain in bed. Now you have overtired yourself. We can only hope you do not have a setback because of it."

Thomas was right. It was beyond all foolishness for a female who had reached her advanced age to go about acting exactly as if she were a schoolroom miss, all blushes and tears. Just because of a big man who could be kind more often than he was cruel.

"And anyhow," she said in a whisper that did not reach Thomas' ears, "I shall never see him again when this charade is over."

At that thought, the tears came harder than before. "Thomas, I want to go home," she moaned into his neckcloth, which had become soaked with her tears.

"We shall, girl, we shall," he said soothingly. He was right, he told himself; it was heartache which ailed her now, rather than mere exhaustion or homesickness. And although she might have deserved some punishment for her reckless masquerade, must it be as painful as this? What could he do to help her? "It will be all right soon. But now you must rest."

He struggled to his feet with her in his arms, much more of a task than it had been when she was a child, carried her to her bed, tucked the covers about her, and wiped away her tears as she fell asleep.

Chapter Fourteen

LUCINDA AWOKE NEXT morning, feeling that all her strength had returned. Her head ached slightly from her weeping, but she told herself it was no more than she deserved for behaving like a sentimental fool for no reason. Her own future was quite unimportant; what mattered was that she should secure the inheritance for Lucien. She rose and dressed, thinking that a drive in the fresh air would put everything aright. And it was past time that she called upon Evita.

At the customary hour of eleven, the urchins who played in the street near Evita's lodgings saw the curricle approaching. The one who had earlier defeated his companions for the privilege of holding the captain's horses dashed to their heads, eager for the reward he knew he would receive.

"We missed yer, Captain," he called.

Lucinda grinned at him. "What you mean is that you have missed the blunt I give you."

He laughed. Most of the gentry who came to this area to pay calls upon their ladybirds would pay no more than a penny to have their prads watched, but the captain was usually good for a sixpence. Sometimes as much as a shilling. Lucinda knew most of these lads would have little or nothing to eat if it were not for the pence they garnered from such tasks.

When she climbed the stairs to Evita's room, finding that she must rest several times even during so short an ascent, she was greeted with some reserve by the Spanish girl. The reserve melted immediately when Lucinda explained the reason she had been absent.

"*Ay, pobrecita,*" the dancer exclaimed, flinging her arms about Lucinda and drawing her into the room, seating her among the cushions piled upon the bed. "What a terrible experience you have had! And I have been ungrateful enough to think you had repented of our friendship. Even that you might have become angered when I hurried you out of here that last night."

"Never that, Evita. But I had no way of letting you know what had happened. In fact, much of the time, I did not know." She recalled her fevered dreams in which Mark had become confused with the doctor, but did not speak of that.

"I understand. Who in your house would have thought me important enough to be told. *Digame,* do you think that the shooting was deliberate?"

It was the same question her grandfather had asked. The same question which had been in her mind when the incident had happened, but which she had carefully put down during her convalescence. Since she had seen Albert's callous attitude, she had wondered at times. However, since he seemed to care for no one, she supposed this was natural to him.

She shook her head. "No. I am certain—at least, I am almost certain—that it could not have been other than an accident. The two of them were struggling with the pistol when it discharged. I know, at least, that *Mark* would never have done such a thing."

"Of a certainty, it could not have been the so-handsome Mark of whom you have told me so much—the giant of a man who was so taken with you at Vauxhall?"

"Not with me—he was taken with 'Margarita,' your cousin from Spain," Lucinda retorted. "And I . . . I do not think one could exactly call him *handsome.* Do you?" She blushed at the expression in Evita's eyes. Had Mark's name truly been on her lips as often as that in their talks? She had not realized it was so, but of course, he had been in her thoughts more and more as the days went by.

"He is not the man I should like for myself. But, yes, I think one might call him handsome. At any rate, to you, he is exactly what a man should be, is he not?" Evita asked slyly, and laughed heartily when Lucinda nodded, feeling foolish. It was the first time she had ever owned her emotions, except to herself.

"But that is how it should be," the other girl told her, "when you love. For as long as it lasts, he must be all things to you. No, I would never believe your Mark would shoot you. But your little snake of a cousin—"

"I own I have wondered about him." Lucinda was glad of the opportunity to change the subject. Not even to as close a friend as Evita had become would she reveal the warmth of her love for Mark. It was hopeless anyhow, for he would never know that such a person as Lucinda Warne existed. "I think Albert is a sneak about many things, but, to be honest, I do not think he has the wits to plan anything so elaborate. He could not know that Mark would load the pistols or that he would try to step in to deflect the pistol's aim."

"But if he suddenly saw the chance—"

Lucinda shivered. She feared that was exactly the way Albert might act. Not deliberately, but if an occasion presented itself, he might try to rid himself of a rival without a thought to the fact that the blame might fall upon him. He would try to shift the fault to someone else, such as Mark, as he had tried to blame her for his curricle wreck.

With an attempt at lightness, she said, "Poor Albert—it would have been a failure, just as is everything he tries. Think what a blow it would have been to him if he had been able to kill me, only to discover that the real Captain Warne was still very much alive."

Evita caught her arm with both hands.

"You—you must not even think such a thing as that. It is a bad—what is the English word for it—*un mal aguero*—"

"A bad omen?"

"Yes, I think that is the word—a thing which brings bad fortune just by the speaking of it. We must truly give thanks that it was not worse and that you have recovered. I feared, when you had not called for so long a time, that I might never see you again. It saddens me to say this for you know how very precious your visits have become to me—more than I can say. But this must be the last time you come to visit me."

"But why? Now that I . . . Oh, you mean that your Robin has—"

"Yes, he has returned to me—to me alone. Since that night at Vauxhall. He is so ardent now. And so generous. He has given me a number of gifts and is furnishing a little house for me—and I did not even tell him that I wished to have one. I think he wishes to have a place where he can call upon me without being plagued with unwanted visitors. I am certain it is because I have been seen with you that he has become jealous. He has insisted that I cannot see you again. It means, *mi amiga*, that you may not come here as a gentleman. And if you return to London as a lady, no one would permit me to see you. I am not respectable enough to be a friend to the granddaughter of an earl."

"How foolish that is, for you are more of a lady than many I have met about the City."

"Lucinda, you know that is not true—at least not in the eyes of the world."

"No, you are right. I shall miss our visits, it has meant so much to me to have someone who knows me as I am. Although, I do admit I'm sick to death of this masquerade."

Forcing a smile, Lucinda went on, "Still, we must not complain. This is what we planned, to bring your Robin back to you. And to reinforce my position as the captain."

"Of course that is so. And I am so happy that it has come about as I wished. But you? What shall you say now to those so-fine gentlemen who are your friends?"

Lucinda placed her hand over her heart and heaved a mock sigh. "I shall, of course, mourn the fact that all females are fickle. And the more beautiful they are, the more fickle they prove. It is only to be expected. They will laugh, but it will not be for long. I shall be going to join my brother soon." Impulsively, she bent to kiss the dancer's cheek. "Now, farewell, my friend. Be happy. I know you will."

Lucinda caught up her curly-brimmed beaver hat, set it at the proper angle, then paused at the door to turn back and ask, "By the way, Evita, your Robin—he is Lord Byrne, is he not?"

"But yes, that is his name. Why do you ask?"

"No reason. I thought I recognized him that night at Vauxhall. One sees him from time to time. However, I had not heard his first name, except from you. And he was so eager to get you alone that I only caught a glimpse of him."

"And you—or I should say, 'Margarita'—were swept away from me by the so-big and so-handsome Mark. If it were not for my Robin, I think I should be jealous of my tall 'cousin.' "

"No reason, for since you told him I knew no English, we could not exchange a word."

"Words are not needed at times, *mi* Lucinda."

"True enough." Lucinda tried to speak lightly, to hide the feeling always aroused by the memory of Mark's arms and lips. But those embraces were not meant for her, but for an unknown Spanish girl. "Now I must go. Farewell once more, my friend."

She would not wound her friend by repeating any of the gossip she had heard about Lord Byrne. There was no need, for Evita would always know the truth. His lordship might be a victim of her charms, but the "protection" he offered could be only a temporary thing. His name and title would be given to a lady of quality—either the one he was now pursuing or to some other. Never to a dancer of the theatre. He would be ostracized should he enter into a *mesalliance*.

"I should wager, however," she said softly, "that many of the private conversations of the 'gently bred ladies' would be quite as much of a shock to their escorts if they should be overheard." Evita's lapses, at least, were unintentional, the fault of her background, while those which the ladies uttered were deliberately planned to titillate their friends.

Yes, she would miss Evita, but she knew she could not long have continued to meet with her, even if Lord Byrne had not been brought to heel. The two months' test arranged by the earl had almost come to an end, and she would be able to put aside her masquerade. It was odd, she thought, how eagerly she had gone into this scheme, disregarding the advice of Thomas and her brother, yet how irksome she found it now. It had begun to pall even before she realized that she was in love—hopelessly—with Mark.

She wondered what the outcome would be. Privately, she thought she had made a better showing as a gentleman than her cousin. The welcome she received from various hostesses proved this to her. Still, there was no hint as to whether this was what his lordship intended. She hoped she had won, for Lucien's sake, but the pleasure she had first taken in the contest had long since faded.

Winning the inheritance for Lucien was the only thing that mattered. The only thing that could be allowed to matter. It made no sense for her to go on mooning over a man she had not known two months ago. Surely, her listlessness was merely an aftereffect of her illness, and the hollow feeling within her was due to nothing more than hunger, although it persisted no matter how often or how heartily she had eaten.

The affairs of Polite Society, which she had found quite intriguing when she first came to London, now held little interest for her. The *ton* was no more than a theatre for gossip, and the stories which were only whispered were worse than anything Evita and her sort would have dared to do. She thought of Lady Melbourne, whose six children were rumored to have been fathered by a half-dozen different gentlemen of her acquaintance. One presumed that at least the eldest would have been her husband's son. And even her ladyship was shocked at the behavior of her daughter-in-law, Caroline Lamb, whose scandals had ruined her marriage even before she began chasing Lord Byron all about London.

Gaming had also lost its interest for Lucinda; even winning meant little. From time to time, she had drifted into a party along with Neddy Fenley and several of his friends who were content to play for chicken stakes. In the last few weeks, it had seemed to her that Neddy had become almost embarrassingly solicitous about her well-being. Any suggestion by one of their friends that they ought to move along to some hell or other or that the stakes in their game might be raised to make it more interesting would quickly be squelched by Neddy. Not having heard the others commenting about this change, Lucinda began to be of the opinion that his family must have suffered severe reverses. By his own admission, Neddy had always been a gamester; she could not imagine that he had suddenly come around to his mother's dislike of the pastime. One did not change the habits of a lifetime within a few weeks. In fact, she had begun to wonder if there was some way she could offer a loan without insulting the marquess. She was certain her grandfather would have no objection to her lending a reasonable amount to the son of one of his old friends.

Although they were overjoyed to have the captain up and about again, it did not take his companions more than a few days to be aware that he was no longer driving about the countryside in the company of Evita Montez. As she had told Evita she would do, Lucinda answered their chaffing by bemoaning her loss, but refusing, with many thanks, all their efforts to help her find another *chère-amie*.

"No, gentlemen, not yet. It is too soon," she told them, sighing heavily. "At the moment, I am too disillusioned with all of them. 'Tis the first time a female has ever deserted me. I had thought her fond—but how can a mere captain compete with a viscount?"

Everyone laughed at this, for all knew that Captain Warne was actually Viscount Willetts, to become Earl of Brayling upon the death of his grandfather.

"Of courthe, being a foreigner, maybe the wench did not know your future is brighter than Byrne'th," Ferdy Maupin said thoughtfully.

"And to a ladybird," Mr. Atwood put in, " 'tis now that is important, not the future. It may be she thought that Byrne has more of the ready."

"True. Perhaps I should have been more generous. Or, since she and I both have dark hair, it might have been Byrne's fair hair which drew her."

All doubted this was the reason; they had heard of some of the gifts Byrne had given the dancer. As Warne said, he ought to have been more generous; they told one another that he would not make the same mistake again.

Lady Leatheringham sent cards for another of her well-attended rout parties. Having endured an overabundance of such affairs, Lucinda was at first tempted to send regrets. Still, if the family was in financial difficulties, as she suspected, it would appear an act of desertion if she did not attend.

In the emerald satin coat she had so much admired when Thomas ordered it for her—the first garment which had not belonged to Lucien—she bowed dutifully over her ladyship's hand and made appropriate replies to the conversational gambits of her fellows. From the enormous quantities of food and drink offered to the crowd, it would not seem there was any lack of funds here, but it could be that the marchioness and her family were merely showing a bold face to the world.

Lucinda wished that Mark had come tonight so that she might see him, although it would pain her to watch him dancing with another woman. Then she accused herself of moongazing again. After all, she could see him every day in her grandfather's house. It was only that no event seemed complete for her if he were not there as well.

The crowd in one corner of the room told her that Stella Proctor was holding her usual court, but Lucinda did not approach her. That jest had long since lost its savor, and whenever she saw Stella with her host of admirers, it was only with a feeling of envy.

"How I wish *I* could be the one having all the beaux vying for my favor," she muttered, knowing that there was only one she wished to attract. "I could do so if I were properly gowned. But it can never be—not in London. I have spoiled my chances with this plaguey charade."

When she returned to Lucien's side, she knew she would have admirers aplenty, as she had had in the past. They had meant little to her then; now they would mean less, since Mark would not be among them.

Turning away, not noticing the groups of eager-eyed young misses, to whom she usually gave some attention, she decided to join Neddy and his friends in the card room. Perhaps she might contrive to lose some money to him, but it would have to be skillfully done, for Neddy's luck was notoriously bad. And with the low stakes the marchioness insisted her guests play for, whatever she could lose would do him little good. However, if she could arrange it so that he won, perhaps she could invite him to accompany her to White's where she could lose a larger sum to him.

Planning this strategy, she almost collided with someone in the doorway. Recognizing Lord Byrne, she would have passed him with a cold, "Good evening," but he put out a detaining hand.

"A word with you, Warne, if you please," he said, and led the way to a deserted niche a short way from the ballroom door.

Lucinda shrugged, then followed him. Had he heard about her latest visit to Evita, and was he about to warn her away from the dancer? If so, she would take pleasure in telling him the Spanish girl had already dismissed her. She wished she could also tell him the girl was too good for him, but she had no wish to begin a brawl under Lady Leatheringham's roof— and who knew how the hot-tempered Byrne might react to such a statement?

To her surprise, he did not mention Evita. Instead, he said,

"It has been some time since we have seen you at one of these affairs, Warne."

"Yes, I was not going about for a time." Why should she tell him any of the details? Even her friends did not know them, and Byrne had never been a friend.

"Yes . . . well, I merely thought . . . since you have been one of Miss Proctor's admirers—"

"I was new in London. And it seemed the thing to do—for a time," Lucinda said lightly and received a frown. So he still had a *tendre* for the Belle, had he? And what of his renewed pursuit of Evita?

"What I meant to say was . . . that is, it is not generally known as yet—but Stella, that is Miss Proctor, has promised to be my wife. The announcement will be made just as soon as we receive her uncle's permission."

Lucinda had never met Miss Proctor's uncle, but she strongly suspected that the ambitious aunt would be the one to decide her niece's future. She recalled the terrific scold she had been given for daring to speak to the girl aboard the Channel boat and her complete *volte-face* when the captain was presented to her at a ball. The dragon gave no hint that she had seen him before, for she would not wish a breath of scandal about her niece, but Lord Brayling's grandson would be quite acceptable to her.

Anyone wed to that formidable female would live under the cat's paw. With her disapproval, did the pair think there would be a chance of their getting permission to wed? Byrne might be a viscount, but he had no money. There were men in plenty with more wealth and higher titles, and Stella's aunt would aspire to one of them.

Wondering if all the other members of Stella's train were also privately advised of the situation, she thrust out her hand. "In that case, I can only wish the both of you happy."

"Thank you." Byrne took the hand, somewhat embarrassed at having discussed something so personal with one to whom he was little more than a stranger. But the fellow *had* dangled after Stella for a time, and it was as well to warn him that the field was no longer clear.

As his lordship turned away, Lucinda said, "Byrne, I must suppose you are warning me not to encroach upon your territory—here, and in another direction, as well."

Byrne turned back, saying in a fierce undertone, "I beg of you, Warne, to say nothing of that *here*. You are too much of a gentleman, I am certain, to hint of such a thing to Stella. She is so pure, so innocent. I doubt if she even knows that such females exist."

"Such females?" she asked, knowing that ladies *did* know of such things.

"What do you mean? You know females of her sort. What more may she expect than I have already done for her? I have been generous with her, far more so, in fact, than I can afford to be. She will amuse me until I am wed—and doubtless for some time afterward, as well. After that, she will have no trouble in finding someone to console her. Her sort always does. You spent some time in France, I know, so you must be aware of how these matters are handled. It is the same here. If you are still in London, you may wish her. If not, there will be another, you may be certain."

He turned away and Lucinda wished that she *were* a man so that she could give him the leveller he deserved. Of course, if she were a man, she might well feel that he was doing what was expected of him. Would Lucien do so? She hoped not. And Mark? But then, Mark had liked "Margarita," so he must be as bad as the rest.

She glanced into the card room, but was suddenly sickened at the sight of all those useless men enjoying themselves so cheerfully. Why were they not defending their country, as Lucien was doing? There was not a one of them who could have earned his living had he been forced to do so. Even Neddy, good friend that he was, was as bad as the others in this respect.

Bidding her hostess good night, she walked home, hoping her mood would be dispelled by the night air. It was not, and she snapped an answer at Mark when he came to the door of the library to ask if she had enjoyed her evening.

He looked so surprised that she was contrite at once, saying, "I must beg your pardon. I fear it is still too soon after my— my illness—for me to find enjoyment at balls. I tire too easily." And you were not there, so how could I enjoy it? But of course she could not say that aloud.

"Yes, you must take care of yourself. You were . . . Thomas tells me you were quite feverish for some time." Perhaps some day, he could tell her how he had held her, had given her the medicine the doctor had left, had overheard her feverish remarks which had given him such hope for the future. "It has sapped your strength. Perhaps a drink—"

"I think not, thank you. You know how prodigal with her refreshments her ladyship always is. And I do not think it wise to take too much until I have regained my full strength. But I wished to ask you how my grandfather finds himself."

"Much better," Mark told her with a smile. "The news of your recovery did much for his health as well. Not that we can expect he will ever be entirely well again. He is an old man, as you know, and frail."

"And doubtless having us here—my cousin and I—has only added to his burdens."

"On the contrary, he has taken quite an interest in what you have been doing." The little I have told him of your escapades, Mark said to himself. What would your grandfather have done if he knew you were consorting with an opera dancer? "Both you and young Albert. It was only his worry about your illness—"

"I told him," she tried to speak lightly, "that a soldier must expect to be shot at."

"But not in London, you added. Oh yes, he told me that. He is right, and so are you. It is something which should never have happened."

"But Albert is such a nodcock that I suppose it could not have been otherwise. It is over now, and no harm was done."

"Well, nothing of the sort will happen again. We shall see that it does not. You have come to mean a great deal to your grandfather—and to me." As he spoke, Mark smoothed back a lock of her hair and rested his hand for an instant against her cheek.

Startled, Lucinda looked up, and the expression in his eyes made her break away from him and dash up the stairs, slamming the door behind her. Mark stood in the doorway, looking after her, shaking his head. Had he been too precipitate? Had he given away his feelings and allowed her to know he was aware of her secret?

Thomas heard the slamming door and looked into Lucinda's room to find her facedownward across the bed, trying to stifle her sobs in her pillow. "What is it, girl?" he asked, coming to her at once. "What has happened?"

"N-nothing," she hiccupped. "Nothing at all."

How could she tell him what she had just learned? It had been bad enough when she saw Mark's reaction to "Margarita," but this was worse—so much worse that she could never tell it.

Mark had developed a *tendre* for *Lucien!*

Chapter
Fifteen

WITH HER MIND—and her heart—in such a turmoil, Lucinda was certain she would never be able to fall asleep. At last, she did so, although her sleep was troubled by terrifying but unrecognizable images.

When she finally began to sleep soundly, she did not waken until late, still feeling somewhat dragged and wondering what in the world she was to do. It was doubtful that she could avoid Mark during the rest of her time here, but how could she face him, knowing what she now knew about him? From things let slip by some soldiers, she had heard this was something which happened at times. But she had never believed it was true—until now.

Thank goodness, her time here was running out. "In another two days," she said to Thomas, "the two months will be ended, and grandfather will make his decision. I hope it will be in favor of Lucien. It should be, for I think Albert has made a poorer showing than I have done."

"You would not have to do well to best him," Thomas replied, "but you have done well, Lucinda. Very well, indeed, although I did not think when we came that you would be able to go through with it."

"Thank you. Praise from you, Thomas, is truly praise. For the first time since we left the Peninsula, you have not said this is a feather-brained scheme."

"Oh, I still think it is that—but you have carried it off in great style."

"Then, if I have done, it is only right that grandfather should name Lucien as his heir. As soon as we hear, I shall tell him we are leaving, that I must return to my post. Oh, I shall express my thanks quite properly for the inheritance and for his kindness while we have been here. I never thought I could call him kind, but he is. Anyhow, the explanation that I cannot be spared any longer should be enough, for reports we have read make it seem the war is worsening. He should certainly understand that I may be needed."

"I thought you could stay here forever," Thomas said with an innocent air hiding what he thought to be wrong with the lass. "Did you not tell me after your first ball that you enjoyed London and this sort of life?"

"I hate it! Not London, of course—it is wonderful, and I shall miss it when we go home. But this masquerade. It is dreadful and I wish it had never been started."

Thomas had seen for some time that she was dissatisfied with her role and wished he could assure her that all would be well. Still, his lordship had ordered him to remain silent. And if he did let it slip to Lucinda that she had fooled no one, her wrath would doubtless fall upon him as the one who was nearest to her. "Certainly, Lucinda, we shall leave whenever it pleases you," he said.

"It would please me to leave this moment, but I suppose 'twould be best to wait two more days and hear what my grandfather says. He might change his mind at the last moment if I should leave suddenly. If it had not been that Lucien was so eager for this inheritance, I should never have come here at all," Lucinda declared, unfairly throwing the blame for the deception upon her innocent brother, since she could not tell the reason for her unhappiness.

Studying her, Thomas asked, "Are you sure you ain't sickening for something, girl?"

"Must you talk like an idiot!" she snapped and flung herself out of the room, banging the door. Yes, she thought, I am sick, sick at heart. If Mark is the way he is, *I* am the one to blame with my pretence of being Lucien.

Rather than being worried or angered by this unusual behavior on Lucinda's part, Thomas began whistling cheerfully, as he set about brushing coats and polishing boots. Now and then, the whistle gave way to a deep chuckle. He was certain he knew what was ailing the girl, and her reaction to his questions only strengthened that certainty.

He decided the ailment would not be fatal; he had never known it to be. Had he any inkling of what was truly preying on Lucinda's mind, he would have been less cheerful and—his lordship's orders or no—would have put her unhappiness to rest.

Lucinda made her way to the library and flung herself into a chair. Then, unable to be quiet, she began prowling about. The thought of seeking out any of her usual companions of the past weeks and joining their pursuits had no appeal for her. She had begun this scheme by envying them their freedom to indulge themselves, but had come around to the belief that most of them frittered away their time in boring activities. To many of them, the fit of a coat or the proper arrangement of a cravat could waste hours. Of all the people she had met in her time in London, none of them did anything half so useful as Thomas and Lucien and their friends.

Except Mark.

Whatever she did, it seemed her thoughts always came back to Mark. She wished they would not, for she would have to learn to forget him. But how could she do so, even knowing what she now knew? If only she could talk to Evita—but not even to Evita could she tell the truth about Mark.

Trying to find something else to occupy her mind, she wandered about the house, looking for some sort of amusement. The staircase with its intricate carved posts, the paintings—most of them of ancestors whose history she did not know—all the possessions which had meant so much when she arrived, she counted for nothing now. Mark, flawed though he might be, seemed to come between her and everything she saw.

She picked up several of her grandfather's books which she had hoped to find time to read, leafed through them, then laid them aside. Today, even they could not hold her interest. Two more days, she thought. Only two more, and she would see Mark for the last time—not that she wanted to see him *now*. She would rejoin Lucien, and everything would be just as it was before she came.

"No, it will not," she told herself fiercely. "Nothing can be the same for me. Whatever happens, I cannot forget. I can only hope that *he* can forget . . . Lucien . . . and live the sort of life he should have."

She was standing at the window, twisting the cord of the drape in her hands and gazing unseeingly into the garden when Albert came to her side. In a low tone, he asked, "Coz, if you will not be using your greys this afternoon, will you let me take them out?"

"My greys? Oh no." The refusal was automatic. She would not have trusted him to tool the most sluggish pair of job horses. Then, thinking of how ungracious her reply must have sounded to him, she added, "They know my touch now, you see, and no other. Not even Thomas has driven them." Of course, Mark—*Mark*—had done so the first day. "I have never thought it wise to allow different persons to handle the ribbons. It confuses the cattle."

It sounded reasonable. In fact, she knew most drivers felt this way about their horseflesh. Yet, in another two days, she must give them up—as well as everything else. Perhaps Mark . . . "Why do you not use your bays?" she asked.

"I thought that one of them seemed to be a bit lame."

This would not surprise her. She knew Albert's habit of springing them regardless of the condition of the road. Just as he had done on the day of their race. That, and the way he had of sawing upon the lines, were two good reasons why she did not intend to permit him to handle her pair. They were too good to be ruined by mistreatment. When she left, she might make a gift of them to Mark. He would handle them with care, as they should be handled.

But was it wise to give Mark a reminder of—Lucien?

Accustomed to being given his way, Albert sulked for several moments, then brightened and suggested, "I have it. Why do you not come with me? I can promise you some rare sport. You will enjoy it."

"What sort of sport?" Doubtless, this was merely a ploy to get her to drive him somewhere, since his own pair was unable to carry him.

"Oh, but it must be a surprise—but it is one I am certain you will like." Then, as she hesitated, he added, "If you do not come, I shall believe that you do blame me for the accident, that you think I meant to shoot you."

"No, I do not think that." He had merely been a sulky boy, determined not to give up his toy. "But—"

"Then say you will come."

Albert looked so young and defenceless at this moment, so far from his usual haughty self, that Lucinda felt a stab of pity for him. Perhaps it was too much to expect that this boy—his mother's darling, who had been petted and spoiled all his life—could behave other than as he did. Would she and Lucien have been any better if they had been raised by their light-hearted, and light-headed *Maman?* She would have spoiled them outrageously. Instead, they had Thomas' common sense to guide them. Of course, Thomas frequently told her that she had learned nothing of sense, but she thought herself better than her cousin.

It was true that Albert had been careless in his manner of handling the pistol, but perhaps no one had taken the trouble to teach him proper respect for firearms. At least, it was certain that whoever had taught him to fence had made a muddle of the task.

If, as he complained, Mark had been lecturing him about the accident all the time she had been ill, it was little wonder that he felt resentful. She could remember just how resentful she had felt whenever Mark had taken her to task about some of her starts, although she could own that he had usually been in the right. And he had kept his . . . his secret feeling under control, never permitting a hint of it to escape. Until last night.

Lucinda did not doubt that whatever Albert had planned for the afternoon would be foolish, but it would certainly be better than sitting about feeling sorry for herself. It would also mean that, for several hours, she would not have to see Mark.

"Very well, I shall go with you," she said with as much enthusiasm as she could put into her voice. "But I think you should tell me where we are going."

"No—it must be a surprise. But you need not worry; I have been told the way and shall guide you."

In that case, there is no doubt we shall be completely lost, she said to herself. But even that would keep them away from the house for a time. She shrugged and gave orders to bring out her curricle and greys. Albert mounted to the seat at her side with difficulty, because of the bulk of his many-caped riding coat. He fondly hoped the garment would lead people to

think he was a member of the famous Four-in-Hand Club, but
no one who had seen him handle the ribbons would have been
fooled for an instant.

Following his directions out of London along roads which
did not look as if they were well travelled, Lucinda hoped he
was not mistaken in the route they were to take. It would be
all too easy for them to become lost in some of these by-ways.
Still, it would serve to pass the time and, if they did become
lost, they had only to drive long enough to find someone who
could set them on their way.

After a time, the road became better, and Lucinda could only
think Albert had been given these roundabout directions for
some purpose. At last he cried, "There it is. I told you I knew
the way."

He pointed to a mean-looking building surrounded by a
number of sporting vehicles. When Albert led the way into the
building, she saw that a crowd of men had preceded them.
There was a low ring in the center of the building with gentry
and workers crowded about it. The air was filled with unpleasant odors, and the shouts of many voices naming their wagers
was not enough to drown the sound of excited chickens.

Of all the harebrained schemes of which she had thought Albert capable, it had never occurred to her that he would plan
to attend a cockfight. Lucinda could not repress a shudder.
This was certain to be worse than the mill Neddy had been
planning to attend before Mark *(dear mixed-up Mark)* had
come to her rescue. She had no doubt this would prove to be
a gory spectacle—and she had reason to know Albert's aversion
to the sight of blood.

"Albert," she ventured, "are you certain this is what you
wish to do?"

"Oh yes, cousin. I have never seen one, but I hear they are
most enjoyable."

His eyes shone with excitement. Lucinda had no way of
knowing that, for all her cosseting him in other ways, Lady Sophia would never permit her son to attend any violent sport.
She knew his weakness in this area much too well.

This meet had all the lure of the forbidden for Albert—and
since his cousin had agreed to come along, the blame could always be shifted to the captain if her ladyship found out where
he had been. He could claim that Lucien had suggested the out-

ing, but had not told him what to expect. After all, it *was* Lucien who had driven here.

"All my friends tell me these fights are most diverting," he repeated. "In fact, I intend to have my own cocks to train and fight." Lady Sophia would never permit him to do anything of that sort, either, but his cousin would not know the truth, so he felt it safe to boast.

Lucinda tried again to make Albert leave, but it was too late for them to move. The wagers of the first fight had been laid, and the bettors fell silent as the handlers faced each other, one holding a grey bird, the other other a bronze. Bred for this pastime, the cocks eyed one another fiercely. When released, they flew to the center of the ring as the crowd began cheering loudly, some urging on one bird, the others favoring his opponent.

Unaware of what the cousins were doing, Mark drove slowly along the winding lanes. He let his horses choose the way they would take, keeping only enough control upon the lines to let them know their driver was still with them. His mind was busy with memories of the preceding night, recalling how Lucinda had fled from him. Had he been too abrupt, had his gesture revealed to her that he knew her secret? Was that what had frightened her into flight?

He had intended to go slowly in revealing the truth, perhaps allowing her grandfather to tell her. After that, he would approach her, convince her of his love, and beg her to stay with him. From the things she had let slip in her fever, he knew she was not indifferent to him and did not resent him as she had done at first. He was not certain that she loved him, but he felt she would soon do so.

The nickering of several animals, greeting the approach of his own, aroused him from his thought. He recognized the low building and knew from the vehicles surrounding it that cockfights were taking place today. His gaze flew to a certain curricle, little different from the others, but with a pair of prime greys he could not mistake.

Lucinda was here! He knew Neddy's predilection for such affairs and supposed he must have persuaded her to accompany him. "If he has brought her to a place like this," Mark vowed, "I shall flay him, friend or no."

Quickly tying his own cattle, he entered the building and began to search the crowd for Neddy and Lucinda. Halfway across the room, he saw the unmistakable yellow driving coat with its many capes. Pushing his way through the crowd, ignoring the complaints of those in his way, he grasped Neddy by the arm.

"Where is she?" he demanded.

"Where is who?" Neddy shouted back. "There's no females here today. You know they ain't permitted."

"You know whom I mean—where is Lucinda? Did you not talk her into bringing you?" Although they were straining their voices, the din was so great that no one else could overhear them.

"Of course I did not," Neddy protested. "I'd never do such a thing—now that I know. I came here with Ferdy Maupin; he's about somewhere."

"But I know those were Lucinda's greys outside. If you did not bring her, how did she get to such a place?" At that moment, he spied the cousins across the room and groaned aloud. "I do not know which of them has the least sense. It would be Albert's idea to come here, of course, but why did she let him? I must get her away from here at once!"

"That will not be easy. You cannot even reach her. Best stay and watch awhile. What do you think of the chances of the black bird over there?"

"The black bird be hanged. I am thinking about Lucinda."

On the far side of the room Lucinda tried to look away as the birds ripped at one another with their spurs. The thought of any bird or animal being hurt had always sickened her. And these men were actually enjoying the spectacle!

One who was not enjoying it was Albert. At that moment, he clawed at her arm, gasping for breath. "I— I—" His face had taken on a greenish hue, and he could not get out more words. Thankful that he had not swooned and happy for the excuse to leave before she herself had broken down, Lucinda caught his arm and dragged him through the crowd to the door, ignoring the catcalls which followed them.

Mark saw them go and caught Neddy's arm once more. "Come with me. We must follow them."

"Leave go, Mark. I cannot go now. I have a wager on the

black." Then, as Mark dragged him forward despite his protests, he said, "What about Ferdy?"

"Let him find a ride with someone else."

"But he is the one who drove."

"Then he will be all right." Mark pushed on. One man, thrown from his place, began to dispute his right, but a quick look at Mark's size and his determined expression changed his mind.

Outside, Albert leaned against the side of the building, struggling for breath, one hand across his stomach, the other holding his head. Lucinda realized that, in his desire to have a share in the excitement of watching a cockfight, he had not thought that the birds might shed each other's blood. What *had* he expected? she wondered.

She stood near him, making an effort to control her own nausea, made worse by the sight of his affliction. As soon as she was able to speak without her voice trembling, she said, "I think it best that I take you home at once."

He nodded weakly. When they reached the curricle, he seemed unable to climb up to the seat without assistance from her. She headed the greys back along the route they had come, stealing occasional glimpses at her companion. He was sitting limply beside her, head lowered, eyes closed. She remembered how he had swooned when she was shot and was again glad he had not done so beside the cockfight ring. How would she have managed to get him out of there unaided? If he were to collapse now, she must see to it that he did not fall from the vehicle.

The curricle and greys were out of sight by the time Mark had pulled Neddy free from the crowd. "Why are you in so great a hurry?" the smaller man asked between gasps for breath. He was unaccustomed to such haste.

"Can you not understand? If it was Lucinda who became ill indoors—and she might well have done—it will be *Albert* who is driving. And I should not trust him to go half a mile without overturning the curricle." He almost threw Neddy to the seat of his own vehicle, loosed his pair and jumped in, pulling the animals' heads about and slapping the lines down upon their backs in an effort to overtake the other two before something should happen to his darling.

Lucinda, meanwhile, had drawn her pair to a walk as they

crossed a stretch of road so strewn with large rocks that she feared to lame one of the animals or break a wheel. As she allowed the greys to pick their own way through the rocks, Albert caught at her arm, causing her to pull them to one side. She looked at him to warn him not to do so again and could see that the motion of the curricle had added to his earlier nausea.

"I . . . I must get down." He was again gasping for breath.

She halted her cattle, quickly snubbed the lines about the edge of the seat, and jumped to the road. When she hurried around to Albert's side and helped him to the ground he clung to the side of the curricle.

"Do not look at me," he begged.

Obediently, she turned her back and tried to close her ears to the sound of his retching. It was only natural that he would not wish his cousin to witness his weakness. It would be embarrassing enough to have anyone know of it, but especially the one with whom he had been in competition for the past two months. She would tell him that she understood, that men were often affected in this manner.

His spell of sickness ended, Albert leaned against the side of the vehicle again, staring at his cousin's back. He was certain the captain must be secretly laughing at him for what had happened. Doubtless he could hardly wait to spread the tale to his friends for them to share his mirth. It was not *his* fault that his system had always been delicate—but a soldier, a man accustomed to killing, would not be expected to know that or to sympathize with it.

At the moment, he had no thought of his grandfather's fortune. There had been no doubt in his mind from the start that it would come to him, no matter what the old gentleman had said. That was only his way of excusing himself because the next earl would be left with so little.

What moved him now was something entirely different. It was solely a desire to rid himself of a witness to his shameful weakness that made Albert bend to catch up the largest stone he could lift.

The greys, knowing there was no hand upon the ribbons, began to move about restlessly, and Lucinda stepped forward to quiet them. Her consideration for the animals' well-being was uppermost in her mind. Still, it would not do to have them run off and leave her in this lonely spot with a sick man on her hands.

As she reached out to grasp the nearest bridle, the blow upon the back of her head sent her sprawling to the ground. Unaware that her movement toward the horses had saved her from the full force of his blow, Albert dropped the stone. He was secretly thankful that no blood had been shed, for that might have made him ill again, and he had no time for illness now. Catching his cousin by the arms, he began to drag her toward a deep ditch which ran along the side of the road.

Chapter Sixteen

ONCE THE BODY was at the bottom of the ditch with more stones thrown upon it and the curricle overturned, perhaps with one of the wheels smashed, who would not believe that the captain had been killed in an accident? Albert had not seen anyone he knew at the cockfight, so he did not think he had been recognized.

Everyone would think that Lucien had been alone at the time of the accident. If anything should be said to him later, he would tell them he *never* attended such events and knew his mother would say the same. It was a pity that he would have to walk such a long way back to the City, but it would be worth it. The greys would have to be left here—or perhaps, after he had smashed the wheel, he could make them drag the wrecked vehicle farther along the road, as if they had been frightened. That would explain the accident.

As he struggled toward the ditch with his cousin's form, there was the sound of approaching hoofbeats, and another curricle swept around the bend of the road. Before the team had been pulled to a halt, the driver had leaped to the ground, saying, "I feared something like this!"

Albert was caught by the collar and flung to one side so violently that he lay stunned for a moment. Mark knelt beside Lucinda, raising her head, probing with gentle fingers at the bruise. The skin on the back of her head had not been broken, thanks to the protection of her hat, but there was a sizeable lump.

How could she have been thrown from the vehicle in such

a way as to strike the top of her head? The crushed hat and the large stone lying near it would have told the story if Albert's expression had not done so.

Lucinda groaned, and Mark uttered a fervent, "Not fatal, thank God." Picking her up, he placed her upon the seat of her own vehicle and swung himself up beside her. Looking over his shoulder, he asked, "Can you manage my pair and bring him along, Neddy?"

Neddy, who had been nervously holding the lines since Mark had tossed them to him, swallowed several times, then said, "I can do it. Get along, Mark, and do not trouble about me." It seemed that he would have less trouble with Albert than with the cattle, for the young man was cowering against the side of the curricle, as if expecting another attack.

"Get up there with Neddy," Mark ordered. "I have no time to bother with you—now." The threat implied in the last word made Albert cringe, then quickly obey the order to mount to the vehicle's seat.

One of Mark's arms pinned Lucinda tightly against him as he brought the whip down smartly upon the backs of the greys, sending them to a gallop. She half-stirred to find herself lying across a broad chest as the curricle racketed over the uneven road. Mark had dropped the whip in order to hold her safely, but she had caught a glimpse of it. "Not the whip," she murmured. "Do not let them harm themselves."

"Do not mind the cattle," he told her. "We must get you home as quickly as we can."

It was then that she realized who it was holding her. What was he doing in her curricle, driving her greys? The jolting of the vehicle over the stones made her head ache abominably. She put up a cautious hand and felt the painful lump on the back of her skull. Then she remembered. "Albert—he tried to—"

"I know. We caught him preparing to throw you into a ditch. I had thought at first that you had an accident and that he was only taking advantage of it. But you could not have fallen on the back of your head. There is nothing to worry about now, though. You are safe with me."

"Safe . . . with you," she murmured bemusedly. Mark had said they had come upon Albert trying to dispose of her.

But what was Mark doing here? She did not think he cared for cockfights, so was it merely an accident that he had been there? She could not believe that Mark was capable of scheming with Albert to remove her. Remove Lucien, she amended. If Mark had planned such a thing, he would have attended to the details himself and things would not have been bungled. But if he had saved her from Albert, how did he happen to be on hand? And where was he taking her now? "Always safe with you," she managed before darkness enveloped her again.

Halting the sweating animals outside the house, Mark bellowed until several servants came running to see what was amiss. "Someone hold these cattle," he ordered, "and see that they are cooled properly. They have had quite a run."

"But that is the captain's rig," Fenton exclaimed. "Did you—" Then he saw the inert figure in Mark's arms. "The captain? What has happened to him?"

"Never mind now. Just go to their heads, one of you, so that I can get down," Mark said in a tone that sent Fenton, who ordinarily would never have demeaned himself by doing a groom's work, running to the horses' heads, while a footman went hotfoot in search of a stable boy.

Mark jumped to the ground and lifted Lucinda's limp form in his arms. As he did so, she stirred slightly and asserted, "I can walk," although the dizziness still threatened to overwhelm her and she knew she would rather be in his arms than anywhere. Then a sudden memory caused her to try to pull away from him.

"Be quiet," he ordered. He strode up the stairs with her cradled against him. Thomas met them at the head of the stairs, but Mark elbowed him aside. Carrying her into the bedchamber, he laid her on her side on the bed, putting a pillow at her back, so that she would not turn and lie on the bruise.

"I do not think it is anything serious, after all," he told Thomas, throwing the crushed hat upon the bedside table. "This seems to have taken the worst of the blow. And we were in time to prevent anything more."

"What . . . ? That scheming cousin?" Thomas enquired, and Mark nodded.

"Yes, I left him with the marquess, who is bringing him in— if he doesn't wreck my vehicle upon the way. I wish to be there to receive him." He hurried from the room, and Thomas came to the bedside to examine Lucinda's injury.

She longed for the feeling of Mark's arms holding her as he

had been doing, but as Thomas bent her head forward to get a closer look at the lump which Albert's blow had caused, she protested, "Do not fuss so greatly over me, Thomas. There is nothing wrong with me."

"Of course there is nothing wrong," Thomas said tightly, clearly worried. He brought a cloth which he had dipped in cold water and applied it to the back of Lucinda's head with what she thought was unnecessary force.

"Your head is much too hard to break," he continued scolding, "and you've given proof enough you have no brains to be spilled. I cannot understand you, Lucinda Warne, giving that whelp of the cousin a second chance—"

"Evita called him a snake," Lucinda said, "but I did not think he had either the wit or the nerve—" Suddenly, all that had occurred seemed very comical to her.

"Poor Albert," she chuckled. "Unable to do anything right. Cannot even murder—" Then, exhausted by all that had happened, she curled herself into a ball and went to sleep, while Thomas stood over her, shaking his head.

She roused some time later to find that Thomas—or had it been Mark before he left?—had propped more pillows behind her so that she would not turn upon her back and cause additional pain to her bruise, which was now pounding as if someone were raining blows upon it.

"Poor Thomas," she said half-aloud. "What a burden I must be to him." And not just with today's trouble, she thought, but so many times. I wonder I have not exhausted his patience years ago.

She realized now that it had not been the pounding in her head which had awakened her, but a series of loud noises from below stairs. Remembering how quietly the servants usually moved about, she sat up to listen.

There were certainly blows being struck, but not upon her head, as she had thought. Someone or something downstairs was being systematically beaten. She could hear yelping, as if some animal might be in pain. But what would any animal be doing in the house?

Lucinda saw that Thomas had not yet heard her, for he was standing at the opened door of her room, a broad grin upon his face as he listened to the uproar. She wondered that no one stopped it, getting gingerly to her feet, driven by curiosity.

What would her grandfather think of such a hullabaloo? Why doesn't Mark make them keep quiet?

When she attempted to pass Thomas into the hall, he caught her arm and held her back. "Best stay here, girl," he warned. "Down there is no place for you just now."

"Thomas, I am tired of being forever tucked up here as if I were a child," she protested, well aware as she spoke that she was being unreasonable. Everyone had only acted out of kindness toward her. Everyone except Albert. But she was so wrought up about all that had happened today—and last evening—that she no longer cared. "If you do not let me go, I shall . . . I shall scream."

Lucinda was not given to such female tricks as screaming merely because she was denied her way about something. The threat so startled Thomas that he dropped her arm. Before he could make a recover, Lucinda slipped past him and started down the stairs. Thomas followed to the head of the stairway so that he could see what happened below, ready to dash down if Lucinda needed him.

The sounds from below ceased as she descended the stairs and, as she reached the hallway, she was almost bowled over by Albert, who ran from the library and out the front door, slamming it behind him. She doubted if he had even been aware of her, and she was sorry. She had wished to tell him what she thought of the way he had treated her.

At the library door, she stopped, staring at the usually neat form of her grandfather's secretary. Now his neckcloth had been pulled awry, his black hair was badly mussed, and his face was flushed. He held a heavy cane in his hand, swinging it as if he planned to strike someone—or something. However, when he saw Lucinda, he laughed and tossed it into a corner.

"Come in, little one," he called pleasantly. "I have just allowed myself the pleasure of giving your cousin the thrashing he should have had years ago."

Her heart gave a lurch at the thought that Mark had done this for her benefit. Then, like a pail of cold water thrown over her, came the thought that he had done it because of Lucien. Or at least, that was what he thought. Once more, the memory of last night's revelation of his true feelings sent a knifelike pain through her.

On the other hand, perhaps what he had done had no bearing

on Albert's treatment of her. He might only have been thinking
of the distress the younger man's behavior had caused their
grandfather. Quite as gruffly as her brother might have done,
she said, "Do you think I am incapable of avenging my own
wrongs, cousin?"

"I am quite well aware you can do so, young fire-eater, having crossed blades with you, as you will remember. But would
you really wish to cheat me out of some of the most enjoyable
moments I have had in many months? Since the day I first laid
eyes upon that cur, I can tell you my hands have itched to dust
his coat for him."

She gave him a surprised look, then joined his laughter. After
what Albert had done to her—or, at least, what he had tried
to do—she felt she would have enjoyed witnessing the beating
he had received, although under other circumstances, the idea
of such violence would have revolted her.

Still, it was not merely Albert's actions of today, but everything he had done in the two months she had known him. His
superior attitude toward Mark, who was, after all, as well-born
as they. His rudeness toward hostesses. Mark was right. He was
a cur.

Thoughts of her own behavior toward Mark during these
months sobered her, and she said, "The pair of us have given
you some bad moments since we came here, have we not?"

"You have," he agreed so readily that she felt some of the
old resentment stirring. At least, he might have said that she
had been less troublesome than her cousin. Or had he found
her so? Considering what she knew about him . . .

"You might be interested to know," Mark was saying, "that
your cousin was . . . er, persuaded to own that, although his
shooting you was only an accident and his attack today was,
according to him, only because you were witness to his weakness and—"

"You mean he would have tried to kill me because of *that*?"

"I think it was an instant decision of the moment. He felt
that you would once more have something about which to
laugh at him. However, he doubtless thought that if you were
removed permanently, there would be no other claimant to the
money he has always considered his own. He never believed,
of course, the earl was serious when he said he might leave everything to a mere servant."

"But you are not—"

"In your cousin's eyes, that is what I am. So, to him, the contest was between the two of you. In addition to what happened today, he has so many reasons for disliking you. You have beaten him at racing, at fencing—and he resents it that you do not faint at the sight of blood."

"But certainly, none of these are reasons enough for him to want to—"

"All I know is what he said. I am not certain that even he knows the true reasons for what he has done. It is unfortunate for your cousin that he has never been denied anything he wished until now. He would not know how to accept the idea that you would be more successful than he."

Lucinda nodded. If he had been less spoiled, Albert might not have been so reckless.

"But I had the greatest of pleasure in being able to tell him that—even if he had been successful in putting you out of the way without ending his life by the hangman's noose, which certainly would have been his destination since he planned so poorly or not at all—he still could not have convinced your grandfather that he ought to change his will."

"Then Grandfather . . . has decided?" Now, at least, she could end this masquerade. Even if it meant going away, never seeing Mark again. Which, of course, she must do as quickly as possible. It would be heartbreaking to go—but worse to stay under the present circumstances.

"Yes. He called in his solicitor several days past to draw up the final papers. Although I think that, for some weeks, he has been certain what he would do. He has decided to give Albert an allowance from the estate—one which your cousin will doubtless think is pitifully small."

"He will not like that." But what of the rest? Would it go to Lucien or to Mark? Why must he be so slow in telling her that?

"You may be certain he will not. With the allowance goes the provision that should his mother give him more than five pounds in any one week, whether for clothing or amusements, the allowance will be immediately discontinued. Since she has already permitted him to fritter away almost all of his inheritance from his father, thinking as he did that he would be the one to receive his lordship's fortune, I fear young Albert's Dandy days are over."

So Albert had lost the wager he offered the first day. Lucinda could not pity him for that when she thought of what he had attempted to do to her. But why did Mark go on about Albert instead of telling her whether or not Lucien would inherit? Had her masquerade been worth the while—worth all the heart-break she would suffer through the coming years? She would have liked to ask, but that might seem greedy. Surely, he would tell her before much longer. Perhaps if she offered to congratu-late him . . .

It seemed, however, that Mark had not finished talking about Albert.

"I had warned your grandfather that he must not be overset by any noises he might hear, that I had matters to settle with his grandson. He did not say so, but I think he did not disap-prove. I have not told him everything which has occurred in the past weeks, although he wanted reports from me. I did not wish to appear a talebearer, but it was not possible to evade all his questions. For his lordship's sake, I preferred to handle the matter myself, rather than turning your cousin over to the law for what he did today."

"Many would have done so."

"True. And he certainly deserves that I should do so, but it would result in a scandal. I fear it would be harmful to your grandfather in his state of health. However, if you wish me to do so, I can tell him what has happened—you can understand why I have not already done so—and I am certain Albert's al-lowance will not be made."

Scandal indeed! It would be far worse than he could imagine. If Albert were to be arrested, her own masquerade would be certain to come out. The combination of events would set Lon-don to buzzing with the sort of gossip it most enjoyed and might well destroy her grandfather's failing health, as well as putting paid to Lucien's career.

She had never considered that her indiscretion might reflect upon the old gentleman. His welfare had been the furthest thing from her mind at the beginning. In fact, she had given little thought to anything except the excitement of disguising herself as Lucien for a time. Even helping her brother had taken sec-ond place to the pleasure of her escapade. Now, her own heart-break must be her payment for such foolishness. No one else must suffer because of her.

"No," she said quickly. "As you say, it would cause my grandfather great pain to know the truth. And we have brought him enough worry, the pair of us, without adding to it. If the allowance is as small as you say, that would be the worst punishment you could give him."

"Many people would consider it to be quite liberal. I, for one, do. But I am certain the young man will not, for it is only a small part of what he now fritters away." He seated himself upon the edge of the desk. "Now, your grandfather has given me permission to tell you about the balance of his will—"

At last it was coming! Lucinda tried not to appear too eager. On the other hand, to pretend indifference would be out of character.

There was a tap upon the door, and Fenton looked in to say in apologetic tones, "If you please, Mr. Warne, Colonel and Mrs. Stoneback have called and insist that they must see his lordship."

Mark frowned. "They cannot be friends of Lord Brayling, for I do not recall hearing him speak of them. He would have been certain to have done so at some time. Nor have they called here before or written. You have told them, of course, that his lordship's health does not permit him to receive visitors."

"Yes, sir." Fenton looked hurt, as if no such reminder would have been necessary. "They say, however, that this is not a social call, and they refuse to leave until they have seen his lordship. Shall I call one of the footmen to put them out?"

"The idea is tempting, but I suppose it would not be for the best. If not a social call, then why? We have done no business with anyone of that name. Since they are so insistent, I suppose I must speak to them. You do not mind?" he asked Lucinda.

She, indeed, did mind greatly at having strangers interrupting them at this moment, but it would do her no good to complain. The callers, whoever they might be, would hardly be expected to wait until her curiosity had been satisfied. Not if they were as insistent as Fenton said. She shook her head and retired to a far corner of the room, biting her lip in vexation.

His stiff back registering silent disapproval of the callers who had overriden his refusal to allow them to see his lordship, Fenton ushered in a large, belligerent lady, whose bonnet, topped with many plumes, and her billowing pelisse nearly hid the small gentleman who looked as if he would have been anywhere but here, had he been given a choice.

Lucinda did not recall having seen him before, although he would have been an easy person to overlook. The lady was a far different matter. Lucinda recognized her at once as the dragon from the Channel boat, who had been more forthcoming when seen at various functions. Stella Proctor's aunt. What purpose could Stella's guardians have in calling upon her grandfather?

The lady regarded Mark haughtily and firmly prodded her husband forward. Doubtless overawed by the greater size of the man confronting him, the colonel nervously cleared his throat two or three times, then said, "Sir, I do not know who you are, but we told the servant quite plainly that our business is with Lord Brayling."

"And I believe you have already been informed that, in his present state of health, Lord Brayling is not receiving visitors. However, I am his secretary, Mark Warne, and if you will inform me as to the business you have with Lord Brayling, perhaps I can be of some help."

"Mark Warne?" The colonel was obviously startled to learn the young man was clearly a relative of his lordship. One must deal more circumspectly with members of the Quality. In a far different tone, he began, "Well, Mr. Warne, the matter . . . the fact is—"

Mrs. Stoneback was made of sterner stuff. Completely unimpressed by any connections the large gentleman might have, and seeing that her husband appeared to be unable to remember his instructions to come to the point, she pushed him rudely aside and said, "The matter, Mr. Warne, is a serious one concerning my niece, Stella Proctor, and *Captain* Warne."

"Really? And may I ask in what way, madam?" Lucinda thought she heard a hint of mockery in his voice, but she doubted either of the Stonebacks would detect it. She could not know he was asking himself what sort of scrape the girl had begun in this case.

"I am correct in assuming Captain Warne is the grandson of Lord Brayling, am I not?"

"Quite correct, madam." It was only Mark's tone which appeared to add, And what has that to do with you? He was accustomed to persons who attempted to claim acquaintance with the earl and had no hesitation in putting their pretensions to naught.

"Then I think, Mr. Warne, that it is only proper that Lord Brayling should be informed that the captain has led my niece to believe—" She broke off with a delicate cough.

Lucinda gasped. Certainly she had joined the crowd of Stella's admirers from time to time, thinking it a good jest, but she had scarcely spoken to the girl in weeks.

Controlling his laughter with an effort, Mark allowed his eyebrows to shoot up questioningly. The lady nodded, the plumes on her bonnet waving so violently that Lucinda feared they might fly off.

"Of course, the proper thing for the captain to have done would have been to approach her uncle first, but since he did not—"

"I understand the situation perfectly, madam." And he did understand very well. The old witch clearly had her eye on his lordship's moneybags. "And is it not fortunate that Captain Warne is here at the moment?"

Turning his back upon the pair, he crooked a finger at Lucinda, ordering, "Come here, Captain," in a tone whose sternness was belied by the grin he gave her. It was plain that the scene was affording him a great deal of amusement, but none of the others had the faintest idea of the source of his enjoyment.

Mrs. Stoneback was clearly taken aback that the captain was present. She doubtless had intended to complete her scheme with no chance of her charges being denied.

Lucinda obeyed Mark's gesture slowly, struggling between laughter at the lady's obvious chagrin and apprehension at the possible outcome of this confrontation. She had always been aware that Stella had no more interest in Captain Warne than in any other of her crowd of admirers; it was only her wish to capture as many hearts as possible, thus arousing Lord Byrne's jealousy. From what Byrne had said last evening, she knew he and the Beauty were betrothed. However, the betrothal was dependent upon the consent of the pair who had called here today.

Their presence showed how little chance that consent had of being received. Lucinda could see clearly, and she did not doubt Mark realized as well, that the dragon had her eye on Lord Brayling's fortune for her niece and was determined to get it any way she could do so. If she persisted in her claim that the captain had insinuated himself into Stella's affections to a point where the girl considered herself to be promised, Lucinda might be forced, even at this late date, to reveal her identity.

Chapter
Seventeen

SHE WAS CERTAIN Mrs. Stoneback would be so angered when she learned there had never been a chance of Stella's getting the fortune that she would broadcast the scandalous details—including whatever number her imagination would supply—and it was not yet too late for Lord Brayling to change his will.

"It would appear, my dear Captain," Mark said in the same stern tone, having composed his features by the time he turned to face the visitors, "that your attentions to this lady's niece have been so pointed that the poor young lady seems to have developed a *tendre* for you."

Who could have foreseen that her jest of joining the train of Stella's admirers would have pitchforked her into a situation such as this one? "I fear," Lucinda said desperately, all too well aware that—to the Stonebacks if not to Mark—this must sound exactly like a young man's attempt to avoid a compromising situation, "that Mrs. Stoneback is in error concerning Miss Proctor's true feelings. Lord Byrne—"

"A nobody." The dragon dismissed the viscount's ancient heritage with a wave of her hand, for she could see no good in a title without the money to support it. "I assure you my niece has come to see him as he really is and has confided her change of feelings to me. After all, I have stood mother to her these many years, and should know—"

Mark laid a hand upon Lucinda's shoulder, but whether the squeeze he gave it meant encouragement or commiseration, she could not tell. "If you have contrived to involve Miss Proctor's affection to such an extent as that, my young fellow," he told her firmly, "you must realize there is only one course for you to take in the matter."

As she tried to think of some way of escaping from this coil without revealing her true identity, Mark had turned once more to the lady, who was smiling broadly at the thought of her success. Perhaps it was better that they had not seen his lordship, who had a reputation for being hard-hearted. This secretary had been easy to convince, and the captain would not be able to evade the net. Stella would do as she was told, weep though she might.

"I must commend your niece," the secretary was saying, "upon having a strength of character which is much too rare in these days. There are few young ladies—no matter how sincerely in love they might be—who would be willing to give up the pleasures of London for life in an army camp."

"Army camp?" Mrs. Stoneback screeched. It was clear that she had been picturing a far different life for Lord Brayling's heir.

"Yes, of course, since Captain Warne is upon the point of returning to rejoin his outfit on the Peninsula and will be there for some time, I fear. I assume that Miss Proctor will be prepared to follow him there immediately after the ceremony. We shall have to arrange for a special license so that the marriage can take place before the captain leaves. He can stay away no longer, and I am certain you would not wish the young lady to wait—perhaps for several years—until the war is ended and he can return home."

"But . . . but—" the dragon began to sputter, but Mark pretended not to hear her.

"In the circumstances, there will be no time for Miss Proctor to purchase bride clothes. However, such things as she could purchase in London would not be suitable for her life in Portugal or Spain. She will need things more fitting for the rugged life of the camp. Heavy boots, I should imagine, for there will be a great deal of walking, and other clothing of a similar nature."

The large lady was now gasping, as if in pain, but Mark went on ruthlessly, "You can appreciate, of course, that a soldier's pay—even that of a captain—is not enough to allow Captain Warne to provide a separate establishment here in London nor

will he be able to employ servants to assist his wife. But if her
uncle makes her a sufficient allowance, she might be able to
manage quite well. I do hope, however, that she is a good cook,
for Captain Warne's appetites nearly equal my own.''

"I do not understand." Although she seemed dazed by all
this information, Mrs. Stoneback's voice had returned. "Lord
Brayling *is* a wealthy man, is he not?''

"Certainly—one of the wealthiest in the country, unless I
am mistaken. But I do not think I am.''

"Then—''

"Oh, I understand. You have been leaping to a conclusion
which is quite erroneous. I can assure you, and as his lordship's
secretary I am in a position to know, this young scamp will
not receive a penny of Lord Brayling's fortune.''

At this further set-back, Mrs. Stoneback stared at him, open-
mouthed until her husband tugged at her arm.

"Come along, Lydia," he ordered. "I told you how it would
be, but you were set on coming. Now, will you believe me that
the old man is naught but a clutchfist and that we have wasted
our time?''

With unaccustomed meekness, his wife allowed herself to be
guided to the door, then recovered herself sufficiently to turn
and deliver a parting shot.

"The announcement of my niece's betrothal to Lord Byrne
will be sent to the *Gazette* immediately. He may have no
money, but at least he is honest about his prospects and does
not attempt to lead an innocent girl astray.''

The door closed behind the indignant couple, and Lucinda
stared at Mark. He had collapsed against the table helpless with
laughter.

"Piqued—repiqued—slammed—and capotted!" he got out
between whoops. "And I wish I might have had a sketch of
your face as well, when I told you you must do the honorable
thing. Did you really believe I would be so heartless as to toss
you to that old she-wolf?''

"I fear I am unable to appreciate your humor at this moment," Lucinda said somewhat sourly, but found his laughter
infectious, especially when she recalled the many different expressions which had crossed Mrs. Stoneback's face—her trium-
phant smile at such an easy victory giving way to astonishment,

then to indignation at seeing that coveted fortune being snatched from her grasp.

The last memory brought the end of Mark's speech to the dragon to her mind once more, and Lucinda's laughter vanished as she asked, "Were you bamming us or was it the truth? Under my grandfather's will, am I to receive nothing?"

"Not a penny," Mark said, wiping tears of mirth from his eyes, but continuing to laugh inwardly as he understood the reason for her questions. "I must tell you that your name was not even mentioned."

Not even an allowance, she thought weakly. Albert had been given that much, despite his behavior. So her entire masquerade had been for nothing. Or perhaps she had even worsened Lucien's chances by the escapades into which she had fallen. Oh, Lucien, she said beneath her breath, truly I thought I could be of help.

Still, she thought, she was far more unhappy for her brother's sake than he would be. He had never held much hope of getting the money and would not miss it. As for Mark—whatever his faults might be, he deserved every good thing the fortune could bring him.

"So it seems that both my cousin and I lose our wagers," she said finally. "And I must congratulate you on becoming my grandfather's heir."

She thrust out a hand and Mark grasped it, holding it as he said, "Only in a small way."

"I . . . I do not understand."

"You are thinking of what his lordship said the day you came, but that was merely to test the pair of you. I was never a candidate for his fortune. It was decided long ago that I was to have one of his small estates. I plan to retire to it when it is mine, for, although I enjoy the life of London now and then, I truly prefer country life. There will also be what you might call a competence. It will be enough to provide a comfortable living—but my wife can never hope to be one of the Belles of London Society."

Lucinda felt as if the floor had suddenly dropped from beneath her feet.

"You are to be married?" It was odd that she had never thought of such a thing. Although he was popular enough at the balls he attended, Mark had never given any indication that he was interested in any lady . . . but of course, any girl would consider herself fortunate—

"I plan to be very soon," he said with a grin, having felt the tremor in the hand he still held.

"Then I must wish you very happy." He would never know the great effort it cost for her to say those words.

"I think I shall be."

Must he sound so certain of it? she thought, freeing her hand. She wanted to shriek or throw something—anything to relieve her feelings. Unhappy as she was at his announcement, another thought came into Lucinda's mind.

"But if Albert nor you nor I inherit grandfather's money, where is it to go?"

Mark began to laugh once more. "You cannot guess?"

She shook her head. With Lucien, Albert, and Mark ruled out, who else was there? Only Lady Sophia. But if the money were left to her, she would let her son have what he wished of it, and Lord Brayling clearly did not intend that. Was he perhaps planning to leave it to some charity?

"You should know." Mark's laughter grew heartier. "It will go to the *real* Captain Warne, of course."

Lucinda stared at him, the words echoing through her mind but making no sense to her. After all, to everyone in this house, to everyone in London—with the exception of Evita and Thomas—*she* was Captain Warne.

"The . . . the real—?" she said at last.

"Yes, of course." Mark was thoroughly enjoying her look of amazement as he said, "To the real Captain Warne. Your brother, my dear Lucinda."

"I . . . I do not understand. You mean that you know—and grandfather, also—"

"From the very first. Of course, your grandfather might have been easier to mislead. But do you think, my darling idiot, that I could have been under the same roof with you for a single day without being certain you were not what you seemed? Then, of course," he owned, "there was your brother's letter."

"Lucien's letter?" She knew she must sound lack-witted as she echoed everything he said. It was only that she had been so certain all this time that she had been successful in her disguise, that she had been able to fool everyone. It was difficult for her to comprehend this change in the situation, to realize that *she* had been the one who had been fooled.

"Yes. Your brother wrote to your grandfather on the day you left because he was worried about the many things which could happen if anyone discovered your secret."

"Lucien did *that*? How could he?" She had known her brother did not wish for her to come to London, but to betray her in this fashion . . .

"He also told his lordship that you would never have attempted so daring a thing if it had not been that he could not leave his post—that you have gone into the affair only because you wished to help him. The letter was delayed along the route and arrived just after your first call."

"You mean you have known all this time?" The accusation in her tone made him grin—that grin she had come to love, but now faced with fury.

"I was almost certain the moment I saw you that you must be an imposter. Believe me, you do not look in the least like an officer."

"But I *do!* I—"

"Oh, I do not doubt you resemble your brother—a bit. But scarcely enough to fool anyone for more than a few moments. When your brother's letter arrived, it merely confirmed my suspicions." During the past weeks, he had convinced himself this was so. "Your grandfather was quite angry at first—understandably so—both with you for attempting to dupe him, and with your brother and Thomas Abbott for allowing you to do so."

"They were not at fault—either of them. They did not wish me to come, but I said I would come alone if they did not agree to help me."

Mark nodded. "Yes, I can believe you would have done exactly that. You wished to help your brother, of course, but I believe you thought it was more of a lark than otherwise. Lord Brayling, however, was so angry at first that he wished to have you arrested for your masquerade—it *is* a crime, you know—and to disinherit your brother of everything which was not included in the entail."

"That would have been unfair! To blame Lucien for—"

"After giving the matter more thought, he decided that a young man who would put his duty to his country—especially a country he had never seen—above his chances of a fortune, and his sister's welfare above all else, would be the best man to receive that fortune. As I told you, we had no way of knowing what would influence him."

So perhaps her coming to London had been of some good, after all, for it seemed that Lucien's concern for her had played an important part in her grandfather's decision to leave him the money. But surely this decision would have been the same two months ago, and she need not have played out the masquerade for the full time.

"If you knew all this from the beginning," she demanded, "why did you not tell me? Or why did Grandfather not send me some word?"

"Your grandfather wished to do so," Mark owned, "and to send you back to your brother at once. But he had already made his arrangements for the two months' contest, so he allowed me to have my way when I begged him to permit you to continue. I told him I would keep an eye upon you, not realizing what a difficult task that would be. To tell you true, your foolishness in attempting such a disguise intrigued me, your presumption in believing you could fool anyone—"

"But I did fool them—any number of people. Both men and women," Lucinda protested, thinking of how Mrs. Stoneback had been taken in. If she would pass as a gentleman under *those* sharp eyes—

"I grant that you did so. We have evidence enough of that. Although I cannot understand how it could happen. Do you believe that, even if I had not been told who you were, your brother's clothing could have fooled me, any more than a green mask and a red wig could do?"

"Do you mean that—"

"That I knew you were 'Margarita,' the cousin who spoke no English? Certainly I knew. I have been observing you closely enough that I know everything about you. Your Spanish is quite good, by the way. But I suppose that is only natural if you have spent much time in the country."

"You understood?" Color flooded her face as she recalled some of Evita's comments and her own whispered plea not to be left alone with him. "But you said you did not—"

"I can understand a bit, although I am not as fluent in the language as you. But almost as much—no, much more—than

I enjoyed watching you trying to play the man, I enjoyed your performance as the unwilling coquette. That is, you were unwilling at first, but . . ." He broke off, grinning at the expression upon her face. Lucinda was recalling how willing she had become under his caresses.

"That was abominable!" she said with a gasp.

"No, enjoyable. Most enjoyable." Then in a different tone, Mark continued, "No, you did not fool me for an instant. Byrne did not notice, I own, but he had other matters on his mind. And, of course, he had less reason for watching you than I did."

What reason, she wondered, could he have for so close a watch? He had called her "darling," but he had also said, "idiot." And he had told her he was to be married. The "darling" had meant nothing.

"At any rate," Mark was explaining, "I was amused, and his lordship agreed to allow you to go on with the charade when I promised to see that you got into no trouble on account of it. He feared a scandal if you were exposed. You may be certain he combed my hair thoroughly each time you contrived to slip away from my watch to commit some new foolishness."

"It was *not* foolishness. And I wish I might have heard him bear-jawing you." She smiled at the thought of anyone, even the earl, daring to speak so to Mark.

He grimaced. "Had he been a younger man, it doubtless would have been more than a tongue-lashing I received from him. Especially on one occasion. And there were many things he never knew about—your curricle race, for one. And your friendship with that opera dancer. I feared that would send him into an apoplexy. But I wanted to see how much of a mull you would make of things—and I must own it was better than a play to watch you go on."

"You might have told me at once that you knew. You did not need to let me go about—"

"As I said, I enjoyed watching you play the man."

"To get shot . . . "

"No one thought such a thing could happen." The laughter was gone at once. "That was a bad time for all of us, as well as for you. Your grandfather almost turned me off for my carelessness in allowing it to happen."

"But you could not—" It had been long since she had any

suspicion that he might have been the one to wish her out of the way.

"In a way, I was. I should never have loaded the pistols and permitted them to lie about—although I could not have been expected to think that even Albert could have been so foolish as to play with them. Of course, when I summoned the doctor for you—"

"You! Thomas told me the man was a friend of my father's!"

"I suppose he felt he had to tell you something, for you would not have let it be. I know how determined you were at the time that Thomas alone could care for you. His lordship and I decided that we must tell Thomas we knew the truth, but we swore him to secrecy. We did not wish to spoil your plot when you were so weak. And I will say"—he was grinning again—"I found some of the things you said in your fever to be most interesting."

What *had* she said? Surely she had not revealed her true feelings. She had a dim memory of now and then seeing someone she had thought was Mark, but had decided that was a dream. *Had* he been there? Had Thomas allowed him into her room?

"*Almost* as interesting as our encounter at Vauxhall," he was continuing.

Her embarrassment over that meeting was forgotten as she recalled that he and her grandfather had told Thomas they knew the truth about her. And Thomas had not told her!

"You . . . you persuaded Thomas—my *friend,* almost my father—to deceive me, too. And all this time you have been sitting back, watching me to see if I made some mistake. You were laughing at me, just as you did when the old dragon came. You thought *that* was a good jest, too. I think you are *odious*! You . . . you . . ."

Her anger was growing by the minute. No longer able to find words strong enough to express her fury for the ordeal to which he had submitted her, she slapped him with all her strength.

Chapter
Eighteen

MARK DID NOT attempt either to halt or avoid the blow, but seized her by the shoulders. Too late, she remembered the many times when he had expressed a wish to beat her. But surely, he would not—

He did not strike her, but, helpless in the grip of those large hands, Lucinda found herself being shaken so fiercely that her head jerked back and forth upon her shoulders and her teeth rattled. Her tears of outrage had given way to those of pain by the time he released her, and she felt as if she could scarcely stand.

Mark unclenched his teeth to say harshly, "From the first moment you walked into this house, I have been wanting to do that." Then, catching her in his arms, he continued, "Almost as much as I have wanted to do this," and his lips crushed down upon hers.

For an instant, Lucinda tried to struggle against the embrace she thought must certainly crush her ribs, then owned to herself the last thing she wished was to be released from it. Mark was behaving exactly as she had dreamed he might do, but had despaired of ever having happen.

Not even the kisses she had received from him that night at Vauxhall prepared her for the fact that a caress so different— almost brutal—could send sparks dancing along every nerve until her entire body was tingling. Her lips parted beneath his, and she returned his kiss fervently.

When he relaxed his embrace long enough for her to make a move, she ran her hands lovingly up his chest, remembering the effect the caress had that other time. His grasp about her waist and shoulders tightened painfully once more and, as she raised her face, his mouth sought hers another time. This kiss was gentler than the earlier one, but just as satisfying and disturbing to both.

They did not hear the opening of the outer door or the sound of footsteps. Thomas had ascended the stairs as Fenton went to the door and was unable to come down again quickly enough to wave Neddy away from the open library door.

"By the way, Mark, something I forgot when I was here this morn—" He broke off at the sight of his friend and the slight, pantalooned figure in his arms.

"Oh no, can't have that, my dear boy," he exclaimed in shocked tones. "That sort of thing won't do at all. Simply not good *ton*, you know, to have anything like that going on. Can't think what m' mother would say, nor Lord Brayling, for that matter."

Conscious of the picture the pair of them must make—and entirely forgetting the similar suspicions she once had about Mark—Lucinda began to giggle. Mark, however, merely raised his head long enough to say scornfully, "Must you always be such a gudgeon, Neddy?"

The marquess took a closer look at the smaller figure, then a happy smile spread across his plump face. "Oh— Yes. Yes, of course. Ought to have known, oughtn't I?" he murmured and walked out.

Drawing as far away from him as the circle of Mark's arms would allow—which was not far, as he had no intention of letting her go—Lucinda demanded indignantly, "Do you mean to tell me that *Neddy* has known who I was all this time, too?"

"Not at first. But after he tried to take you to that mill—"

"And how many others did you tell?"

"No one. My word on it. You apparently fooled the greater part of the crowd, even Brummell, who prides himself on the sharpness of his eyes. How I wished I could tell him what a cake he had made of himself, lecturing you on the proper costume. But I thought it best to take Neddy into my confidence. I could see at once that you would become suspicious if I insisted upon accompanying you everywhere."

"Yes." She thought of her anguished suspicion when he had

caressed her cheek the night before—and she had thought he was thinking of Lucien. If he had never left her alone—

"Yes—especially after you had made a point of telling me forcefully that you did not need a nursemaid. Since it would be necessary for me to attend to his lordship's work from time to time, I decided it would be wisest to have someone to help me keep an eye on you—to try to keep you out of trouble when you went racketing about the countryside."

"I did not racket!"

"What would you call it if not that? Neddy was nearer your own age than I and had no position to keep him busy. And no one—especially not you—would suspect Neddy Fenley of being a watchdog. Still, I own you had the both of us at Point Non Plus most of the time."

While delivering his scold, he had discovered a spot directly under her left ear that seemed to have been made for kissing. His experimenting to see if that was so made it difficult for Lucinda to keep her mind upon the questions she wished to put to him. She found that wherever his lips touched her, it caused the most delicious sensations to run through her until she could barely think.

Still, she persevered. "That is why . . . why he did not want to gamble where the stakes were high. I thought his pockets must be to let—and you mean he was doing that only to protect me? When he enjoys gaming so much?"

Mark had changed his objective to the spot beneath her right ear, so merely made a sound which Lucinda understood to be an affirmative.

"Poor Neddy! What a sacrifice for him to make, just for friendship. Friendship for you, I mean. Not for me, although he has been kind to me from the first time we met. But you say he did not know about me when he was going to take me to the mill?"

Having found that her cravat, which Lucinda had tied as inexpertly as always, was preventing him from kissing her throat as he should have liked to do, Mark grumbled a bit, then whisked off the obstructing cloth and tossed it aside. He spread her collar wide with both hands and his lips sought the hollow of her throat. Momentarily, Lucinda forgot what she had been saying and gave herself over to the thrill of his caresses.

"I must say," he commented, "that, aside from looking

much better on you than this outfit, the green gown was much better suited for such pastimes as this. Not that I cared overmuch for the mask."

"Um," Lucinda murmured in agreement. Then recalling her earlier questions, she asked, "How *did* it happen that Neddy was about to take me to a mill?"

"Must we talk about Neddy? Well . . . as I said, that was before he knew about you. I was forced, you may recall, to come up with the tale that the mill had been cancelled—and almost lost Neddy's friendship as a result."

"I remember how he stalked out of here to pay off wagers on a match he had not seen—because of you."

"Yes. But when I asked for his help and he realized that he had nearly taken a female to a prizefight, I had to restrain him almost forcibly from coming to apologize to you. Also, I gathered, because of some of the things his friends might have said in your presence. That gave me some concern—and your grandfather, as well."

"Thomas, too, but I told him I was accustomed to hearing soldiers talk."

"And he doubtless told you they did not talk the same in the presence of a lady as they might if you were not there. The worst, of course, was when you began jauntering about the country with a Cyprian in tow. I did not dare to tell your grandfather about *that* escapade. I could see at Vauxhall that she had learned your secret, but how long did it take and what did she say when she learned she had been fooled?"

"Evita? She was not fooled for a moment. So I had to tell her the truth. She is not a bad person—only an underpaid dancer and must seek other support. She agreed to help me with my masquerade if I would help her to regain a man she wanted, one who is not nearly good enough for her."

"That is the kind of men most females prefer, I gather. I hope that is the kind you wish, for that is the kind you are getting."

"You mean you have decided *that* for me, as well."

"Yes. Neddy has made sense—for once in his life. No one must be allowed to see us like this—nor must they learn who you really are. I have talked the matter over with his lordship and have been in correspondence with your brother. We have decided that Captain Warne will be called back to the Peninsula at once. I shall accompany him on some business for Lord

Brayling, and there I shall fall heels over head for the captain's lovely sister—for you are lovely, you know. Then I shall bring you home as my wife—that is, if you will agree to have me."

There was nothing in the world Lucinda wished more than to become his wife, but even that last phrase had sounded as if he were too assured of success. Saying petulantly, "You appear to have settled everything among yourselves," she tried to pull free from his arms, only to be drawn so tightly against him that she could scarcely breathe.

"Certainly—and why not? I have had two months to make my plans, for I knew from the beginning that I wanted to marry you."

"That is not so. You did not even like me."

"I did not like the young braggart you pretended to be. I know your brother is not like that, so I suppose you were put into that position by Albert. I *did* want you from the moment I knew who you were, although I received the impression you disliked me. But I did not believe 'Margarita' could behave as she did without being serious. Unless . . . unless you might have behaved that way with any man you met."

"Why that— How can you say—"

"Tell me, why were you at Vauxhall that night dressed as you were? It could not have been to meet me, for you did not know I would be there. Were you planning to meet someone in particular?" He gripped her arms, shaking her gently. "Or were you merely looking for anyone who attracted you?" He shook her again.

"Why I— Certainly not! You are insufferable!"

"Then why were you there?"

"I do not see why I should tell you. Still, I had told Evita how tired I was of going about in men's clothing, so she found the gown for me and took me with her. It *was* nice to be admired for myself, instead of as Lord Brayling's heir. But that you would think—"

"No, I did not—not truly." He drew her close once more, determined she must never know he *had* doubted her, if only for a moment. "And I was as certain of your feelings as I was of my own, after hearing some of the things you said in your fever when you had been shot. Oh, my dear, when I think I might have lost you then . . . But I do not intend to let you out of my sight ever again, for who knows what starts you might be in when I was not looking? My only regret is that we cannot be married here with your grandfather to watch. If he wished it, however, we could have a second ceremony when we return—with all the pomp due an earl's granddaughter."

Secretly delighted, Lucinda said with a show of reluctance, "Well, since you three gentlemen have arranged my life, I suppose I am left with no choice but to go along with your wishes. And after all, as a married woman, I shall have a great deal more freedom. I can visit Evita when I—"

Mark took one arm from around her long enough to deal her a light box on the ear. "You can do nothing of the kind," he said sternly. "My wife shall not jaunter about with a dancer from the opera no matter how nice she may be. And as for having freedom, you have had far too much already."

Then, seeing her grin, he said, "You, my dear one, are a complete rogue, and I should know better than to be taken in by any tale you spin. But from this moment, I shall have my eye upon you every moment of our lives."

"I hope so, my darling," Lucinda said happily. "I truly hope so."

As Mark gathered her into his arms again, he caught the library door with one foot and swung it shut to prevent any other interruptions. And Thomas, with the same thought in mind, came down and planted himself firmly before the portal, his arms folded and a wide smile on his face as he murmured, "We shall have no more worries about our girl, Philip. She is in good hands now."